THE
Cemetery
OF
Untold
Stories

ALSO BY JULIA ALVAREZ

FICTION

How the García Girls Lost Their Accents
In the Time of the Butterflies
¡Yo!
In the Name of Salomé
A Cafecito Story
Saving the World
Afterlife

NONFICTION

Something to Declare
Once Upon a Quinceañera: Coming of Age in the USA
A Wedding in Haiti

POETRY

Homecoming
The Other Side/El Otro Lado
The Woman I Kept to Myself

FOR CHILDREN

The Secret Footprints
The Tía Lola Stories
Before We Were Free
finding miracles
A Gift of Gracias: The Legend of Altagracia
The Best Gift of All: The Legend of la Vieja Belén
Return to Sender
Where Do They Go?
Already a Butterfly: A Meditation Story

THE
Cemetery
OF
Untold
Stories

A NOVEL

JULIA ALVAREZ

ALGONQUIN BOOKS OF CHAPEL HILL 2024

Published by
ALGONQUIN BOOKS OF CHAPEL HILL
Post Office Box 2225
Chapel Hill, North Carolina 27515-2225

an imprint of Workman Publishing
a division of Hachette Book Group, Inc.
1290 Avenue of the Americas,
New York, NY 10104

The Algonquin Books of Chapel Hill name and logo are registered trademarks of
Hachette Book Group, Inc.

Printed in the United States of America.
Design by Steve Godwin.

The publisher is not responsible for websites (or their content)
that are not owned by the publisher.

This is a work of fiction. While, as in all fiction, the literary perceptions and insights
are based on experience, all names, characters, places, and incidents
either are products of the author's imagination or are used fictitiously.

Library of Congress Cataloging-in-Publication Data
Names: Alvarez, Julia, author.
Title: The cemetery of untold stories : a novel / Julia Alvarez.
Description: First edition. | Chapel Hill, North Carolina : Algonquin Books of
Chapel Hill, 2024. | Summary: "When celebrated writer Alma Cruz inherits a small
plot of land in the Dominican Republic, she turns it into a place to bury her untold
stories—literally. She creates a graveyard for manuscript drafts and revisions and the
characters whose lives she tried and failed to bring to life and who still haunt her.
Alma wants her characters to rest in peace, but they have other ideas, and the cemetery
becomes a mysterious sanctuary for their true narratives."— Provided by publisher.
Identifiers: LCCN 2023032944 | ISBN 9781643753843 (hardcover) |
ISBN 9781643756066 (ebook)
Subjects: LCGFT: Novels.
Classification: LCC PS3551.L845 C46 2024 | DDC 813/.54—dc23/eng/20230720
LC record available at https://lccn.loc.gov/2023032944

10 9 8 7 6 5 4 3 2 1
First Edition

Anon

Tell me a story.

THE
Cemetery
OF
Untold
Stories

 I

➤ Let's go to Alfa Calenda

Alma once had a friend, a writer, who for years before she died, relatively young, was always talking about this one story she had to write down.

Over the course of their thirty-plus-year friendship, Alma's friend became quite famous, winning major prizes, garnering important interviews, awards left and right. A TV movie based on one of her novels was in the works with well-known names even Alma, not a big Hollywood person, had heard of. And yet her friend dismissed these achievements as "incidentals." The real deal was this one story that would not be hurried.

The story possessed her. She could reel off its characters, complete with their names and histories. Periodically, they compelled her to go to one or another part of the world: a gravesite in Sweden, a fishing village in Liberia, the outer islands off South Carolina where she bought a house and lived for a spell. These characters had secrets she was listening for, and the reception was better in some places than others; their voices would break through, until she'd lose the connection and it was time to move on to some other place.

Alma had stopped counting her friend's many addresses, switching to pencil in her address book. A migrant storyteller, to be sure, Alma told her. Her writer friend liked that description, and from then on, she used it for interviews and at readings, insisting she was not a writer, or a novelist, but a migrant storyteller.

Alma wasn't so sure it was a great thing for her friend to be so rootless. A writer needs to be grounded or the force that through the green fuse drives the flower is going to incinerate it. But instead of pointing this out, Alma held back, celebrating her friend's lilies-of-the-fields attitude. Her friend could be fierce, bristling at the slightest hint of criticism.

In one incident—and Alma was at the reading to verify it—a woman during the Q and A mentioned the difficulty of understanding some of the dialogue. Did the writer ever worry about her audience? Alma's friend leveled one of those if-looks-could-kill looks at the woman. I'm not writing for white people, she said straight out. This before people were saying such things, except for Toni Morrison.

One of the protagonists in the unwritten story was a likeable white guy from Sweden (thus the trip to Sweden?), a sailor, with ropey arms like the rigging of a ship. Kristian, whose name changed over time—Kristofer, Anders, Nils—falls in love with the enslaved female protagonist, Clio—her name did not change over the many years her friend talked about the book.

Alma sometimes wondered if her friend had befriended her in part to find out more about white people. If so, Alma was not the best choice: she wasn't 100 percent Caucasian, if such a critter even existed. Her family came from an island where, the popular saying goes, *Everyone has a little Black behind the ears*. Even the pale members of her mother's clan who claimed their ancestors had come over on the Niña, Pinta, or Santa Maria would occasionally spawn a dark seed they blamed on the in-laws. Her father's family couldn't hide their racial mixture: the dark-skinned matriarch with the French surname, Rochet, meant roots in Haiti; probably a slave owner helping himself to his property.

Whatever her friend's reasons for befriending her, Alma was flattered. Being the chosen one was something that rarely happened to her. It was as if a bad-tempered toddler who bawled when others approached had smiled and lifted their little arms to her. The two women spoke often by phone, exchanged long, thoughtful letters. After Alma moved to Vermont for a teaching job, her friend would take the train from the city every summer. Before one visit, Alma asked Luke, her then boyfriend, to plant some sunflowers, knowing her friend had a thing for them. He didn't sow just one or two, but the whole back pasture—a bumper crop of yellow suns.

Alma took her friend out to the back deck and gestured grandly. Your welcome bouquet!

Her friend kept shaking her head with wonder. Did you do that? Alma gave credit where credit was due.

You keep this one, you hear, her friend said bossily.

Along with a green thumb, Luke also had cool tattoos. Her friend spent the afternoon sketching them in her journal. They're perfect for my Kristian, she said.

But it takes more than a green thumb to keep love growing. Several months later, Alma discovered Luke was sowing his wild seed in other fields. When she broke up with him, her friend was pissed at Alma.

Over the years, Alma began to feel anxious before each visit. Her friend had fallen out with most of her friends as well as with her family. She was mistrustful, increasingly paranoid. She was being watched. The Feds were after her. Her sister was hitting her up for money for drugs. She had pulled all her titles from her publisher. She recounted angry scenes. Alma began to wonder when her own banishment would come.

Of course, her friend had reason to be wary. All sorts of people courted her, their motives never completely free of that pursuit of celebrities that her writer friend considered an affliction in the culture. Don't ever forget, she often coached Alma, we're just the literary flavor of the month or at most the year. More and more, publishing houses were being bought by huge conglomerates who also dealt in fossil fuels and breakfast cereals and pharmaceuticals. Like all their other assets, their writers had expiration dates.

Alma listened, but she was not yet ready to dismiss fame and fortune. Easy enough for her friend, already a big deal. Just you wait, she kept saying to Alma. But Alma didn't want to wait. They were the same age, and Alma was still struggling. Her friend was super generous, inviting Alma along as her sidekick at conferences where she was giving the keynote, introducing her as "one of my favorite writers," advising Alma about where to send her work and whom to trust, this latter a very short list, and getting shorter.

Finally, Alma's writing started gaining some traction, but this caused fallout she hadn't foreseen. Her mother took issue with her daughter's "lies" and threatened to sue if Alma didn't stop publishing her shameful stories, defaming the family name (naughty girls having sex, using drugs). She was going to disown Alma and write her own version of events. Since Mami was not speaking to her, these ultimatums were delivered to Alma via her sisters.

Alma was distraught. How could her own mother attack her? Even hardened criminals had mothers who said, He's an axe murderer, but he's my baby.

So, change your name, her writer friend suggested. You're always talking about *The Arabian Nights*. You can be Scheherazade from now on.

No one will be able to spell it, Alma noted.

Their problem. You're not writing for them, are you?

Who is *them*? Alma didn't ask, for fear she'd get an earful.

It's all settled, her friend said, ignoring Alma's reluctance. Only two months older and her friend was bossier than Amparo, the eldest of Alma's three sisters.

At a conference where her friend was giving the keynote, Alma overheard a writer on the staff describe her friend as "a piece of work."

Alma might have dismissed the comment as typical of what happens at these conferences—contributors and staff afloat in alcohol to get through all that contained intensity and ambition—but Alma was especially sensitive to the phrase. Both Luke and, before him, Philip, Alma's former husband, had said the same thing about her. The idiom always sounded off. Didn't anything worthwhile involve work?

A number of such expressions still eluded her. She knew their dictionary meanings, but she didn't get that *Ah ha!* feeling that came from a word or idiom touching bottom inside her. Perhaps because English wasn't her original language, its root system didn't go deep enough in her psyche, a troubling thought for a writer.

Of course, Alma knew the term wasn't intended as a compliment, especially when used by a man toward a woman he's losing interest in. The end is nigh. Her friend had never met Philip, but she had a lot to say about men in general, not usually positive, which was why it had been unusual when she advised Alma to keep her sunflower fellow.

For her part, her friend never mentioned any passionate attachments, male or female. She did leave a message one time on Alma's answering machine. She was in Paris, engaged to be married. By then, both women were in their mid-forties and single. I want you to be my maid of honor. I'll send more details soon. The promised details never came. At their next meeting (another conference where this time they were both keynote speakers—Alma was coming up in the world) her friend never mentioned the fiancée. So, did you just elope with this guy? Alma asked. What guy? her friend batted back. Alma brought up the phone message from a few months ago. A fly-by-night, her friend waved the fly away. But what about the wedding band on her left hand? Just a protective measure, her friend replied. Protection against what? Again, Alma didn't ask.

Her friend seemed to treat her life like drafts of a novel. This plot isn't working. Okay, no problem. Let's take out the marriage and rearrange the sequence, see what happens. Some troubling confusion between art and life.

At a subsequent reunion, her friend cornered her. Will you promise me something?

Depends on the promise, Alma answered in a jokey voice her friend did not appreciate.

This is serious. If something happens to me, promise you'll tell Clio's story.

Alma balked. I can't. I wouldn't be able to do it justice, she added, a compliment to mollify her refusal.

Of course, you can. You've heard me talking about her for years.

One thing is hearing a story, another is writing it down. Besides, it's not for one person to tell another's story. (Like Alma hadn't been doing this left and right in her own writing.) And nothing's going to happen to you, she assured her friend.

I guess you haven't heard the news that none of us is getting out of here alive.

Ha, ha, Alma said the words, too uneasy for genuine laughter. Any moment now her friend might go off the deep end and drag Alma along with her.

Alma began to hang back, afraid of an intimacy that had always been so singular, unsettling. She'd let a few days go by before answering letters or calls. That summer there was no invitation for a Vermont visit. For one thing there was no boyfriend with alluring tattoos and property out in the country. And Alma herself was on the move. After a spate of publications, she'd gotten tenure and purchased a "starter home," so the Realtor called it, though Alma meant the modest cottage to be the house they carried her out of feet first. It's tiny, Alma remarked to her friend, leaving a guest room vague. She would be spending most of the summer away; length and location of her stay she also left vague.

Alma was at the airport, headed for the Dominican Republic, the island she still called home. Her parents had moved back in their old age, and it was Alma's turn to spell Amparo, who had moved down to manage their care. At her gate waiting for the delayed flight, Alma heard the ringing in her handbag. Her friend's name flashed on the screen. Alma debated whether to answer. She didn't need one more piece of work with a whole month of heart-wrenching eldercare ahead of her. But Alma had rarely been able to refuse her friend. Soon she'd be in a whole other country for over a month, so it's not like her friend could easily land on her doorstep.

Her friend didn't greet Alma but launched right into her story. She was locked up in a facility—no, not a prison, but it might as well be—a looney bin somewhere in the city. A family member had obtained a power of attorney, claiming she was a danger to herself. Lies, all lies! You have to get me out of here. It wasn't a request so much as a command.

Alma hesitated, thinking over all the ways she had seen this coming. The signs had been there: over two decades working on that novel, her characters driving her all over the face of creation. Alma had listened patiently to her friend's wild suspicions about outrageous plots to silence her.

It was time to take a stand. Alma couched her refusal in a way that her friend might find acceptable. By getting well, that long-awaited novel might come. We both know, Alma reminded her friend, that we don't get free until we write our stories down. She quoted a passage she often used to rally her students stuck on a piece of writing: *"If you bring forth what is inside you, what is inside you will save you. If you do not bring forth what is inside, what is inside you will destroy you."*

An unsettling silence had fallen on the other end of the line. It's from the Bible, Alma added, knowing her friend had once been a Jehovah's Witness and was still enough of a believer that she didn't like for people to celebrate her birthday. And then, what a mother might say to a daughter or a woman to her lover, Do it for me. I need you to write that story. And no, I can't do it for you, no one can.

I see. Her friend's voice had turned to ice. They've gotten to you, too. And here I thought you wouldn't betray me.

Alma defended herself. It's because I care. I love you! Alma would never know if her friend heard these last words. There was more silence. Then the screen went dark.

Alma tried calling back, but no answer. For weeks, months, Alma kept trying. Her friend's voicemail wasn't set up, her old landline number had been disconnected. Alma didn't know whom to contact. She had never met anyone in her friend's family. She did manage to reach her friend's former agent, who confessed concern about her author's psychosis. The first Alma heard of a diagnosis.

Alma didn't go into the details of their last call. She told herself she had to protect her friend's dignity, her privacy. But it was her own failure Alma was most ashamed of. Not about declining to spring her friend from the mental ward, but about remaining silent all those years when Alma suspected her friend wasn't well. Back in Catholic school, the nuns had called these sins of omission.

For several years, Alma kept an eye out. She'd type her friend's name in search engines. No recent novels, readings, lectures. She had vanished. It was as if Alma had imagined her friend along with the other characters in her books.

The end came as no surprise. The former agent let Alma know.

The official word was that her friend had suffered a massive heart attack. There were conjectures about what had caused it: too high a dosage of some substance or other; a contraindicated mix of medications; overexertion that crashed her burdened vessels. But Alma didn't believe any of these explanations. What killed her friend was that novel she could neither write nor put aside.

Alma vowed that when the time came, she wasn't going to let the same thing happen to her. It didn't seem likely. She was going at a fast clip—a book every other year, articles, talks. It seemed her friend had passed the fame baton on to her.

Years passed. The great mortal migration began

Every month, Alma would get a call: this tío or that tía or older cousin had died. Then came her parents' turn. First, Mami began showing signs of dementia. Surprisingly the erasure of memory brought out the best in her. For the only time any of her daughters could remember, their dragon-lady mother was tender and affection- ate, patting her lap for her daughters to come sit and play kissy games and sing clapping songs together. Alma finally understood what years of writing hadn't unraveled. Her mother needed a mother, too.

She died with her four girls taking turns cradling her like their child.

Papi was bereft. Every day, he'd ask, ¿Y Mami? and every day suffer the fresh blow of hearing that she had died. Did he also have demen- tia, the sisters wondered, or was this his usual disconnect? He'd been detached for years—nothing new there. But after his wife's death, he seemed to sink into a deeper silence. He stopped talking altogether, except for occasional sallies, and then they couldn't get him to stop— like he only had an *on* and *off* switch—reciting long passages of Dante, Rubén Darío, Cervantes, recounting canned incidents of his life, every- thing airbrushed, a firewall Alma could never seem to get through.

After Mami died, Amparo volunteered to stay on managing Papi's care. Management had never been Amparo's strong suit, however. She didn't believe in keeping a budget, a stingy way to live, draining her parents' savings instead. She picked up men, buying them lavish gifts, expensive colognes and clothes, a motorcycle, a washing machine for one man's mother. She fell for every tear-jerking story: my sister is dying of cancer, my brother needs a prosthesis, his kids don't have school supplies. She had a heart of gold, but it was not her gold to give away.

How do we solve a problem like Amparo? became her younger sisters' theme song from *The Sound of Music* for Amparo. What a misnomer of a name: "Refuge," really? ¡Por favor!

Amparo was furious at her sisters' lack of appreciation for her sacrifices, giving up her life to take care of their father. You think you can do it better, go ahead! She was off to Cuba with her new boyfriend. Cuba?! What new boyfriend? Amparo's lips were sealed. She could be as elusive as Papi.

Papi's care now fell on the three younger sisters, all living in the States. The most practical solution, therefore, was to bring their father to live with one of them or in a nearby facility. Yes, they had promised both parents never to bring them back or put them in a nursing home, but what difference would it make? Half the time Papi didn't even know where he was. What was the harm in pretending? We're going to Alfa Calenda, they told him as they packed up his belongings, put the house on the market, and boarded the Jet Blue flight to JFK. Just the mention of that fantasy place he'd invented with his mother in childhood seemed to soothe him. His personal Shangri-la-la land, his daughters had dubbed it.

As the second oldest, next in line to be the "honorary son," Alma took charge of Papi's care. Although the sisters decried the patriarchy in the Dominican Republic, primogeniture and succession still held sway in their psyches. Alma had every intention of keeping Papi at home, but that plan soon proved untenable. Her little cottage with its narrow doorways and steep staircases was not accessible. Her father was not a big man, but he was twice her weight, and a dead weight at that. No way Alma could handle him by herself. In her rural community, round-the-clock care was expensive and hard to find. Sunset Manor was less than five minutes away. It was full of old Vermonters, mostly women who didn't know what to make of this tanned, foreign man, a cigar-store Indian in their midst. Dr. Manuel Cruz became a favorite of the aides, an exotic creature in his Panama hat, gallantly kissing their hands, complimenting them. The women soaked it up, spoiling him with double portions of dessert. His blood sugar was through the roof.

You like it here, eh, Papi? Alma kept asking, trying to assuage her guilt.

He'd scowl at her. Did he realize his daughters had tricked him? Maybe he was just trying to figure out who she was. Amparo? Consuelo? Piedad? He always did this growing up: run through all their names before landing on the daughter in question. It hurt their feelings. Now, he was adding new names to the roll call. Mami? (Did he mean their mother or his?) Belén? (A sister Alma was supposed to resemble.) Tatica?

Who is Tatica, Papi?

Papi shook his head, but his eyes were bright with memories.

Come on, Babinchi, Alma coaxed, using his childhood nickname. You know you can tell me anything? She stroked the hand on her hand tenderly.

Papi patted her hand back, a gesture of affection or was he tamping down her questions? These moments of lucidity were rare. Alma kept trying. Bendición, she greeted him in the old-fashioned way he had taught them. She spoke of Alfa Calenda as if she'd been there. Tricks that almost always roused him. Tatica, she tried several times, which seemed to stir him as well.

Do any of you know who Tatica is? Alma asked her sisters. Papi keeps mentioning her.

Probably someone from Alfa Calenda, Piedad offered. Their code way of referring to all their father's backstory none of them needed to know more about, except for Alma.

Fuck Alfa Calenda. Papi was probably getting something on the side. Consuelo's telenovela imagination had a tendency to go into overdrive.

Amparo, back Stateside after her boyfriend dumped her in Cuba, fumed. So, they were really going to smear their father with conjectures now that he was incapable of defending himself. And for their information, Tatica was the nickname for Altagracia, the national virgencita. It was super common. One out of every thirteen Dominican girls bore her name. In the campo over 80 percent of the women of a certain generation had Altagracia as a middle or given name. Papi was just calling out to the Virgin Mary.

Give me a break! Consuelo scoffed.

There was only one Altagracia in their extended family—so much for Amparo's statistics—their maternal grandmother, whom Papi had disliked. The feeling was mutual. Abuela Amelia Altagracia had never approved of the nobody her beautiful, willful daughter had condescended to marry. No way Papi would be calling out to his good-riddance suegra. Besides, Abuela never went by Tatica. She insisted on the full regalia of her name. Doña Amelia Altagracia. It means "high grace," she bragged to Americanos who asked, as if the name were a title conferred by royalty the island didn't have.

So, who was this Tatica?

Mami must not have known or she would have said so. A direct conduit from her brain to her mouth. But if Mami was an open book, Papi wasn't even in the library. He kept to himself—especially after they came to this country. When he did talk, it was always indirectly: the story of Babinchi, who grew up under two "dictators" (his harsh father and the brutal el Jefe), joined a revolution, escaped as a young man to Nueva York, then Canada, where he had to repeat three years of his medical education, selling his blood to pay the tuition . . .

So is Babinchi you, Papi? Alma kept asking. Did all this really happen to you? Her father would give her an arch smile. Manuel Cruz, aka Babinchi, wasn't talking.

He died in his sleep, taking his stories with him.

After Papi's death, Alma found herself adrift, launching into one writing project after another, abandoning each one when another story began tugging at her sleeve. There weren't enough years left to tell all the stories she wanted to tell.

One night, her writer friend appeared in a dream, thinned down, almost transparent. Her voice a whisper, her touch a breeze. *I should have known better*, she said. *Some stories don't want to be told. Let them go.*

But I can't seem to, Alma wailed. Willpower never worked on her obsessions. Then, burn them, bury them, whatever it takes.

Alma woke up in her small house in Vermont, determined to let the past go, including her sense of blame and shame about her friend. It was time to put her affairs in order, pack up all her old drafts and folders in boxes. Good riddance—an idiom she understood in her gut. She would soon be entering that territory of the old—okay, not *old* old, but the anteroom, no matter what the magazines said about seventy being the new fifty.

She informed her department that she would be retiring at the end of the spring semester. After four-plus decades in the classroom, there were too many déjà vus. Didn't I say all this before? Didn't I teach you twenty years ago where to put that comma? The old strategies, jokes, anecdotes, inspirational quotes bored her, if not her students.

At the parting faculty meeting, her colleagues delivered glowing remarks that made Alma sound like a fictional character. Brilliant, collegial, beloved? Really? Did they not remember the less-than-stellar evaluations from disgruntled students, the legacy parents who protested about "a Mexican woman" (*Dominican*, couldn't they at least get their prejudices straight?) teaching their son English—a son who had earned a D in Alma's class, no doubt the spark that ignited the parental fire. After the meeting, Alma dropped by her office to pick up the last of her files and doorstopper Norton anthologies, only to find one of the grounds crew scraping her name from the door. She had to laugh. *Sic transit gloria mundi.*

Say again? the man had asked.

There was a rightness to these endings, however unsettling. What Alma was finding harder to accept was that aging also happens in the creative life. Maybe not for Yeats, submitting to his monkey-gland treatments. Or for Milosz or Kunitz—interestingly, all males, at least the ones Alma could name—working well into old age. Critics liked to write about the late style, usually a euphemism for a messy grasping for what has passed. The glow of celebrity now tinged with nostalgia might keep the fan fires going, but Alma didn't want anyone's condescension or pity. The time had come to stop beating herself up for not being able to finish anything. She was trying to hold on to the literary version of good looks, the plastic surgeries of astute agents and editors nipping and tucking the flagging work. Every worker knows to put aside her tools at the end of the workday. Even that paramount narcissist, Prospero.

But what had he done when he put aside his rough magic? What did a world without his cloud-capped towers feel like? How did Yeats cope, stuck in the rag and bone shop of his own heart? Maybe that's when he signed up for his monkey-gland treatments.

It was as if her writer friend had passed on another baton to Alma, this one of disenchantment. Perhaps Mami had been right: Alma's "betrayals"—usurping stories from her familia and homeland to serve as savories for the First World's delectation—would come back to haunt her.

Even so, Alma was not about to renege on her craft—it had kept her afloat all these years. She had answered this calling—not exactly with her eyes wide open: Who would ever do anything if they knew what lay ahead? TMI, as her students said, too much information, for sure.

She had plunged into what she loved with borrowed confidence from mentors and muses like her writer friend, editors and agents who told her she had an aptitude for putting words together. What her mother had described as Alma's big mouth. Now it was time to shut up.

The problem was the writerly impulse was still inside her. And if she didn't bring it out, would it destroy her as it had her friend? It wasn't like she had a choice. But one thing she could choose: after spending decades giving characters' lives a shapely form, Alma wanted to close the story of her own writing life in a satisfying way.

She began to toy with the idea of returning to the island. After all these years she still thought of it as home. As young women, Alma and her sisters often spoke of their "dear DR" as a kind of emergency cord, like the ones they'd encountered in subways as new immigrants in Nueva York. If all else failed—their marriages, careers, their medicated peace of mind—they could always go back. Maybe the time had come to bail. Ending up where she began would indeed give her life a pleasing symmetry.

Years ago, in her twenties, she'd written a poem—a draft stored in one of her many boxes of unfinished work—that ended with the line, "Only the empty hand is free to hold." She'd then proceeded to live a life of grab and grasp, mistaking glitter for gold, though obviously she knew better. Now, she was going to take her own advice. She'd let the writing go and stand empty-handed for as long as she could stand it, allowing the fears and disturbances to pass through her, not an easy thing for someone with a craft so ingrained that not to do it felt as if she'd already disappeared.

Alma hired a former student to help organize her boxes upon boxes of rough drafts. Sophie glanced at the ones labeled BIENVENIDA. It means "welcome," right? I'm taking Spanish, she added, as if she were paying Alma a personal compliment.

¡Qué bueno! Alma replied. And yes, that's what the word *bienvenida* means. But in this case Bienvenida was the name of her protagonist in a novel she'd been working on for years, based on a historical figure, one of the wives of a ruthless dictator in the Dominican Republic, Alma's homeland. Ever heard of Trujillo?

Can't say I have.

It was not uncommon for North Americans not to know much about her little half island, except for its awesome beaches and exported baseball players. Besides, the southern Americas were rife with dictatorships. One dictator was so much like another. But Trujillo, aka el Jefe, was one of the most brutal. Thirty-one years in power.

That's older than me, Sophie noted, youth's measure of all things. So, it's a true story, not like you made it up?

It was a question readers often asked. Alma was weary of explaining that a novelist should not subject herself to the tyranny of what really happened. She herself couldn't always separate the strands of real life, as it was called, from pure invention. Her own life, parts of it, happened so long ago, she wondered if she'd made them up. Her father's life, recapped as Babinchi's in his letters, chock full of narrow escapes from the Secret Police, sometimes sounded more fantastical than his childhood fantasy world. Let's go to Alfa Calenda, he'd say before beginning a story. A place that existed only in his head, and now hers, where it had come to a dead end.

Does it matter? Alma answered Sophie's question with a question. Stories move beyond these binaries, Alma went on. She couldn't stop herself. A handicap of having spent over four decades in classrooms, being the one who was supposed to know. So easy to pontificate and so difficult to bring a character to life, the words made flesh. If her readers could only see her on any given writing day, humbled by the continual little failures of getting a sentence right or a character's name or tone of voice.

Sophie's eyes had begun to glaze over.

Anyhow, to answer your question, yes and no. Alma's Bienvenida was closely modeled on the real-life Bienvenida except that Alma supplied all the thoughts, feelings, details that the historical figure hadn't left behind.

So, is that the title, *Bienvenida*? Sophie wanted to know. Can I order it on Amazon?

You can't order it. I never finished it, Alma answered in her case-closed voice. It wasn't coming together. Sometimes you have to be willing to walk away. Like it had been that easy. Like she still wasn't walking around with that ghost book in her head.

Sophie surveyed the shelves. So, are all these boxes stuff you never finished?

Pretty much, yes. Alma pointed to now one box, now another, giving brief synopses of the stories she had abandoned. This one was going to be about a torturer in that dictatorship I mentioned, a Mr. Torres, a blind old man when we meet him, living out his days in Lawrence, Massachusetts. A young Dominican-American girl volunteers to read to him. The girl has no idea that this old man was once a SIM agent who killed her own grandfather, whom she never knew. This other one was about a Wisconsin farm woman who claimed to have visitations from the Virgin Mary. The box beside it was the beginning of a novel about the 1937 Haitian massacre, ever heard of it? Sophie had not.

So, what happened?

Trujillo ordered the slaughter of all Haitians living on the Dominican side of the border. Many didn't even know they were trespassing. The border between the two countries had been changed so many times, the line drawn and redrawn on the maps. Some Dominicans of conscience hid families. But most were too afraid. I guess I abandoned them, too, Alma conceded.

Well, it's not like writing about them would've saved them, Sophie noted reasonably.

Still, Alma blamed herself for these failed stories. Maybe she hadn't loved them enough. Or, a possibility that frightened her even more, maybe she just lacked the necessary talent and scope. But they wouldn't let her go, especially her last two attempts, the stories of Papi and of Bienvenida, in whom she had invested so much time, so many drafts, so many folders full of notes. At readings, Alma spoke about the dictator's ex-wife, read short passages of dialogue and descriptions of Bienvenida's growing up as an upper-class girl in a border town.

Alma had researched every aspect of life in that border town in the late nineteenth, early twentieth century. Monte Cristi had been a boom town back in Bienvenida's childhood, years before the bloody massacre, a major port, where German, Dutch, and Spanish ships docked and loaded up with tobacco, cocoa, coffee, mahogany. The biggest export was something Alma had never heard of: campeche. Back in the days before synthetics, its bark was used to dye fabrics as well as to treat diarrhea and menstrual disorders. Alma had researched that, too.

In her novel, Alma had Bienvenida resort to campeche teas in a desperate effot to prevent her recurring miscarriages. But these fictional infusions couldn't alter the real-life facts: Bienvenida seemed unable to carry a child to full term. After eight years of marriage and miscarriages, the dictator discarded her in order to marry his mistress who had recently borne him a son. This new wife turned out to be el Jefe's match in terms of ruthlessness, stopping at nothing to get rid of her rival. Bienvenida was sent into exile, her name taken off road signs, avenues, clinics, schools. Overnight she disappeared. In an old history book about first ladies of the Dominican Republic Alma inherited from her father, Bienvenida Inocencia Ricardo wasn't even mentioned. In protest, Alma's father had crossed out the name of the new wife and scrawled in Bienvenida's name. Alma was intrigued. Did you know her, Papi?

He knew of her. A kind lady, she had saved a number of dissidents, alerting families about a raid, providing safe passage for them across the border.

Did she help you escape? Alma pressed. She was curious to know more about her father's first exile as a young doctor in the States and later Canada.

She was already banished by the time I had to leave.

Alma's research unearthed several old people still living in Monte Cristi who recalled the sweet girl who'd fallen head over heels in love with el Jefe. Just like her middle name, Bienvenida Inocencia had been clueless as to the monster she was about to marry. Even after he divorced her and banished her, Bienvenida remained loyal, as far as anyone could tell, blaming the cronies who surrounded el Jefe for the worst brutalities, including the massacre.

How could such a good woman end up with the devil incarnate? That was the question that kept coming up. It was also the question that fueled Alma's own obsession with Bienvenida. Beauty and the Beast, all right.

Alma had even visited the cemetery where Bienvenida was rumored to be buried in an unmarked grave. After the regime was toppled, all the statues, monuments, and houses of the dictator and anyone connected to him were overrun by the furious victimized masses. Bienvenida had been quietly interred in an unmarked grave to avoid desecration. No one knew exactly where.

Talking to her father, Alma discovered that his father—Alma's grandfather—had owned property in the outskirts of Bienvenida's hometown. His wife and children were safely ensconced in a large house in a city in the interior. Papi's father spent considerable time away, managing his properties, traveling back and forth, a trip that took two days on horseback.

Just as well he was gone a lot, Alma's father remarked but refused to elaborate. His father was verboten in their conversations. Still, Alma pressed on, each time finding out a little more.

These long absences gave him free rein—not that he needed or requested it—to start a second family on the other side of the border. Curiously, his Haitian children were all born within months of his light-skinned legitimate children, as if wife and mistress were in competition with each other's fertility.

So, what had happened to that other family? Alma had queried her father. She had always wanted to write a novel about the Haitian massacre, and this personal connection added to her interest. But Papi claimed he didn't know any more specifics. All he knew was that shortly after the massacre his father sold off his border properties and turned against the dictator.

All these stories, not yet cohered into a novel, were in the PAPI box. Alma could recite chapter and verse of her father's life, the tired anecdotes he had shared with her and her sisters over the years. But the rounded character, the non-Papi parts of Manuel Cruz, proved elusive. Alma would ask the wrong question or probe too hard, and her father would clam up like those moriviví plants she remembered from childhood that folded up their leaves at a touch.

Maybe his untold stories, blood-soaked and tragic, had sent her father spiraling down into his own world. Alfa Calenda was his emergency cord. Just imagining these stories had also proved to be too much for Alma. A firewall of words had not been sufficient protection from "The Horror! The Horror!"

Papi, Bienvenida—Alma had even tried to write a novel combining their stories. BIENVENIDA + PAPI, that box was labeled. These two most recent failures especially haunted Alma. Bienvenida had been erased from history; Papi had sealed himself off in Alfa Calenda—these were precisely the characters Alma felt drawn to. The silenced ones, their tongues cut off; wives and daughters taking dictation from their husbands or fathers, improving and revising, in fact cowriting the epics, the sonnets, the ballads, with never a credit to their names. Generations of Anons.

To close a story, the old people back home would utter a chant. Colorín colorado, este cuento se ha acabado. This tale is done. Release the duende to the wind. But how to exorcise a story that had never been told?

With the death of the second parent, Mami and Papi's lawyer, Martillo, dubbed the Hammer by Alma and her sisters, a bilingual name swap that made them feel empowered in the face of the bureaucratic nightmare of the Dominican legal system, could now begin the long process of settling their estate. Retitling, reporting to tax authorities, submitting apostilled documents, birth certificates, passports.

The four daughters learned they had inherited a dozen or so parcels of real estate. The lots were scattered throughout the capital—wedged between office buildings, on a hillside with no street access, downtown on a busy street—nothing substantial, at most a few tareas, unfortunately no beachfront. There was also one large lot in the outskirts of the city.

According to Martillo, these little pieces of real estate were a form of currency back in the old days when people paid their bills with land, livestock, labor. Papi would remove a tumor, an appendix, save someone's crushed leg, and next thing he knew, the grateful patient would show up in the waiting room with a goat tethered outside or a campesino with his hat off would be at the back door of the house offering his services for the day, his pickaxe ready to excavate the stone pond Papi was making for the ducks another campesino had gifted him.

The sisters had never been a harmonious foursome and deciding what to do with their shared inheritance was no different. They argued about whether to sell, how much to charge, who would take on the legwork of implementing decisions. Finally, they consulted a mediator, who suggested they divide the real estate into four equal parts and be done with it.

The problem was that the parcels were assessed at different values, so how to fairly divide them? The sisters each wanted the most unloadable and best priced of the properties. At first, everyone eyed the largest of the lots, fifteen-something tareas, located outside the capital. Valuable country property, they all surmised. But it turned out that whoever greedily grabbed for it would be falling for the old childhood trick of being conned of their smaller dime by an offer of a bigger-sized nickel. The lot was worthless, Martillo told them, near the city dump, surrounded by the poorest of barrios. Overnight, the once-appealing parcel became the hot potato everyone wanted to pass on.

On the mediator's suggestion, the sisters decided to toss a coin on an online app. At first Amparo tried to discredit the app, as she didn't believe in the Internet. *How do you solve a problem like Amparo?* her sisters sang in frustration. But short of them all hopping on a plane to an agreed-upon location, which would require the kind of group cooperation that was precisely the problem, this was the best option. They would each take a turn, the winner getting the first pick. In the next round, another toss among the remaining three losers, the previous winner going to the end of the line, until all dozen lots were apportioned.

Alma won the first round. She surprised her sisters by choosing the worst lot, north of the capital. Because it was the largest, she said she would relinquish her share of the rest of the real estate.

That's not being fair to yourself, her sisters protested. They could fight to the bitter end, pulling each other's hair as children, spitting out the meanest putdowns as teens, hanging up on calls way past the age when hormones could be blamed, but let one sister go down, the others dropped everything to pick her up and attack whoever had dared break her heart.

Hey, guys, trust me, Alma assured them. This is the one I want.

But why? I thought we all agreed it was worthless.

I've changed my mind, okay?

From protectiveness, her sisters shifted to suspicion. Maybe Alma had discovered that the lot was actually worth more than the appraisal? Why else would she want a place next to the dump, surrounded by a barrio full of crime? Did she intend to move "down there," the term the sisters used for their former homeland, always accompanied by a snicker, as that had been their mother's way of referring to their private parts.

What do you want it for? her sisters would not let it go. They were in a Zoom meeting, a gallery of little frames interrogating Alma.

Look, if you guys don't trust me, then forget it! She was ready to click the *Leave the Meeting* button, but Consuelo stepped in. I'm fine with letting Alma have it. A few grumbles later, the others followed suit, and Alma was now the owner of fifteen-plus tareas of abandoned land north of the city next to the town dump.

Later that evening, Consuelo called to complain about the bickering that had ensued after Alma left the meeting with her single pick. What parcels each one had gotten. Who wasn't talking to whom. Alma was relieved not to have gotten embroiled in what she was not above hearing about. The dirt they all loved. It gave them common ground where they could sink down roots and still be a family now that Mami and Papi were gone.

So, tell me, Soul Sister, Consuelo said, digging for more dirt. What is it you *really* want that lot for?

Well, Consolation, Alma bantered back. Like I said on Zoom, I'm not really sure. Alma went on to explain that she was having all these dreams. In the latest one, she was standing in a place, lush with vegetation, a landscape that suggested the DR. A woman approached, wearing a long skirt and tunic with lots of tiny reflecting mirrors, like the outfits from India they used to wear as hippie teens that drove Mami bananas. (I'm going to Bellevue! she'd threaten, the place she'd learned was for crazy people in this country.) As this woman drew closer, Alma could see it was Scheherazade.

You mean *you*? Consuelo asked.

I guess so.

So, what did Sherryzad want?

It was almost thirty years since Alma had adopted the pen name, and her sisters still stumbled over Scheherazade. To be fair, so did most folks, a Middle-Eastern bazaar of sounds and consonants consorting and clanking with each other.

She wants me to bury my abandoned drafts. Stories I've failed to bring to life.

Ohhhkaaay . . . Consuelo said with the intonation of an aide handling a deranged person at Bellevue. But you haven't *failed*? You've published a ton of books.

Hardly a ton, but for a sister who preferred her stories in movie or gossip form, Alma's production seemed monumental. Okay, forget failure. Let's just say, she was ready for whatever adventure lay on the other side of her written narratives. Anyhow, you wanted to know why I wanted the lot? It's a place to put those stories to rest. Better not mention that she was thinking of moving there herself.

I'll pay for a storage unit if that's all you want it for.

Not the same. If Gunnar died, would you put him in a storage unit?

I'd put him in a storage unit now if I could get away with it!

Alma laughed. Ay, 'Manita. When affection brimmed over, it spilled into Spanish.

Anyhow, Soul Sister, wherever you end up, I'm counting on you to stick around and help clean up all the meltdowns. Promise you'll be careful.

There followed some horror stories Consuelo had heard from the homeland family about the increase in crime. The cousins were hiring bodyguards.

I'll be fine. It's not like I'll be tooling around in a Mercedes with a chauffeur.

Just don't break my heart and get yourself killed, Consuelo said in closing.

I'll keep that in mind when the grim reaper comes. I'll just tell him, I can't break Consolation's heart.

That's right. Tell that fucker I'm first! A new competitiveness had arisen among the sisters. Instead of who was the favorite, the prettiest, who got a window seat in the car or the aisle seat on the plane, now it was who would get to die first.

Alma went down to sign the papers on the property division and look over her lot. The fifteen-plus tareas turned out to be a mess, overgrown weeds, broken bottles, the smell of urine and feces overwhelming. Skinny mongrel dogs roamed. Across the street from the lot, a woman entering a pink-and-turquoise casita turned and waved. That was the extent of neighborliness. Mostly the barrio residents watched her, the usual Dominican friendliness on pause, probably waiting until they figured out what she was up to.

Maybe Consuelo's horror stories were not just stories. Maybe her neighbors were sizing her up like el Cuco in their childhood fairytales.

Alma forged ahead, a habit developed over years of writing. When a manuscript wasn't going anywhere, you stayed with it. You loved it into being. It worked, until it didn't.

That said, as one of a sister pack, Alma tended to be braver in plural numbers. She needed a collaborator, someone who knew the country she hadn't lived in for most of her adult life. Years ago, at one of her Dominican book presentations, she had met an artist who had approached with a large portfolio of prints, photos of her sculptures, gallery flyers, blurry copies of articles about her work. It was annoying when people at a signing didn't show consideration for those waiting on a line. But Alma knew better than to be ungracious. Most of the fans who came to these events claimed to be related to her, not a stretch on the small island.

Brava, the woman introduced herself. No last name, no claim to blood. Her work was her calling card.

Alma had fallen in love with Brava's wild and fierce creations, towering carvings and large paintings that belied their creator's petite size. But like her art, Brava's personality was larger than life, a fireball throwing off sparks. None of the anguished and torturous revisions and self-doubts that besieged Alma. Brava joyed in her work like a little kid stomping in puddles, trying to pour the ocean, cupful by cupful, into the moat surrounding her sandcastle, believing she could.

Brava's small two-room apartment was crammed with oversized canvases stretching from floor to ceiling, prints that could have wallpapered a suite of rooms, papier-mâché sculptures, whose parts had to be assembled outdoors. Alma found Brava on a ladder, detailing the fingers of a woman who was peeling back the flesh on her chest. Inside her ribs was a trapped bird, wings spread out, desperate to get out.

Brava came down from her ladder to stand beside Alma. If it hadn't been for her Afro, Brava would not have cleared Alma's shoulders. Unlike her North American friends, her Dominican friends made Alma feel normal-sized; sometimes, as with Brava, even tall. It was a good feeling to experience equality literally in the flesh, not just as an abstraction.

Alma shared what she remembered of her dreams as well as what she was vaguely planning. She needed a place to bury her unfinished work, a space honoring all those characters who had never had the chance to tell their stories. She wanted to bring them home to their mother tongue and land. What do you think? she concluded, finally looking at Brava. She had avoided glancing in her direction so as not to be deterred by an eye roll or a condescending smile.

Brava instantly got it. No need to explain, quote Yeats or the Bible, no danger of being called loca to avoid using "crazy," as if insults were okay if delivered in their native tongue. Why, oh why, couldn't Brava be her sister instead of her sisters?

Brava was already sketching on the paper spread out like a table-cloth on her worktable. I can do plaster tumbas, markers for each book, write your characters' names on them, with excerpts from your drafts, lo que tú quieras. We can bury the boxes under them. ¿Qué te parece?

I have a lot of boxes, Alma warned. It was part and parcel of being an obsessive reviser, nothing pleased her. So many characters abandoned mid-narrative because she couldn't perfectly describe the curl in their hair, the freckles in an old man's hand, or the twists and turns in a life. Sentences deserted for lack of the spot-on verb. Didn't she know art could also be forgiving?

I don't want to take you away from your own work. Alma gestured at the towering woman with the half-formed hand.

My work, your work. Querida, it's all of a piece. Brava was ready to throw herself into the deep end while Alma was still hesitating, dipping a toe into the shallow end. You'll be doing me a favor. Look at this closet. Brava gestured, the hands at the ends of those arms seemed to belong to a bigger person. I need more space for my work. For your characters, it will be un cementerio, for mine, a gallery garden.

Instead of a handshake, the two women fell into an abrazo. It was like hugging both a child and a genie stuffed in a bottle. They held on to each other until that suffocating self-consciousness set in, *You are you—I am me.* They pulled apart, laughing.

Before returning to Vermont to pack up her old life and put her house on the market, Alma needed to find a place to live. She considered asking Brava about being housemates. But two genies stuffed in one bottle would not work. Why not build a house on the property? Brava suggested. Construction was a lot cheaper here than in the States. Brava must have seen the uneasy look on Alma's face, because she added, una casita, the diminutive making the house sound reassuringly small.

But it wasn't the size of the house that worried Alma. The specter of all the kidnappings and rapes and murders that Consuelo had summoned in their phone call filled Alma's head. That was the problem with stories. Once they got in there, they were like a digital footprint, you couldn't erase them. Her cousins had hired guachimanes to protect them. Alma wouldn't be driving a Mercedes, but she was an Americana with a big dollar sign like a scarlet letter on her chest and a blue pasaporte in her satchel. Is it safe? she wondered.

Brava laughed incredulously. Mujer, who do you think lives there? The old syllogism the privileged ensconced in their gated communities often forgot. People live there. You are a person. Ergo: you can live there, too. Alma bowed her head, chastened.

Still, her style had always been to take her time, second-guess. Revise, revise, revise, as a way of life, not just writing. But borrowing Brava's bravado and contacts, Alma consulted an architect about maybe/perhaps/quizás putting a small house on the newly acquired property. Nothing fancy, something sweet and simple, like a child's drawing, a front door, a window on either side like two eyes, vividly colored walls—like the pink-and-turquoise casita with the woman waving she'd seen across the street from the property. Above it all, a perennially smiley-faced sun beaming down its blessing. See? The world is safe, the people are happy.

In the meantime, Alma asked her wealthy cousins if she could crash at their beach house. I'd only need one room for a month or so, she added, embarrassed to be imposing. As long as you want to stay, they reassured her. No big deal. We hardly ever use it. Hey, maybe you'll get inspired and write up a storm. Her familia still imagined Alma turning out a novel every other year. None of them were big readers, so they wouldn't know the difference. Her books were paperweights on their coffee tables.

Alma felt reluctant, occupying her cousins' getaway and further increasing her debt of gratitude. What could she offer in return? Her little clapboard house in Vermont would hardly meet her familia's standards, adequate perhaps for their maids and gardeners. Not to mention, she would soon be selling it.

You don't have to pay us back. We can put up a plaque at the door. Instead of "George Washington slept here," we can say our famosa prima wrote her novels here. They were proud of Alma. She had made a name for herself in the First World they all aped and aspired to. Too bad the pen name didn't rebound to their shared surname. Mami's small-mindedness had gypped la familia of a feather in its cap.

Though she didn't always agree with their politics, Alma availed herself of the perks that came with being a part of an extended family. She had grown up with the cuzzes, as she and her sisters referred to the cousins, their blood coursing in her veins, bone of her bone, flesh of her flesh, their stories circulating inside her story.

Back in Vermont, Alma was swamped by the volume of details that ending one life—while still alive and starting another—entails. Every time she'd feel an attack of panic or indecision coming on, she'd calm herself with a line from a favorite poem, *Practice resurrection.* A useful skill to master for the hereafter.

Her mind sort of made up, her bridges not burned, not Alma's style, but blocked off, Alma set up a Zoom meeting to announce to her sisters that she was indeed moving to the DR—a trial move, she hedged, so as not to start up the chorus of warnings.

Which started up anyhow. Be reasonable, her sisters argued, as if their lives were examples of that approach. Alma knew better than to point this out.

Every time we've tried going back, it never works. Piedad cited any number of instances. As Mami always said, Piedad should have studied law. Argument was her native language.

But those earlier homecomings had taken place in the thick of their lives, Alma argued back. As hippies in their jeans and peasant blouses, they didn't fit in with the "hair and nails" cousins. The oppressive poverty was demoralizing. They couldn't find jobs unless they were willing to tap the nepotism network, and what jobs they could land were as receptionists, trophy secretaries with their pale skin, fluent English, and "good hair," window-dressing up front. They had discovered that indeed they couldn't go home again. It was easier to love their dear DR from afar, preserved in memory and scented by nostalgia. An Eden they had lost and could take into therapy as a way of explaining failure, depression, mediocre marriages.

Now closing in on old age, going back to the DR no longer seemed a defeatist move, but the best option. What if?—Alma didn't want to mention the dreaded word, but—face it, two parents with dementia, one a certainty, Papi a question mark but likely—what were the odds? Alma had read and shared with her sisters a clinical study by Columbia Presbyterian doctors that found a genetic propensity for Alzheimer's among Dominican participants. All that intermarrying of cousins, trying to keep the bloodlines pure. Should Alma follow in her parents' footsteps, she'd be much better off in her native land. Even if it wasn't first rate in terms of social services, that world had been her first world: her senses, her body's rhythms, her psyche were all steeped in it. The weather, the smells, the sounds of Spanish, gestures understood without explanation. Life was also cheaper there. Her social security checks could be forwarded as well any royalties and permissions fees that might trickle in—the safety net of el Norte, should Alma's emergency-cord experiment fail.

Not to mention that Alma didn't have a passel of Stateside kids to tether her here.

You have us, her sisters argued. Don't say we didn't warn you, they added in their mother's you'll-be-sorry voice.

It's just a temporary move, Alma repeated with less assurance. They had succeeded in seeding her mind with self-doubt. Maybe she'd rent, not sell, the house in Vermont until she was sure. You can always visit, she added. Come winter, it might be nice to have a sistercation in the tropics.

Where would she host them?

Alma didn't dare breathe that she was planning to build a small house on that dangerous property. Their cuzzes had offered the old family beach house. There was plenty of room.

Alma stood her ground, albeit on shifting sand. The Zoom meeting was drawing to a close. The sisters grew quiet. The imminent parting. The end of something.

We still have no idea what you're going to do down there. Piedad would have to pick that bone again.

Jesus, give her a break. I hope you meet a really hot guy, Consuelo said, trying to put a positive spin on Alma's decision. That illusion they still clung to, that they were beautiful and young with romantic choices.

They said their goodbyes. Love you! they called to each other from their small boxes. Love you more! About that, too, they would have to compete.

The last tough call was to her literary agent. Alma informed him she was closing up shop, no longer accepting invitations to blurb, perform, or give opinions on any number of topics from the death of the novel to the importance of multicultural representation in school curriculums. She was shipping her old manuscripts to the homeland, putting them to rest there.

Her agent tried dissuading her. Alma could sell these additional boxes to the university library that bought her papers years ago. The Scheherazade Archives would want them.

Maybe they would have in the past, back when Alma was in her flush period, actively publishing book after book. Introductions at her readings often mentioned "the prolific author," a phrase that carried a whiff of the pejorative, as if fertility in female writers was a kind of indiscretion, the way her mother's family regarded the campo custom of having large families as a lack of self-control, breeding like animals, all those mouths to feed. Don't they have any sense?

TMI, she told her agent. Too much information already out there about me, my books, articles, opinions. Storytellers should learn when to shut up.

Her agent disagreed. There were young critics making their academic careers studying the multicultural boom in American literature. Scheherazade had been part of that abriendo-caminos pack. In fact, there was a pesky young professor—a Dominican-American, her agent added as bait—who was writing a book about the influence of canonical and classical texts on Latinx literature. Because of her pen name and avowed connection with the *Arabian Nights*, he wanted to interview Scheherazade about her work.

It speaks for itself, or not, Alma said. She was done. Period. Colorín colorado. End of story.

II

≈ Chismes

When activity begins on the abandoned property on the north-
ern edge of the city, the residents in the surrounding barrio wonder
what will be put there. Many fear that the land will be used to extend
the nearby landfill, where big belching trucks dump their loads of
trash: mounds of discarded wrappers, broken bottles, plastic contain-
ers, rusted cans, rotting food scraps, all heaped as high as the nearby
hills. Some days the stench is so bad, the locals are forced indoors,
shuttered inside their casitas, sweltering in the heat, burning yerba
buena and dried sábila stalks to offset the putrid smells.

Excavators and bulldozers move in, clearing and cleaning the
grounds, alongside a crew of Haitians, which signals new construction. The people breathe a sigh of relief. Rumors of what is being built
begin circulating.

One chisme has it that the place will be a resort, which would
provide employment for maids, gardeners, waiters, cooks, watchmen.
Many resorts now organize field trips to nearby barrios, the tourists
arriving in minivans loaded with supplies for projects subsidized by
their churches and clubs back home. They take selfies in front of the
new playground or clinic with the names of benefactors from Omaha,
Akron, Danville: the Herbert & Mary Lou Huntington-Maxwell
Parque Infantil, the Clínica Johansen, the Patterson Family Centro,
where teenagers can hang out, playing pool and drinking refrescos

(NO ALCOHOL ALLOWED). And once the turistas are paying attention, the politicians become more attentive to the barrios' needs. A
gaze from el Norte makes those in power more accountable.

An *inland* resort? ¡Qué ridículo! Tourists to a tropical island want
to be on the beach. More likely, the property will be turned into a
grand house, complete with a swimming pool, a tennis court, a mini
putting green, all of which require maintenance, fewer jobs than a
resort, but work for a lucky handful. Before anyone can begin planning what they will do with steady earnings, someone points out that
no rich Dominican would be fool enough to build his pleasure palace
so close to the city dump.

Better an industrial park. The new international complexes offer
enticing perks: breakfast, almuerzo, and for those on night shift, cena
at a reasonable cost; clinics and daycare for the children. Baseball
games between the employees of different companies. Pfizer versus
Johnson & Johnson, Fruit of the Loom versus Champion. There's also
the opportunity for a little skimming on the side, but you have to be
careful. No stashing a bunch of brassieres and panties in your satchel
only to be caught by the inspector at the gate. Next thing you know
you're out of a job and locked up until you've paid for the underwear
as well as the fine for stealing.

But that lot is too modest for such an extensive enterprise. So,
maybe a single factoría, with a small workforce. Rubber gaskets.
Bricks. Handbags.

Those who already have steady jobs would prefer a mall with
brightly lit shops and establishments strung along air-conditioned
corridors, punctuated with benches and bubbling fountains like an
indoor park. Piped-in music, tantalizing smells from the repostería.
A nice place to stroll down the hallways on a Saturday afternoon,
away from the heat, and window-shop the displays, if the stores don't
permit loitering inside.

A call center is another possibility. The hours are long, weekends, night shifts, as consumers insist on complaining at all hours—but the pay is decent and at least it's a desk job. The hardest thing is learning English. After a month-long training session, memorizing and practicing a list of phrases (*I do apologize for your trouble, I am so sorry for your inconvenience, Is there anything else I can do for you?*), you're hired, but with no guarantees. You can be fired if a certain percentage of callers complains that your accent is too thick or your attitude surly. Callers are easily infuriated, shouting as if their wrong-size shirt or twisted mixer blades are your fault. Worse than Dominican doñas talking to the help.

A baseball academy would be a dream come true for the tigueritos roaming the streets. Keep them out of trouble. A few might make it, become millonarios, come back and help their barrio.

After several weeks of bulldozing and clearing, a stucco wall goes up, topped, not with the broken glass or concertina wire, but with fanciful ironwork, butterflies perched atop flowers, birds taking flight, dolphins leaping into the sky. A children's theme park? A private primary school? An art academy?

The foreman seems to be the only person the locals can find to talk to them. He knows very little, but he tells them what he knows. The place is to be un cementerio.

A cemetery! Muertos and zombies roaming the streets at night, encampments of the homeless defecating behind mausoleums and burning their cooking fires on Abuelita's gravestone. And what jobs will a cemetery provide that anyone but the desperate would want? The people in the barrio may be poor but they have their pride. Insulting enough that the city dumps its trash in their backyard, without now adding to that injury with its dead.

The foreman reassures them, bunching his lips at the fanciful wall with its playful sculptures. This is not to be a run-of-the-mill cemetery, but a place of mucho respeto y orden. No riffraff, no free-loaders. As for spirits and ghosts, there'd be none of those either, as this is not to be a cemetery for people.

¿Para mascotas, entonces? Those who work as maids and gardeners know firsthand how attached the rich are to their pets. When their little dogs die, the owners mourn them more than they do other people's children. But generally, these pets are buried on the grounds of their owners' estates.

The foreman shakes his head. No, the cemetery is not for pets either.

But if not for people or animals, who is it for?

This is as much as the foreman has been told. All he knows is that he has never felt happier in a job. For the first time since he became a foreman, he pitches in, working the backhoe, removing stones alongside his Haitian crew. He leaves the job refreshed, no need to stop on the way home at the barra or colmado and pick up a bottle of ron and drown himself in forgetfulness, ignoring his mujer and swatting at his kids if they make too much noise. Instead, he converses openly with his wife and children, remembering things he has forgotten. Amorcito, his wife teases, did you eat parrot for your almuerzo today?

The owner stops by to review the progress of her project. A skinny woman with a lined face, graying hair, and an unpronounceable name that sounds like Che Guevara. Doña, he addresses her by way of avoiding it.

No doña. Just call me Alma, la doña says, shaking his hand like a man.

She is accompanied by a small, energetic woman with the easier name of Brava, about the same age but half the size of the other. One would think she is a dwarf, but all her body parts are in the right proportions, except for her large workman hands. She talks a mile a minute.

The locals continue to pester him, so the foreman decides to go ahead, phrasing his question as a community request. The people in the barrio would like to know who this cemetery will be for, if not for people or pets or toxic materials?

The owner laughs, a bright, sharp sound, which ignites the small one's laughter. Perdón, she apologizes. I don't mean to be secretive. Just that people never understand when I tell them. It's going to be a cemetery for stories.

The foreman shakes his head the way he does at the beach to get water out of his ears. Cuentos? he repeats.

The women laugh again. Yes, he has heard correctly.

Interesting, the man says, so as not to appear ignorant. Next time, someone asks, he says the cemetery is for los locos, the crazed, deranged.

But wait, aren't locos people, too?

I'm just the foreman, he shrugs.

A sign goes up on the wall at the main gate. EL CEMENTERIO DE LOS CUENTOS NUNCA CONTADOS. A cemetery for untold stories. The only way to enter is to speak into a small black box at the front gate. Cuéntame, a woman's soft voice requests. *Tell me a story.* Only then does the door open, or not.

First visitor

The first to gain entry, once the construction is done, is Filomena. She lives alone in the tidy pink casita with a turquoise trim across the street from the back of the property. During the week, the house is closed up, as she is a sleep-in caretaker for an old woman in a nice recinto in the capital. Filomena, un alma de Dios who cleans the church on her days off, is none too bright, or so it's said, as she seldom speaks. She has never married and is now on the achy side of middle age. She still maintains the slender figure of a girl, so that she often gets whistles and catcalls from strangers until she turns around and the hecklers are surprised by the lined, seasoned face.

As far as anyone knows, and the barrio prides itself on knowing everybody's business, Filomena has no living relatives, no former husband or lover who left her for another woman, no kids gone to el Norte for opportunities. It happens with women: they close down before they ever open up. Some flowers never bloom. Or bloom too soon or late in life. Only God knows why; Padre Regino has delivered several sermons on this observation.

Saturday afternoon, heading home for her day off, Filomena stops at the front gate. She doesn't know what comes over her. She looks left, right, then presses the button. A woman's voice asks for a story. Filomena is used to obeying orders. My name is Filomena, she begins. Soy Católica. I dress the saints at church. I take care of a viejita in the capital. I have a sister, Perla, in Nueva York. Tesoro, her husband, is a good-for-nothing sinvergüenza. Also, I have two nephews, Pepito and Jorge.

Filomena has run out of things to say. The gate remains locked. Obviously, what she has reported is not a story. She squeezes her eyes shut as if she could wring one out of her head. From the mango tree just outside the gate she hears a bird singing. *A little bird told me*, the old people in the campo say before sharing a juicy piece of gossip that lures even the most indifferent to listen. Maybe that's what the voice box means by a story, something more like a chisme.

Filomena recalls the story she told Perla years ago on the eve of her sister's departure with Tesoro for Nueva York. The story caused a rupture between the two sisters. Perla accused Filomena of jealousy. Her little sister was just wanting to hold on at all costs, thereby soiling Perla's chance at a better life. Don't ever talk to me again! Perla shouted. That was thirty years ago. The two sisters have not spoken since.

Perla's words sealed Filomena's mouth shut. Except for her confessions to the priest, and necessary phrases and quiet replies at work and in the daily commerce of life, Filomena has nothing to say. Did the rats eat your tongue? the locals tease her.

But now, standing in front of the gate, the rats return her tongue with interest. For the second time, she tells her story, an outpouring into the little box. Colorín colorado, este cuento se ha acabado, she closes with the incantation. Es verdad, she adds, as she doesn't want to be accused again of lying.

Lo and behold, the gate swings open.

Once inside, Filomena runs into the woman everyone calls la doña, who greets her warmly and compliments her on her story. Filomena feels emboldened to inquire. She has heard that the cemetery is not for people.

That is so. Hasn't Filomena read the sign?

Filomena is reluctant to admit her ignorance. Once people know, they dismiss her as someone not worth their while, or worse, they pity her. The daughters of her viejita have caught on, but instead of firing her, they color-code all of their mother's medications. Give Mamá a pill from the bottle with the blue mark and a spoonful of the jarabe with a red mark for breakfast, for her lunch, the yellow tablet, and on it goes, a rainbow of cures throughout the day and night.

Filomena gestures at the sculptures of birds, butterflies, a fish with a belly full of letters, bypassing the question of what is written on the sign. Is it a camposanto for animals?

It's a cemetery for stories, the woman replies.

Con su permiso, how does one bury a story?

If a story is never told, where does it go? the woman answers with a question.

The story she told her sister, where has it gone all these years of her silence? It's a question Filomena has never asked herself before.

She exits the cemetery with the shiny eyes and the ethereal smile of the santos she dresses in the church. A few neighbors have gathered outside the gate. Rumor has spread that Filomena, of all people, has gained entry.

Did you talk to la doña? Did she say who is to be buried there? What do the tombs say? Her neighbors pepper her with questions. Filomena is not about to admit to them either that she can't read. All she will say is that there are boxes everywhere, filled as far as she can tell with papers. She does not confess, lest her neighbors think her possessed, that as she strolled the pebbled walks, she was accosted at every turn by voices, young, old, rich, poor, male, female, telling tales.

≈ Nothing stands in the way

Every time someone catches sight of Alma's pickup entering the cemetery, the word goes out. A crowd gathers at the gate waiting for la doña's exit. A few intrepid ones approach the intercom. *Tell me a story.*

A little bird told me. Había una vez. Cuentan los viejos. Some scandal on the news, who is sleeping with whom, what fulano has done or said to fulana, a juicy chisme, a hot rumor, or a telenovela storyline (this last one never seems to work).

The moment the gates open, the petitioners surge forward, bodies pushing, jostling, claiming to be first, surrounding the pickup. The shouting starts, ¡Doña! ¡DOÑA!, as if a job will be offered to whomever hollers the loudest. I need work! Por favor, doñita.

The locals have persisted in calling her doña. The pen name has proved to be impossible with its entangling syllables and tongue-twisting consonants. Call me Alma, she keeps telling them, just plain Alma, please.

Have pity on me! a toothless half-drunk man pleads. I have eight mouths to feed.

Eight mouths, yes, but one mouth drinks up all he earns, a neighbor snarls, necessity also being the mother of meanness.

Each time they accost her, Alma explains she doesn't need a work crew. When the time comes, she'll hire someone to keep an eye on things, weed and sweep the paths, scrub the bird shit off the tomb-sculptures. No need for that, Brava intervenes, dismissing Alma's squeamishness. The birds are just "baptizing" her work.

Alma laughs, relishing her friend's playfulness. A groundswell of yearning draws her to the other woman. Is this what she would have been like had her family stayed in their homeland? Some innate sense of safety and belonging, which releases the duende to frolic and create. In fact, Brava reminds Alma of her younger self, before she ever thought of publication, when she relished writing for its own sake, before her career took off and she got the fame her writer friend warned her about. Maybe this new project will return her to that core self—the psychological task of old age, according to sisters Amparo and Piedad, both former therapists and experts on all matters psychological. More likely, Alma will just grow old, too worn out to keep surmounting whatever lowly self or emptiness lies at her core.

Brava sees something else in her friend's future. Alma is a storyteller in her bones. Don't let anyone tell you otherwise. Brava jerks her head in the direction of el Norte. What? You're only a storyteller if *they* say so? Remember when we were girls in Catholic school and the only books we could read had to have the bishop's imprimatur, *Nihil Obstat*, "Let it be printed. Nothing stands in the way"? Remember how boring they were? Books don't always tell the best stories. It's why Brava never became a reader. She much preferred sitting at Abuelita's knees, listening and drawing pictures with a stick in the dirt of the characters in her grandmother's cuentos. Word of mouth, Radio Bemba, was her library.

Doesn't that count? Brava challenges. Or is a story untold just because it isn't published?

Well, if it's not written and not published, it'll die with its teller. Alma thinks of all those poems claiming immortality, and in a way, it's true. Here she was reading and teaching them to the next and the next generation. That's why in certain tribes they say when an old person dies, a library is gone.

But the stories get passed on, Brava is quick to rebut. Las ciguapas, la Vieja Belén, Juan Bobo, Brava lists her favorites, stories coated with Mami's milk, punctuated by Abuelita's cachimbo coughs, known, remembered, beloved on a cellular level, long before Alma ever wrote them down.

☙ Fire hazard

The boxes of unfinished novels and stories are stacked in discrete piles covered with plastic tarps throughout the cemetery. Alma's original idea was to bury them intact, but she decides to burn them instead. More final that way: a period, not an iffy ellipsis, at the end of her writing career.

Alma enlists the woman who gains access every time she tells a story at the gate to help with the burning and burying. Filomena, right?

Sí, señora, the woman murmurs shyly. Para servirle.

Most of the boxes catch fire, crackling and sending up sparks, as if the flames are hungry for stories, even unfinished ones. The stories are released, their characters drifting off to the sea, to the mountains, into the dreams of the old and the unborn, seeping into the soil. A lucky few find their way into books by other writers. Sometimes the fragments are blown back, liberated from their plots. Stray lines and déjà-vu faces.

But neither the Papi nor Bienvenida boxes will burn. It's a sign, though Alma can't say of what. Now that she's given up writing, the world is a clutter of chaotic details—stories, stories, so many stories, and Alma has nowhere to put them except in the ground.

Brava is used to working with different materials. Those particular boxes are probably made of a coated, waxy cardboard that's not as flammable. She suggests they pull out the individual folders and set fire to the drafts piecemeal. But Alma hesitates.

Maybe because these two were her last failed attempts, she isn't yet ready to let them go. Papi and Bienvenida are hunkering down in Alma's imagination, insisting on their stories being told.

Instead of burning their folders, the three women dig two deep holes and line the excavations with garbage bags, burying Papi's boxes first, and then Bienvenida's. When they are done, Filomena kneels at Papi's site and makes the sign of the cross, calling on el Barón to bless this holy ground.

Alma pulls Brava aside. What's going on?

El Barón is the boss of cemeteries, Brava explains. The deity who allows passage between the worlds. The first tomb always belongs to him. Brava recounts a story she heard a few years back. A new cemetery opened, and there were two deceased persons scheduled to be buried that day. Neither family wanted their loved one to be first as that would mean devotees of el Barón would be breaking in to conduct their ceremonies on their beloved's tomb. One of the families actually paid the driver of their hearse to fake a flat tire, so the other hearse got there first. Although this isn't a real cementerio, the rules apparently still apply. People have their stories. Hay que respetarlos.

The other boxes are almost done burning—smoldering piles of ashes to be buried under the signature sculptures Brava has designed for each one. Ghostly plumes lift above each spot, some dark and stormy, others pearly gray, a pinkish-hued one here, a bloody gush above the marker shaped like a machete.

Down the street in his colmado, the shopkeeper Bichán sniffs the air, steps outside and sees the smoke rising from the other side of the wall. He phones los bomberos, and soon, firetrucks pull up at the gates, the firemen ready to axe the door down, as the intercom won't accept their barked orders as a story. Alma lets them in, but by this time there's nothing left for them to put out, only clumps of ashes, a few stray sparks, which the women instantly stamp out.

The captain is shaking his head in disbelief. What are you doing here? Before the women can answer, he informs them, You can't do this!

It's just trash, Brava asserts.

We're being very careful, Alma adds, holding up the fire extinguisher she and Brava brought along. The captain keeps shaking his head as he fills out a citation. It turns out they need a permit.

Where does one obtain a permit?

The captain is glancing around at the strange shapes. What is this place anyhow?

If they confess, the captain will probably tell them they need a permit for a cemetery and give them another citation. Brava flashes Alma a look. *Let me handle this.* I'm an artist, Brava says. This happens to be my showroom. My clients come here to view my creations and order from these models. She rattles off a bunch of her credentials, prizes she has won, exhibits featuring her work. The captain is not impressed. Rules are rules. They still need un permiso.

Okay, Brava changes tack. She proposes a "solution." Can we just purchase the permit from you?

The captain's face sharpens with self-interest. He orders his men to wait for him outside in the air-conditioned trucks. A welcome order. They are suited up in rubber boots, Kevlar jackets, helmets: a portable sauna bath. Sweat is pouring down from all their faces. Fighting fires in the tropics is no joke.

The captain sizes up the two women, one in sweatpants and a T-shirt, the other in a cotton tunic and flowing pants, an Americana to be sure. The price of permits is climbing. Forty dollars, he quotes, watching their faces, ready to give them a discount should they balk.

Brava is about to protest, but Alma steps in. Will the permit cover any more fires we might set? Just in case she decides to burn the Papi and Bienvenida drafts.

The man firms up his face: he has fish on the line. Absolutely, a forever permit. He smiles, flashing a mouthful of gold-capped teeth, and pocketing the bills. In the future, so as not to run into problems each time they're going to be burning, they should alert los bomberos. He'll send a fireman over to supervise. In fact, one of his men lives right in this area. Florian. For a small propina for his cigarettes, Florian will keep an eye on any fire.

The captain spots Filomena patting down the mound under which the Papi boxes are buried. He bunches his lips, lifting his chin, the Dominican way of pointing, Alma has noted. Filo work for you?

Alma hesitates in case the man might levy another penalty, for hiring a local under the table. She's just helping out. Why do you ask?

She knows Florian, don't you, Mami? The captain winks at Filomena who scowls back.

Once the trucks have left, Alma asks Filomena if she indeed knows the local fireman. Yes, doña. Florian lives next door to her casita. The guarded look on Filomena's face suggests a story is being withheld.

Alma wonders but does not ask what the woman will not say. In time, it will probably come out. She has been piecing together Filomena's story from the tales she tells at the gates.

⁓ Filomena and Perla

Before moving to the capital, Filomena and Perla lived up in the campo with their father in a wooden casita consisting of a large room in front and two side-by-side rooms in back—Papá's room and their room with the double bed they shared. The roofed kitchen with its wood-burning fogón was out the back door, and down a well-trod path, the latrine. The house sat on a small plot their father claimed was his, but he had nothing in writing. Any day a big-man tutumpote might show up in a fancy SUV with a deed their father couldn't read and a revolver to enforce his claim of ownership.

The two sisters were eleven and sixteen when their father died. Their mother had already been gone for years, disappearing one night while Papá was off on one of his wild parrandas. Filomena, the younger sister, had been six at the time. Whenever she'd ask about her mother, Papá would say Mamá had died. If Filomena persisted in her questions, her father would threaten a beating and, if he'd been drinking, give her one. Filomena learned not to ask, hiding the few of her mother's belongings her father had not trashed in a cigar box under her mattress.

You better not let Papá catch you with that, Perla warned. She, too, refused to talk about their mother. Only after their father died did Perla admit the truth. Mamá had not died but taken off to seek her fortune en la capital.

So, they weren't total orphans after all! Filomena felt a rush of joy. Remember that time Mamá came to say goodbye and promised to come back? Why did you say it was just a stupid dream? Why didn't you tell me the truth then?

And get beaten? Perla's frown was as big as the world. Filomena couldn't bear upsetting her big sister, who was both mother and best friend. Don't you remember how Papá got every time you brought her up?

But why didn't Mamá take us with her?

¡Ya! Perla yanked extra hard as she braided her little sister's hair. When Filomena yelped, Perla quoted the familiar saying, El que quiere moño bonito que aguante jalones.

Why should it hurt to look pretty? Perla wouldn't say. She was like that, rain and shine at the same time.

Where in the capital could their mother be? And why hadn't she come back like she promised? Every time Filomena forgot and started in on her questions, Perla would shut her up.

Someday, Filomena promised herself, she would go to the capital with her sister and find their mother.

After Papá's death, the sisters managed to keep up with his conuco, the neighbors lending a hand, planting plátanos, víveres, habichuelas, enough to feed them both and still have something to barter at the colmado for whatever else they needed. During harvest season, the girls earned a little money working in the larger fincas, picking coffee. They had sold off the ox team to pay for Papá's funeral and kept what was left in an old sock stowed under the mattress por si acaso. Between them, they owned a handful of work clothes, chancletas they washed and propped up in the sun to dry, their father's work boots for clomping into the fields, and a couple of dresses and a pair of closed shoes each for going to church or the nearby town. You didn't need much if your ambitions were as small as your means, which was the case for Filomena. But Perla had been born with richer endowments than her younger sister, so naturally, she had bigger expectations.

The sisters looked alike, same basic features, but with the slight tweaks and refinements that made one face pretty and the other less so, one head a cascade of curls, and the other a knotted bird's nest. Perla was a beauty with a womanly shape that elicited clever piropos, each young man vying to outdo the other, as if they were all troubadours in a court competing for the princess's hand.

So many curves and my brakes are shot!

Did it hurt when you fell from heaven, angel?

The old people in the campo often commented that Perla was the spitting image of her mother, a compliment Perla bristled at. She did not appreciate looking like esa sinvergüenza, who had abandoned her family, leaving her two young daughters behind with a violent father.

Ay, Perla, she's still our mother. A mother who, in Filomena's dreams, wore her older sister's face.

⟳ Elections

Every election cycle, politicians and their followers came up the mountain in their pickups and Jeepetas, proclaiming how their party would help the campesinos. The locals accepted the bottles of ron, packets of cigarrillos, sheets of zinc emblazoned with the names of the candidates. In exchange, they promised to vote purple or red or green—whichever party offered the best perks. On election day, these campaigners returned with a belching bus to ferry everyone down to the municipal trailer, reminding them of the color to vote for. Inside, their right forefingers were dipped into a jar of indelible ink that wouldn't wash off for days, so unless a man was fool enough to cut off his finger, he couldn't get away with casting a second vote.

One Saturday afternoon, Perla and Filomena joined other vecinos in front of the colmado, to hear the bombast and blasting music and collect the free baseball caps and notions that were being handed out. They still couldn't vote, as Perla was only seventeen and Filomena had just turned twelve. But up in the mountain villages, without television or movies or nightclubs or stores, any diversion was welcome. Walking back home in their church dresses, sporting their new red baseball caps, they were tailed by one of the young men who'd been manning the noisy speakers mounted on the flatbed of the camioneta.

Oye, mamacita, he called after them. They ignored him, holding tight to each other's hands. Ay, angel, don't be like that. My soul needs salvation!

Perla kept walking, her chin at a dignified angle, yanking her sister's hand every time Filomena twisted her head to look back at the pesky young man.

Do you have an extra heart? he pleaded.

The sisters had attended school sporadically whenever el profesor came up the mountain. Unlike Perla, who had learned a little more as the teacher was more patient with pretty girls, Filomena had never learned to read and write. But she knew a few things, and one of them was that every person was born with two eyes, two ears, two hands, but only one heart. Didn't the young man know that? She turned around to inform him that what he was asking for was impossible.

I'm going to die, he wailed like a hurt child. I can't live without a heart.

Filomena glanced down at his shirt to check. There were no stains on the pristine guayabera.

Perla had swiveled around, ready to give the man a withering look and scold her gullible little sister. But the young man flashed her a billboard smile, ear to ear, a dimple holding down each side of his mouth. Pale skin and bootblack hair and thick lashes, eyes like two shiny pebbles at the bottom of a river.

Please angel, do you have an extra heart?

Perla drew herself up, her hands akimbo. Why are you asking me that?

Because someone seems to have stolen mine, he replied, doubling his assault by winking an eye as well as flashing his dimpled smile again.

¡Vámonos! Perla ordered, hauling her sister away.

Filomena knew Perla's tones and moods as if they were her own. Her sister was only pretending to be cross. That night when they were both in the bed, Perla got up to shoo away an intruder who was pelting their shuttered windows with pebbles. Filomena heard her sister unlatch the front door and whack at the bushes with a broom. A while later, Filomena heard her sister in the main room and called out, Is everything all right?

Yes, yes, just a big rat. Now go back to sleep.

Early morning when Filomena woke, a faint light seeped in through the window slats. She was alone in bed and whispers were coming from their father's former room, now used for storage, on the other side of the wall.

The rat's name was Tesoro, and he began to pursue Perla. Weekends, he'd arrive from the capital, his pickup stocked with beer, rum, a cooler with ice, as well as gifts for Perla: scented talcos in round boxes with fluffy powder puffs; cheap perfumes in tiny doll-sized bottles that made the whole house smell like a garden; skimpy underwear that didn't cover anything. The storage room was converted into a lover's nest with a pink mosquitero hanging from a hook in the ceiling, tied up with a pink sash during the day. All week, Perla talked of nothing else but Tesoro, reminiscing about the previous weekend: what Tesoro had said, how handsome he looked, what he had given her. The minute he stepped in the door, it was as if Filomena had disappeared. She was forlorn and jealous at being replaced as the focus of her sister's attention.

After supper, and sometimes before, the lovers headed to their nest, hand in hand, a hand, Perla's, that for years had been only Filomena's to hold.

You can't go in there, Filomena would protest. It's Papá's room!

Perla would glare at her. Papá is dead. He doesn't need a room.

From then on, Filomena avoided the storage room, even when she needed to retrieve a tool or a cup of sugar—though soon all these supplies had migrated into what had now become just her room.

There was really nothing wrong with Tesoro. He brought Filomena gifts, too, but she tossed them aside, refusing to be won over. She had recently turned señorita, and those days of her menses, she malingered in bed, complaining of cramps, moaning like a woman in labor, hoping her sister would call down to the capital from the colmado, canceling weekend plans. She sulked, accusing Perla of just thinking about herself, whereas Filomena would give up anything for her sister. She had even let her big sister have her own name. Filomena hadn't been the one who decided this, as she'd just been a newborn when it happened. But she had heard the story so often that she was convinced she actually remembered it.

Their mother had chosen the name Perla for her second daughter, but the older sister wanted it as her own. She pouted and stomped her foot until her mother finally agreed to an exchange. The first child had already been registered as Filomena, the second as Perla, but what difference did it make what a document said? In their house and around the campo, the eldest became known as Perla and the youngest as Filomena. This was nothing strange: the people in the campo often used chosen names that had nothing to do with their formal legal ones.

If you're going to be that way, then I want my name back! Filomena threatened her sister.

No way Perla was going to give up her precious name. She had become even more attached to it now that Tesoro called her his pearl of great price.

I am the world's richest man!

And you are mi tesoro.

All kissy, kissy—disgusting! They headed for the bedroom, leaving Filomena to clean up, crying into the dishwater, and later into her pillow. Except for Papa Dios, she was nobody's treasure. Everyone in the world had deserted her.

≈ A proposal

One weekend, Tesoro surprised Perla by inviting her to come live in his house in the capital. Perla was thrilled. This was indeed a welcome sign as Tesoro was always so vague about his plans whenever Perla brought up their future, talking instead of his dream of emigrating to Nueva York. Some weekends he didn't show up, and if she complained on a subsequent weekend, he'd threaten to leave.

Perla had broached the idea of marriage, as she would soon be eighteen, the age by which girls in the campo were either officially married or married in the common-law way of living with a man—like her own mother with her father—or they began to be devalued as jamonas. A pretty woman's value lasted a little longer, but not by much. Most men preferred very young girls who were more likely to be virgins and could serve as their caretakers in old age. Perla had always dreamed of a church wedding, a ring on her finger, a long flowing gown like a princesa. Joining Tesoro in the capital was a first step toward that dream.

So, we'll get married there, right? You love me, mi tesoro, don't you? she persisted when he didn't answer right away. You are mi tesoro, aren't you?

Of course, he responded, pulling on his ear, a tick Perla found endearing.

What about Filo, though?

What about her?

I can't leave her behind. Can she come too?

Sure, Tesoro said, shrugging. As the only boy in his family, he was used to being surrounded by females. The more the merrier.

Perla had a harder time convincing Filomena. She wasn't going. She was staying in the campo.

A young girl alone in an empty house, olvídate! Viejos verdes were already sniffing around, as if these dirty old men could tell la señorita had begun menstruating.

Perla tried enticing her stubborn little sister. Do it for me, 'manita, por favor. Just think: you can go to a good school in the capital. Filomena had a curious mind and liked learning things, if she wasn't shamed for not already knowing them in the first place, the pedagogical style of the few profesores who made it up to the local escuelita, a roof over a packed dirt floor, no walls or budget. It's why Filomena had never learned to read or write—the bullying and scorn had convinced her she was una bruta.

Perla tried another tack. She knew about the longing in her sister's heart. In the capital, they might be able to locate tu mamá, as if she weren't Perla's mother, too. Perla could not bring herself to call "that woman" Mamá.

Abracadabra! Filomena ceded to her sister's will. They closed up their casita and the following Sunday, they were off, dressed in their church dresses, fresh and scented like two picked flowers, their belongings in paper sacks crammed in the back seat next to Filomena.

They called to their neighbors as they drove away, ¡Abur, abur! the old way of saying adiós.

En route to the capital, Tesoro disclosed that they would all be living in his parents' house, along with his three older sisters. He was the only son. Por eso soy su tesoro, he added, dimpling up. And actually, his mother needed help with the household.

Perla wondered why with three grown daughters, his mother would need more help. Maybe the sisters had important jobs outside the house. Maybe they were handicapped in some way. We'd love to help, Perla volunteered them both. Right, 'manita? she called to the back seat where her sister sat, sullen and silent, gazing out the window, a bored look on her face, as if a ride in a vehicle were not an unusual thing for her. We know how to do everything in a house, Perla boasted, filling up the silence. Cook and clean and keep a garden.

That's why you're my pearl, Tesoro said winningly.

Filomena sighed audibly from the backseat, thinking, You stole that pearl from me.

The family lived in a nice development, across from a small park full of shade trees and twittering birds. The house itself was not so grand as to be daunting like the properties they had passed on the avenida, large mansions surrounded by high walls, topped with glass shards or concertina wire, guards standing watch at the front gate. Tesoro's was a modest house made of blocks with a trellis of brightly colored bougainvillea up front. They pulled in under the carport, Tesoro announcing his arrival by honking his horn. The front door opened and out poured his sisters, followed by a sweet-faced older woman. How was the trip? Was he tired? Was he hungry? Had he run into any trouble? They sure made a fuss over him.

The sisters acknowledged the two young women with sober nods, looking them over, as if evaluating a purchase they were about to make. When Perla leaned forward to give her future in-laws a kiss of greeting, they drew back as if the young woman had overstepped her place. No one asked for their names. I'm Perla, she offered, hoping Tesoro would add that this pearl was his treasure. But he stood there, grinning and awkward, as if unsure what to do. Of course, city people were different from the campesinos they were used to. No problem. Perla was determined to learn the new ways that would allow her to fit in with a better class of people.

Lena, the oldest, seemed to be the sister in command. Let me show you to your room, she said briskly. Perla glanced over at Tesoro with a puzzled look on her face. She had assumed that, as in her casita, they would be sharing a bed. But that's right, this was his parents' house. The young couple would have to wait until they were officially married to sleep together openly. Perla hoped the wedding would be soon, as she had missed a third period, and some mornings she couldn't keep anything down. She was waiting to tell Tesoro until they were settled in their new life. She had heard stories of men bolting when they learned their girlfriends were in a family way.

They're so young, Perla overheard the mother commenting, as she and Filomena followed Lena inside.

Ay, Mami, remember, they're strong girls from the campo. They know how to work hard.

Perla didn't dwell on the comment. She had so much else to pay attention to as Lena led them down a dark hallway, past the family bedrooms, into and out of the dining room, through the indoor kitchen—an indoor kitchen!—into an outdoor patio, with a laundry room—a machine to do the washing!—and a dark, stuffy room with two tiny windows, eye level, a bunk bed against the wall, a stand-alone cabinet closet, a shelf above a sink, and a small bathroom with a toilet and shower.

Lena gestured toward the closet. When you've unpacked, just come back into the kitchen and I'll show you where everything is. Papi will be home from his farmacia soon, and he likes his supper early.

She was about to leave but turned back. Almost forgot, she said, opening the closet door and pulling out two beige dresses with white collars and cuffs. See how these fit. They might be too big, but we can have them taken in.

We have our own clothes, Filomena spoke up for the first time. Perla had suddenly gone silent.

Lena tilted her head to one side; she, too, was beginning to understand. These girls had no idea that they were the new maids. The previous maids had taken off with the cash and jewelry their absentminded mother had left lying on her dresser.

Back in the front of the house, Lena confronted her brother in the hallway. Her mother and sisters were waiting for Papi in the galería where it was cooler. What did you tell those girls?

Her brother pulled on his right ear, always a sign he was about to lie. I told them the truth that Mami needed help.

What else? As the oldest, Lena was the only one of the sisters who dared defy the scion of the house.

How was he supposed to disentangle what untruths he had mixed with the truth? And really, the truth was complicated. He had told Perla he loved her; he would marry her "someday"; he had promised that the younger one could go to a school in the capital. Peel all these half-truths back and the full truth was that he wanted sex without having to drive up the mountain every weekend, missing all the fun of hanging out with his friends. And Mami did need help. And he did truly have a tender spot in his heart for Perla, for both sisters, for anyone vulnerable and hurting in general. Those poor girls are orphans, Lena, poorer than Papi was growing up. They need the money, even if they're too proud to say so.

Lena suppressed a smile at her charming scoundrel of a brother, then headed for the kitchen to orient the new maids.

≈ Hacer de tripas corazón

When his father found out the young maid was carrying Tesoro's son—an ultrasound had revealed the tiny erection—¡Epa! a macho even in the womb!—Don Pepe insisted Tesoro marry the mother. No grandson of his was going to be born a bastard. He himself had been the product of a husband taking a fancy to the young maid, who had subsequently been turned out of the house. He and his mother had endured some tough years, memories that Don Pepe would recount with tears in his eyes. An innocent child should not have to pay the price of parental indiscretions.

Once the baby was born, Tesoro could do whatever he wanted, divorce the mother, go off to Nueva York, overstay his visitor's visa, marry a gringa, sire babies who couldn't tolerate the hot sun or speak the mother tongue. But this baby, whom Don Pepe claimed as his much more ardently than its own father, this first grandson would be brought up under his roof, a legitimate heir to the small business Don Pepe had struggled all his life to build.

For years Don Pepe had hoped and prayed for grandchildren, mis nietos he called them, as if they were debts his children owed to him. Over time, it became obvious that his daughters were not going to oblige. Now in their late twenties, they were chaste as nuns, and God forgive him, plain as puré de papa. All the good looks unfortunately had gone to the boy in the family, who, given his playboy ways, was never going to settle down. His wife had spoiled their son from day one. Tesoro didn't seem to be very interested in holding down a job. He had no concept of earning his wages with the sweat of his brow— as if the Bible didn't apply to him. He had said no to working at Don Pepe's farmacia. No to becoming a professional. No to anything but politics, which allowed him to strut and drink and sleep around. But in this last election, his partido had lost, so Tesoro's chances of getting a plush government job had vanished. El Norte was probably the best option; maybe the gringos would settle him down.

As for his grandson's mother, Perla could probably be persuaded to let her son be raised in a family where he'd have more opportunities. Young and pretty, she could remake her life. And if she wanted to stay on with her sister, who was turning out to be the hard worker of the two, all the better. They could both help with the household and with bringing up the boy.

You don't even have to continue to live together, his father counseled Tesoro. You can get your divorce there, those gringos dissolve marriages at the drop of a hat.

Papi was funding the Nueva York venture, and since he who pays the perico ripiao calls the tune, Tesoro was forced to comply. As a sign of her changed status with marriage and a baby in the works, Perla was permitted to move into the house proper, to Tesoro's bedroom. When she grew so big-bellied that sex became untenable, Tesoro headed for the maid's quarters in the back of the house, where the younger sister now slept alone. What was the harm? He thought of them as two versions of the same person. You're both my pearls, he wooed the young girl. Filomena resisted at first but finally gave in. More than anything she wanted her big sister's devoted attention, and barring that, she wanted what Perla had, a boyfriend, a baby, someone to love who would love her back.

The next morning there was blood on the sheets as if she was having her period again, though it wasn't time. Maybe something had gotten torn down there? Perhaps it wouldn't hurt so much when she was older? She had just turned thirteen so she didn't know much about it. There was only one person to ask, but of course, she couldn't talk to Perla.

Perla's and Tesoro's marriage took place a few weeks shy of the baby's birth. A civil ceremony, Tesoro had insisted, easier to dissolve than a church wedding, the Catholics being sticklers about what God had joined together let no man pull asunder. Perla was none too happy about getting married in an office. But Tesoro assuaged his pouting bride by presenting her with a sparkly ring and by promising they'd have a fancy church wedding later once he was earning his own money and could do it up real nice. Tesoro's sisters and mother would also have preferred a church ceremony, but God knows what He does—and this was a way to avoid commentaries about a bride in a white gown with her stomach out to there. Maybe the priest could come by later and give his blessing?

José Tesoro Pérez, named in honor of his father and grandfather, Pepito for short, was born the very day Tesoro's visa came through. ¡Mi buena suerte! His good-luck boy. Tesoro wasted no time. Within the week, he was on a plane to Nueva York.

Perla was tragic over her abandonment, as she called it. She cried and wheedled and begged to join him. ¿Tú 'ta loca, mujer? Didn't she know he was planning to overstay his visitor's visa and work his tail off for his new familia? A newborn would make their undocumented lives all the harder. But as the months went by, Tesoro grew lonely for his Perla, his sex, his tasty meals; he was more than ready for her to join him.

From his compadres at work, he learned that there was a shortcut to getting your papers: you could pay a willing American to marry you. Once your green card came through, you divorced and colorín colorado, end of story: you were legal. He presented the plan to Perla.

Perla did not like the idea one bit of marrying other people.

It's pretend, mujer. Everyone does it. Pero cuidao. You better not fall in love with your Americano and leave your old man.

How little he knew her! Perla would rather kill or die than lose her treasure.

Don Pepe agreed to finance Perla's trip north with a caveat: little Pepito would stay behind with his grandparents "until you are settled," was the way he put it. The old man reasoned that two youngsters with no family up in el Norte would be home inside a couple of years.

He was not to live to see that day. When Don Pepe died, Pepito was already four years old with a baby brother he had never met and parents with newly acquired green cards. They came down with a toddler, George Washington, to bury the old man, pick up their son, and take him back to the good life they had managed allá.

It was Filomena's turn to be tragic—her one consolation after her sister's departure had been the little boy, whom she loved more than anything. She had hoped that she, too, would have a baby, thereby giving Pepito a cousin-half-brother, but she had not been as lucky as Perla. After the baby's birth, Tesoro had stopped coming around. Nuestro secreto, he called it. Filomena had kept her mouth shut because she soon had her little Pepito to love.

Now, in her desperation, Filomena told her sister the truth, not so much to end Perla's marriage, but to keep the boy with her. It had all backfired. Tesoro denied it, pulling on both his ears. On his father's grave, he swore. Perla was in a rage. Filomena was thrown out of the house, with no place to go, their parcela in the campo having been taken over by a rich landowner, who came with papers and a revolver to prove it was his. To avoid an ugly scene, he had paid off the sisters, then had torn down their casita, building himself a big block house with a barbed wire fence and a mean police dog paroling the grounds.

Filomena would have been homeless. But after Tesoro and Perla departed with their boys, his sisters begged Filomena to come back. Their mother's dementia was manifesting in a deep attachment to the young maid. Filomena resigned herself to what she could not change. Hacer de tripas corazón, as the saying goes, making the best out of the worst. That's all she could do.

With her savings from her salary and her share of the settlement for the campo property, Filomena looked around for a house she could afford, a home base for her days off and her final years once she got too old and weary to work. She found one near the town dump, a little casita that reminded her of the houses in her campo. A home for when Pepito would be returned to her, something she fervently prayed for.

Even as the years passed, Filomena held on to her hopes of a reunion. In all her dreams Pepito was always a little boy, with his hair freshly combed and tamped down, dressed in his starched preschool uniform, talcum puffing out from under his little white shirt when she hugged him goodbye. When Perla and Tesoro would bring him on their once-a-year visits, the sisters would first send Filomena on her vacaciones. Nuestro secreto, they called it, echoing their brother. A family of secrets.

In the emptiness left behind by the boy's departure and the estrangement from her sister, Filomena rekindled her yearning to find their mother. That had been the enticement Perla had used to lure Filomena to the capital, but once the sisters were ensconced in Tesoro's house, Perla showed no interest in pursuing a search. Filomena had soon been distracted herself by the birth of Pepito and his subsequent care.

But now, the hole in her heart had opened again, and she had to fill it with someone else to love.

Filomena turned to Bichán for help. The colmado owner knew how things worked in the world. He'd have some ideas.

She waited for a time when the store was empty to avoid tongues wagging. Bichán shrugged discouragingly. If a person goes missing it's for a reason. Don't disturb a wasp nest. He himself had been dumped in a garbage can in the middle of the city. It's a good thing he hadn't ended up as landfill in the dump. A kind soul had rescued him and deposited the squalling infant at the Jesuits' door.

Filomena's shoulders fell; she turned to go.

Pero . . . Bichán added, a *but* that made Filomena pivot. You could look this person up in the telephone book. Who did you say you were searching for? The barrio gossip was that Filomena didn't have a living relative. .

Nadie, I was just asking.

Bichán snorted. At the end of the day, every secret in the barrio would end up being told to him. He was a master of interrogation. The Jesuits who raised him always said he would make either a good secret agent or confessor. Here's the book, he said, setting the thick volume on the counter. Of course, cells aren't listed, then again, this person might have a telephone.

But how could Filomena look up her mother in a book when she didn't know how to read? Instead of divulging more to Bichán, who was already peppering her with questions, she decided to enlist Doña Lena's help, saying she was searching for a distant relative who had moved to la capital. She was too ashamed to confess the truth, as if it were the child's fault to be abandoned by its mother. Doña Lena tried, bless her heart, a dozen wrong numbers, before she had to concede defeat. There were hundreds if not thousands of Altagracias, and Almonte, Mamá's surname, was a common one.

Over the years, Filomena became resigned to the crumbs of love. She kept up with Pepito's doings through the stories she heard from Lena and her sisters. After an initial difficult time adjusting and missing his abuelita and his tías—most especially Filomena—the boy had settled down, learned English, made friends. He was a good student, earning a scholarship to a university. ¡Qué orgullo! She had stolen one of the framed photos on the sideboard of Pepito at his graduation in his cap and gown, a theft she repeatedly confessed to Padre Regino, regularly saying her penance, but unable to return the loot. Finally, the old priest absolved her completely—saying God had forgiven her and probably the sisters had forgotten it was missing.

During one confession, Filomena asked Padre Regino if God indeed meant it when He said, Seek and ye shall find?

God always keeps his promises, Padre Regino assured her. But we have to wait until He decides it is time. And remember, he who has faith has everything. As the Bible teaches, that is the pearl of great price.

His mention of *pearl* brought tears to Filomena's eyes.

Filomena had lost her Perla, her Pepito, her mother, her father, but she had her faith! And what a sinvergüenza, that Tesoro, stealing Jesus's own words to woo her big sister!

But God in His great kindness had also given Filomena her vie-jita to care for like her own mother. She fussed over the old woman, painting her nails and toenails, combing and bobby-pinning her hair, feeding her the fruit compotes she loved. If the weather was nice, no threatening rain or torrid heat, Filomena would take her viejita across the street to the small park to visit and feed the birds. Doña Lena often commented that her mother treated Filomena more like a daughter than her very own.

That's where they were sitting that last afternoon. It was a breezy March day—chichigua weather, when children so enjoy flying their homemade kites. Filomena was thinking maybe they should head inside when she heard a strange sound, not a bird, more like the scratching of a blown branch on the cement walk. It turned out to be the old woman's death rattle. Filomena raced the wheelchair back into the house, but it was too late: like a chichigua whose string you lose hold of, her viejita's soul had blown away.

Guardian angel

The last of the ashes from the burnt drafts have been buried; a stick marks the spot where each of Brava's sculptures will go. The Papi and Bienvenida boxes have long been buried, their sculptures in place, Papi's globe requiring the services of a glassblower. Alma gazes at her friend's handiwork wistfully. If only she still had the duende necessary for making the characters in her head as vital and real as Brava's fanciful creations.

Attracted by rumors about the marvels within, locals begin sneaking in at night when the box is turned off, using the cover of darkness and Florian's fire-ladder, which he rents out for a small fee. If they can't get in with a story at the gate during listening hours, they'll find another way. Like the tigueritos at the autocine, climbing fences, scaling walls to watch the dinosaurs devour trees in *Parque Jurásico* or the beautiful Salma Hayek as Minerva get murdered by the SIM in *En el Tiempo de las Mariposas*.

The problem is, these trespassers take whatever is left lying around: garden equipment, the papier-mâché doves perched on one of the sculptures, Alma's water bottle. They dig holes where Alma and Brava have buried the ashes, convinced there is treasure there. They relieve themselves on the statues. One morning, the two women find the Papi and Bienvenida boxes torn open, pages strewn about like politicians' leaflets during election season.

Brava recommends a guard dog, but that would keep Alma away, too. She panics whenever a four-legged creature comes bounding toward her, even if its tail is wagging and its owner calling out, Don't worry, he's never bitten anyone. There's always a first time, Alma hollers back. In fact, Alma has been bitten by a number of neighborhood dogs who never bit anyone before, the owners blaming *her* for being afraid. In her research for one of her novels, Alma discovered that the conquistadores used dogs to hunt down the Tainos who had escaped into the mountains. There you go. Alma comes by her fear honestly and historically. The DNA remembers. The body keeps score.

Better than a guard dog, a guardian angel. Someone to oversee this final resting place for her unfinished stories. A mention to Bichán, and the word spreads by means of Radio Bemba that Doña Alma is looking for a caretaker. Next morning, a crowd of petitioners swarms Alma's pickup as she arrives at the gate.

¡Doña! They call out their qualifications. One can cut a throat as easily as debone a fish. Another boasts experience working en la policia. The toothless drunk is back. Have pity! I have eleven hungry mouths to feed. Less than six weeks and he has spawned three more kids. The barrio is full of wonders.

Alma spots the woman who was the first visitor who had helped them burn the manuscripts. She has returned often, on occasion helping out, refusing propinas. Quiet though she is, it turns out she is packed with stories. Every one of them has won her entrance, a track record no one else can claim. Filomena! Alma calls out, motioning her over. The crowd looks around, unsure they have heard correctly. Filomena?

They should not be surprised, given Filomena's astonishing success. A near mute, yet she babbles away to the intercom and invariably the gate swings open. What is it you tell the box? they quiz her.

Filomena shrugs. So many of the things that have happened in her life—forgotten incidents, feelings she never before put into words—all this and more Filomena has been confiding to the voice box, in small portions, rationing out her life, holding back, afraid she might run out of the stories. But after decades of silence, there is a lot to tell.

Filomena climbs on board and the three women drive inside the cemetery, the gates closing behind them. Doña Alma comes right to the point. From Filomena's last story, la doña knows her viejita has died. She is very sorry for Filomena's loss, she adds sincerely.

I'd like to offer you a job here. I don't know how much you were getting paid, but I'll more than match your salary. The job should not be onerous.

Filomena feels a surge of excitement. Doña Lena and her sisters have been trying to persuade her to stay on, to take care of them.

They are gente buena for the most part, but Filomena needs a change. Thirty years have gone by since her sister and Pepito disappeared from her life. Now her viejita is gone, and the only places she finds solace are the church and in this very cementerio she has been visiting, across the street from her house.

What would be my duties? All she's ever done is take care of a house.

Do you know how to bark? Doña Brava asks playfully. The little trickster is trying to trip her up, yelping hilariously. Filomena looks back calmly at the small woman—an adult waiting for a child to stop its silliness.

You're going to scare her away, Doña Alma chides her friend. She turns back to Filomena and explains. From your stories, I know you know your neighbors: who would be good workers to hire when something needs doing. Who to avoid. And you mentioned that you live across the street? From your own house, you can keep an eye out. Any problems, you can call me, and if I'm out of town, my friend here lives right in the city, you can call her. You fix your own hours. Doña Alma lists a few more tasks and finally stops long enough for Filomena to answer. What do you say? Por favor say yes?

Before Filomena can think through what she will tell Doña Lena and her sisters, she accepts, using the words she has been taught to say whenever a superior makes a request or asks for a favor. Sí, señora, para servirle. This time, however, it's what she wants as well.

⨁ A calling

Filomena wakes every morning, looking forward to each new day. She has her routines. Order is important in a person's life, Padre Regino often says so. Anything done with love is a sacrament. The old priest is very smart. He knows how to say things that Filomena didn't know could be put into words.

First thing Filomena does is pray, consulting the religious calendar Padre Regino gave her in recognition of her devotion to the parish, each day illustrated with its feast-day saint.

Filomena can't read the names, but she knows the look and accessories of each one from dressing the statues in church as well as listening to the priest's stories: Santa Lucía, with her platter of rolling eyeballs; San Francisco, with birds perched on his arms; San Cristobal, with the baby Jesus on his shoulders; Santa Juana de Arco, engulfed in flames; San Judas, patron of desperate cases and lost causes, with a flame flickering on his forehead. Filomena thanks them for putting this new job in her path, without her even asking for it.

She makes her coffee in a sock, boils a plátano, mashes it, and tops it with fried cebollitas: ay, how her viejita—¡Qué en paz descanse!— loved Filomena's mangú! She eats at her table, quietly contemplating her day. Before setting out, she makes sure her fogón is banked. Last thing she needs is Florian, her neighbor, tearing down her door to put out a fire. A final check to be sure her cigar box of treasures is tucked far enough under the mattress that un ladrón won't find it, and she is ready for her day.

Walking past la mata de mango; in front of el salón de Lupita, already doing business, straightening and blowing out hair for la jovencitas who work in offices in the city; past Bichán's bodega, with its aromas of cafecitos and fried salami and queso frito; the repair shop, where one-eyed Bruno can fix anything from worn soles on your shoes to a broken handle on your butcher knife.

¡There goes la jefa! voices call out. Make sure los muertos behave today, you hear? Her neighbors will not be disabused of the idea that dead bodies are buried in the cementerio.

Filomena says nothing, but she smiles as she never did before. Were she to show any signs of pride, her neighbors would take her down a notch. But her happiness is genuine and unadulterated by arrogance or preening, so they settle for teasing. The nosy ask for details about what goes on inside the cementerio. They all saw the smoke rising from behind the walls. What was being burned there? The smell was not that of burning flesh.

Just boxes of paper, that's all, the ashes buried under one statue or another. Nothing much to report. She crosses the street to the back gate and unlocks the door with the key Doña Alma has provided, each time feeling as if she is entering a whole new life.

The gladness in her heart has nothing to do with having landed an important job. After all, Filomena had been running the viejita's household for years, while deferring to her employers, Sí, señora, sí, señorita, para servirle. When she left the household, Filomena recruited a young woman from the barrio to replace her. But the daughters complain. This new girl doesn't know how to do half the things Filomena could do. She needs two full days off, and she won't wear a uniform as she has not joined the military. If you don't attach *please* to a request, she does what you tell her to but with a surly look.

The daughters are lost without Filomena. A life of respectable idleness has rendered the younger sisters rudderless, their middle-class status softening them for truly hard work. Lena, the eldest and most competent, is too busy running their father's pharmacy to also manage the household. Don Pepe's—as it is still called—does a brisk business. The wealthy people in the new developments up in the hills send their chauffeurs down to pick up the orders they call in, knowing that the pharmacist has been instructed—as per Don Pepe's directions and now Lena's—not to deny their clients anything. They want Valium, they get Valium. They want codeine for their cough, no hay problema. Diet pills, sedatives for pain. If they don't get it here, they'll go elsewhere. Prescriptions are worthless: they can be plagiarized, modified, falsified. Don Pepe's is not the police, but a provider.

Periodically, Lena comes over to the barrio trying to lure Filomena back. Is it more money she wants? Shorter hours? Name her terms.

It's difficult for Filomena to explain—even to herself—why she prefers the new job. The only thing she can compare it to is what happened some years back with a neighbor's daughter who decided to join the convent. Her parents were baffled. ¡Qué locura! A good-looking girl who could have any man she wanted. Padre Regino intervened, talking with the parents, explaining that the girl had a vocation, a calling to enter the religious life. Of course, that had been God's doing, but who exactly is calling Filomena, and to what?

Doña Alma is pleased with her new hire. Filomena is doing a great job of keeping everything clean and tidy, including scrubbing the sculptures. Initially, Doña Brava doesn't mind bird droppings, as she likes for her work to look like a part of nature. This soon changes when the artist begins showing her work to potential clients, who do not appreciate art baptized with excrement. Brava suggests getting some cats to roam the property. But Filomena balks. No way she will hurt her little birds.

In fact, she spoils them, requesting a birdbath from Doña Alma, who obliges by asking her artist friend to design several freestanding figures. One is a dreaming girl lifting a bowl to the sky; another, a large lily, its center brimming with water; yet another depicts a woman holding up the lap of her skirt to catch the rainfall. The birdbaths become Doña Brava's bestsellers. With la doña's permission, Filomena also plants fruit trees to encourage the birds to perch and feed there. The place fills with birdsong, and yes, more and more bird shit. But Filomena doesn't mind. It's work she enjoys.

Her duties are so light that Filomena feels guilty getting paid a full-time, generous salary for what amounts to half a day's work. Each day she is finished by noon.

¿Nada más? she asks Doña Alma one day, when she reports that she is done.

La doña studies her a moment, as if assessing Filomena's capa-
bilities. Actually, there is one more thing. Among her other duties,
Doña Alma would like Filomena to visit each grave. Maybe just one
a day—whichever one Filomena feels most drawn to. Late afternoon
is probably best, when the sun isn't too strong, though soon, with the
trees Filomena has planted, there will be increasing shade. La doña
purchases a canvas chair with a sling that Filomena can easily carry
from spot to spot.

And what should I do while I visit?

Doña Alma again looks thoughtful. Just listen, that's all.

Ever since her first visit, Filomena has heard voices rising up from
the markers, joining the birdsong and the breeze. She has not mentioned this, fearing la doña might consider her unfit for the job. Padre
Regino has told her about saints and martyrs who heard voices, but
Filomena is no Santa Juana de Arco or Virgen María, and the voices
she hears are not telling her to fight a holy war or be the mother of
the son of God. They are telling stories. So, is that what Doña Alma
means? Filomena should just listen to them?

Exactly. Just that, no more.

Filomena considers asking for further guidance, but she does not
want to pester la doña with too many questions. Doña Alma seems
heavy-hearted, lingering at one sculpture or another, as if her own
stillborn child were buried beneath it. Maybe the locals are correct in
suspecting that bodies are being dumped here at night, after Filomena
has left for home. But there is never any evidence of disturbance in the
ground, mornings when Filomena arrives.

Doña Alma's sadness feels familiar. As far as Filomena has been
able to piece together, la doña is also alone, childless; she has alluded
to a former husband, always making a face when she mentions him.
Filomena knows all too well what it's like to live with a broken heart,
longing for someone to love.

⚞ Desperate cases, lost causes

Today before setting out, Filomena feels a slight headache coming on, no doubt from worry about having everything look nice and tidy, as Doña Alma is due back tomorrow. She left several weeks ago for the United States to sell a house she owns there. Earlier this week, Doña Brava came by with an architect friend, Doña Dora, who surveyed the grounds, jotting down numbers. It seems Doña Alma will be building a small cabaña on the property.

By now, Filomena has visited every site at the cementerio. She has gone about it in a methodical fashion, beginning with the central marker so as not to anger el Barón, then radiating out to the next and the next, setting up her sling chair at each site, listening, as she has been instructed.

The voices—if that's what they are—are so faint Filomena could easily confuse them for the birds singing in the trees, the breezes blowing through, the murmur of conversations on the street. Sometimes she hears distinct phrases, which fade away as if erased by the breeze. Sometimes disturbing shrieks that unsettle her. Sometimes humming sounds and sweet airs she sways to. *I took the taller one, the most beautiful. . . . She had a dark look full of spells. . . . A man who will save himself above all else. Alfa Calenda . . . Alfa Calenda . . . Give me your hand, I say, have you learned nothing from . . .*

Maybe the rumors are correct and the place is haunted. As a precautionary measure, Filomena wears her rosary around her neck, along with the keys to her house and to the cemetery's back door. She fingers the beads from time to time and kisses the crucifix. Dios me libre. Jesús acompáñame.

Late morning, Filomena is on her knees, scrubbing la tinaja—a large earthen jar; with its lid askew, it tends to accumulate leaves and bird droppings inside. She is finishing up the jar when she hears a voice coming from the white plaster head above the spot where the second set of boxes that would not burn are buried. The woman's head is unsettling: the neck, like a stem, rising out of the ground; the hair arrayed around her face like the petals of margaritas young girls pluck to learn whether their novios love them or not. Words are scribbled across the mouth like thick black thread stitching the lips together.

Filomena approaches quietly, guessing some tiguerito has climbed over the walls and is hiding behind the statuary. But no one's there. Throughout the day, as she goes about her chores, she glances over at the woman's face. Perhaps this is what Doña Alma meant by choosing the tomb Filomena feels drawn to? Late that afternoon, when her cleanup is done, she carries her chair over and sits staring at the scribbles as if by sheer concentration she'll be able to read what is written there.

The swallows are twittering in the nearby trees, punctuated by a loud whistling crescendo. What bird is that? Doña Alma is always asking for the names of things. Neither Doña Brava nor the foreman could tell her. Filomena was pretty sure el pajarito was a maroíta, but it was not her place to know things her superiors didn't. Besides, the names she knows are often nicknames given in the campo to birds that probably have fancier names. Bobo, Cuatro Ojos, barrancolí, and the common cigüitas she and her viejita used to feed in the park. Today, the bird's song fades away, and Filomena hears a woman's voice speaking as if the stitched lips have parted, the sounds clarifying into sense.

She crosses herself in case it is a devil speaking. She looks over her shoulder, lest anyone overhear her talking to the air, and whispers, Did you say something?

Bien-ve-ni-da, the birdlike voice trills. *Bien-ve-ni-da Ino-cen-cia Ri-car-do de Tru-ji-llo.* The voice stops abruptly, as if regretting the disclosure.

Filomena often feels self-conscious herself when speaking up. She waits, giving the voice space to recover.

Don't believe anything you've heard about me, the voice continues.

Filomena can't say she has heard of this woman. Would it be insulting to admit it? She has heard of Trujillo, as her father often spoke admiringly of el Jefe. Filomena settles for the noncommittal, I don't listen to gossip, Doña. That is how the devil spreads its lies.

The plaster face softens with relief, the hair relaxes as if a straightening comb has gone through it. *It's a blessing not to be judged. To be seen with the eyes of love.*

Así es, doesn't Filomena know it. The many years she has lived without a loving gaze turned her way. People always glancing over Filomena's shoulder at her beautiful sister. Or assessing Filomena as they would a machine for a job that needed doing. Only a long time ago on Mamá's face, or on Pepito's, his little arms around her neck, or more recently on her viejita's face, has Filomena felt that cherishing gaze. But in the viejita's case, did it count? She kept confusing Filomena with one of her daughters or some other blood relation. Do people love you if they don't see *you*? A question for Padre Regino.

Perhaps he did love me, the voice continues. *Do you think he loved me?*

Who is "he"? Filomena wonders. And furthermore, who can ever tell the secrets in another's heart? U'te que sabe, Filomena replies, as she has learned to respond to superiors who pretend-ask a question. You are the one who knows.

But I don't know. I misled myself so many times. No one is more blind than the person who does not want to see, the voice quotes the old saying.

That is why Filomena confesses to Padre Regino, sifting her confusion through another's ears, her life through another's eyes, to discover what is good.

The sun is low in the sky, casting strange shadows behind each tomb. Soon it will be dark—a moonless night ahead. But Filomena cannot leave. She wants to hear why this Doña Bienvenida feels so bereft. Who was it that broke her heart?

The knock at the back gate startles her. Filo! She recognizes the voice of her neighbor Florian. You have a phone call at Bichán's. Larga distancia. They'll call back in ten.

Con su permiso. I have to go. Filomena folds up her chair, checks for her keys in her pocket.

No te vayas, por favor, Bienvenida pleads, the very words Filomena used when her sister and then her Pepito left for Nueva York. *Everyone leaves me*, Bienvenida says tearfully. *Even the writer who was going to tell my story.*

But Filomena has no choice. The call is probably from Doña Alma, who always calls at the colmado, as Filomena has refused la doña's offer of a cell phone. No doubt it would be a convenience as the colmado is sometimes closed or Bichán not always amenable. But a phone on her person would mean anyone could summon Filomena at any moment, the equivalent of the little bell Doña Lena and her sisters would ring whenever they wanted Filomena to come clear the table or bring refreshments or sweep a mess la viejita had made.

Mi jefa must be calling me; she is due back tomorrow, Filomena explains to Doña Bienvenida. She tries to think of something soothing to say to the haunted soul. No hay mal que por bien no venga, Padre Regino always counsels. Filomena wonders if that is even true? Good always comes out of bad? Maybe it isn't the words themselves that matter, but the lilt and cadence of kindness and love that carries the sounds from the heart to the mouth and into the world. Even now, she can hear the trees alive with birdsong, the twitter of the cigüitas and golondrinas as they settle down for the night.

I'll be back, she promises. No se desespere. No hay mal que por bien no venga! Every sorrow has a silver lining. Every night has its dawn. I will pray for you to San Judas, Filomena adds.

Bienvenida seems placated by this outpouring of reassurances.

It's a rare feeling for Filomena: saying the words that someone needs to hear, even if they aren't hers.

☞ Long distances

Florian is waiting outside the gate, smoking a cigarette. His on-and-off wife has tried to make him quit. Cigarettes are expensive. Cigarettes are bad for him. Inhaling all that smoke.

Nothing compared to being a fireman. How about he quit his job? How would she like that? She'd have to go back to work like the haragana whore she is.

Filomena hears them quarreling late into the night. Suddenly, they grow quiet, their angry voices morphing into cries and moans of passion. The fighting seems to soften them for lovemaking, like pounding meat to tenderize it for cooking. Periodically, the argument escalates, shouting and screaming, the sounds of glasses breaking, doors slamming, the wife leaves, or is thrown out, un escándalo. The neighborhood has gotten used to it, like the hurricanes every year.

¿Qué hay, Mami? Florian greets Filomena, his voice intimate as if they are in bed together. You've gotten so comparona with this new job. Too conceited to visit me anymore.

Por favor! Filomena has never been inside his house—it's he who has visited her. But that was years ago, when in her loneliness and grief for her sister and for the child taken from her, she did not turn him away.

I heard you talking. You meeting your novio in there?

Better a rumor about a lover than one about hearing voices. Was it Doña Alma who called? she asks, all business.

Mami, how should I know? I was told to get you, that's all.

They trot down the street to the colmado; the phone is ringing as they walk in the door. A buen tiempo, Bichán says as if she has arrived just as a meal is being served.

PERLA?! Filomena calls out her sister's name in disbelief. The colmado goes still. So, there is a person named Perla, who can bestir their taciturn neighbor to cry out. The listening in the room sharpens. Are you all right? Filomena asks, trying to calm her voice.

I'm coming to stay with you, Perla is saying, as if thirty years of estrangement haven't passed since their last conversation. No one must know.

Y Pepito? Filomena can't help asking. Is he all right?

I'm on my way to the airport. I'll try to get on the next flight. Where are you living now? Either Perla can't hear Filomena's questions or she is unwilling to answer them.

If Perla wants to be incognito, better she gets dropped off at the cemetery. Otherwise, if she comes to Filomena's door, all her neighbors will know. What time will you be arriving?

I'll call you when I get there. Perla's voice breaks. She is sobbing as if someone has broken her heart, like Doña Bienvenida just now. Filomena can guess who is to blame.

Filomena tries to soothe her sister as she did Bienvenida minutes earlier. Every sorrow has a silver lining. Every night has its— But before Filomena can finish, her sister has hung up.

The eyes of everyone in the colmado are on her, eager to know what's going on. Doña Alma, Filomena lies, remembering too late she cried out *Perla*. Bichán's eyes narrow, a savvy smile stretching his lips like a rubber band. If Filomena should get another call, any hour, please come summon her? She pulls out some bills from her brassiere to tip him for his trouble. But the colmado owner waves her money away. He'll collect his payment later when he asks for the story Filomena has promised not to tell anyone.

Filomena hurries home, making plans, her head buzzing with details. Perla and she can sleep together in the same bed, just like they did as girls in the campo. If her sister's presence is to be kept a secret, Filomena will have to make breakfast before she leaves for work as Perla can't be stirring in a supposedly empty house or lighting the fogón in the yard. It's going to be difficult hiding a visitor in this barrio full of eyes. What is this secrecy all about anyhow?

The conversation did not last more than a few minutes, and yet Filomena can't sleep all night going over it. Any moment she expects Bichán to come banging at her door. How did Perla know to call the colmado's number? There was no mention of Tesoro or Jorge, and more important, none of her little boy. Man, Filomena corrects herself.

The last time she saw Pepito, Filomena could not believe her eyes. As usual when her sister and brother-in-law were visiting, Filomena had been sent away on an enforced vacation. But daily, surreptitiously, Filomena would stroll by the house, hoping to catch a glimpse of her Pepito. And there he was, a grown man, coming out of his grandmother's house, headed for the car to retrieve some bags from the open trunk. It was a shock when she saw him in the flesh, as the Pepito in her dreams was always a little boy. The way he moved suggested un Americano, casual, self-assured, all in black in his tight jeans and T-shirt with some letters written on the chest. Filomena stopped and stared: he looked so much like his young father.

Pepito turned, a suitcase in either hand. Filomena crossed the street ready to embrace him. But just then, Perla was at the door, calling her son. Dinner was on the table.

The sounds of lovemaking are coming through the cracks in her walls. Filomena has not heard the preparatory fighting, so distracted is she by her thoughts. Finally, she must have dozed off. Next thing she knows, light is seeping in through those same cracks; she can smell the coffee being brewed in neighboring houses. Along with Perla, Doña Alma is due today. There is so much to do. Filomena dresses hurriedly, no time for her routines. In her rush, she forgets to pray to San Judas, whose help she certainly can use today.

Possession

After calling her sister, Perla shows up at the airport wanting to leave the country. Surely the gringos won't object. They're always deporting foreigners. It's getting in that's costly and problematic.

She stands in line at the counter, jittery, rocking from foot to foot, like a child who has to make pipí. She checks and rechecks everything she might need—cell, cartera, cash, rosary, pasaporte—reminding herself that she must now answer to Filomena Altagracia Moronta, the name on her Dominican passport matching the one on her birth certificate.

After their green cards were issued and Tesoro and she divorced their pretend Puerto Rican spouses, Perla had wanted to set the record straight. But their lawyer warned that in trying to correct the error, Perla might end up deported for falsely claiming to have been who she wasn't when she was issued her green card. She could call herself whatever she wanted to at home; however, legally she'd have to be Filomena for the rest of her life.

Perla has renewed her Dominican passport at the consulate in Nueva York every time it was about to expire. She used it recently for going to Greece, so she should have no problems. Of course, she hadn't committed any crime then. She is sure her guilt shows, not just on her face, but on her passport photo. Why else would the attendant at the counter be taking so much time typing into her computadora, shaking her head when Perla puts a pile of bills on the counter. Sorry but she cannot receive cash for the ticket. ¿Y qué lo que? A show of money always works back home. All previous times Perla has traveled, Tesoro—or in the case of this last trip, Pepito—paid with their credit cards. No tengo tarjeta, Perla keeps insisting to the woman who has been joined by her supervisor. This is good money, dinero de verdad.

For years, Perla has been saving these chelitos for the day they can finally retire. Tesoro has always promised to go back and build a big clamshell of a house for his Perla. Now she is returning but not as she hoped, taken in by the one person who has every reason to turn Perla away. Her sister did not set up a single objection, even after thirty some years of estrangement. She has opened her door, without demanding an explanation or insisting Perla tell her story first.

Tesoro is the one who has shut her out. The longer they are together, the more struggles they endure, the more he drifts, searching for other pearls. He's insatiable, no matter that she gives him as much sex as he demands. Now nearing fifty, she doesn't even feel like it most of the time.

Tesoro is always bringing up his sacrificios, working day and night and weekends driving for Ramírez Town Cars. What about her? Perla has kept a good home, economizing (she has a stash of you-never-know cash inside the cover of one of the sofa cushions), cleaning, cooking, washing and ironing his clothes, even his socks and underwear. All this while working as a maid for a Dominican couple on the Upper East Side. Perla could have made more money with Americanos, who pay by the hour, but she likes being where she can understand what people are saying. Even after all these years, she hasn't been able to pick up much English.

Perla suspects Tesoro is up to something. All those late nights and weekends spent driving out-of-town clients or visiting un amigo enfermo in Queens. Of course, it has been convenient for him that her job requires her to sleep in, four nights a week, home for the long weekend, which she spends cooking and cleaning for her own family.

Underlying all her suspicions is the story her sister told of being seduced by Tesoro when Perla was pregnant with Pepito. Every time the specter of her sister comes up, Perla throws another fistful of forgetfulness on the memory. When her mother-in-law died and Perla flew down with Tesoro and los muchachos for the funeral, Lena tried to work a reconciliation, but Perla refused, Over my dead body! flinching when she realized how inappropriate it was to say so at a funeral.

One thing she can be proud of is raising two sons who have turned out so well. She expects it from George Washington, who from the beginning has had a charmed and easy life. No wonder, with the patriotic name Tesoro chose so it would look good on their residency application, a name that Perla couldn't even pronounce. Jorge, she persists in calling him, as do his tías. Pepito, on the other hand, was affected by the early separation from his parents and later from his beloved Tía Filo. There were sessions with school counselors. He has special needs, so she was told. Who doesn't? He's withdrawn, his teachers complained, he doesn't communicate. Of course! He doesn't know any English. How can he speak up? Then one day in class, the silent boy burst into speech, complete sentences in English, as if he'd been learning the language all along. After that, he was always reading, his nose in a book—which his father didn't think was healthy. His teachers couldn't say enough good things about him.

Pepito even persuades his mother to let him teach her to read. I know you already learned a little, but you need to practice. It'll be easy, Mamita. We'll start in Spanish. Maybe someday we'll move on

to inglés. Don't give me that look. I'm going to be a writer. I want you
to be able to read my books.

To please him, Perla makes the effort. She struggles through what
Pepito calls easy books, written for kids with lots of pictures. His
favorite is filled with old stories of the gods and goddesses people
believed in before Jesus came to set them straight. Those gods and goddesses behaved horribly, raping women, betraying their wives, sleeping
with their mothers after killing their fathers and eating their children.

Did these things really happen?

That isn't the point, Pepito explains. These stories are about real
passions in people's hearts. They tell of all that is possible. Look at the
Bible, he points out. You think those things really happened?

Jorge Washington is the very opposite of his bookish brother: out-
going, interested in making money—a more understandable nature
to his father. But Tesoro comes around when Pepito wins a full scholarship to a university, the mention of which makes his boss, Tony
Ramírez, lift his eyebrows, impressed. Pepito goes on to earn a doc-
torate, which baffles his parents, who hadn't known there is such a
thing as a doctor of anything but medicine. After some years teaching, his university gives him a year off. A whole year! He does have
to write a book, he complains. Pobrecito, his father wags his head
unsympathetically. As if confirming his father's opinion that his son
is milking the system—not that Tesoro has any problems with that—
Pepito is headed for Greece for several months on his sabbatical to
do research.

Pepito invites his parents to visit him while he's there. Tesoro begs
off—too much work, they're down several drivers. So, Perla takes
two weeks off. You should see that part of the world, her employers
encourage her. The cradle of civilization. Perla is surprised, as these
people claim to be Catholics, whose origin story starts with a cradle
in Bethlehem.

Perla has the time of her life. Islands, boat rides, meals she doesn't have to cook. Every night Pepito squires her to tiny restaurants, ordering tasty dishes for her to try and vinos that make her head and heart light. She feels like gente rica, her food brought to the table by attentive waiters, her glass filled when it's only half empty. They visit a bunch of ruins—which would be tedious, but Pepito tells her stories like the ones in the picture books they used for her lessons. This is the temple of so and so, this is where a god rained down a shower of gold or defeated a monstrous serpent or was gored by a gang of drunk women. ¡Dios santo! The things people do!

When she flies back to Nueva York from Greece, Tesoro is not at the airport to pick her up. Perla keeps trying his cell phone, no answer. Finally, she calls Ramírez Town Cars, only to learn that Tesoro has taken the last two weeks off. Tony dispatches a car to pick her up. The minute Perla opens the door of the apartment, she knows. His clothes are missing in the closet. His toiletries gone from the bathroom. No note, no nothing. What a coward: moving out in her absence!

But you can't hide the sun with a finger, not among Dominicans anyhow, even in a foreign country. Turns out his coworkers at Ramírez and his cronies at the barra and bodega know about Tesoro's other pearl. An address in Queens. Sick friend! ¡Qué desgraciao! The woman is una Cubanita, figures, no shame—the informer snaps her fingers. Adding further salt to the festering wound: Tesoro has started another family, a little son. At his age!

This time, instead of calling Ramírez Cars, Perla takes a taxi to the address. She doesn't know what she's going to do. For protection, she has wrapped the kitchen knife she uses to debone chicken for sancochos and asopaos in a towel in her work satchel. Cubanos are fighters—look at that barbudo Castro standing up to the gringos long after every country in the hemisphere had signed on to the USA team.

Perla stands staring at the small house with a front lawn, surrounded by a chain-link fence, a little dog barking away like a toy gone rogue. All those years Perla pushed for their own house instead of the cramped apartment in the Bronx, Tesoro talked her into saving their chelitos to build a house back on the island when they get ready to retire.

Perla walks by several times, hoping to catch a glimpse of Tesoro before she confronts him and his puta. She has her knife to defend herself. On the radio years ago there was a story about the woman who cut off her abusive lover's penis—maybe that's the way to go.

The front door is open, but the screen door blurs the interior. The dog's barks grow louder, more vehement, as if Perla is trying to break in from across the street.

A woman appears at the door and descends the front steps. Vitalina López—her informer gave out the name. Something familiar about her, a face Perla has seen before, maybe in a photo on Tesoro's cell phone. She's young enough to be Tesoro's daughter, blanca with dyed blond hair—Perla can see the dark roots even from a distance. Vitalina scolds the dog, yanking it inside by the collar, and disappearing back in the house. As the screen door is closing, her toddler slips out, descending the three steps, butt first. Perla crosses the street.

Hola, chichí precioso, Perla croons, squatting to be eye level with the little boy. The toddler comes right up to the fence, his chubby fingers wrap around the links as she offers him one of the menticas in her satchel. Oh my god, there is no denying this is Tesoro's son.

Before his little fists can grab the candy, she withdraws it. You have to tell me your name first.

The boy looks up, his bottom lip thrust out, his eyes blinking back tears.

No, no, no. Don't cry. I'll unwrap it for you. Here. He nabs it—greedy like his father—and stuffs it in his mouth.

His mother's voice is calling from inside the house. Oro! Oro!

Oro, Tesoro's golden treasure. Each time the woman cries out the name, Perla feels as if she is being stabbed in the heart.

She unlatches the gate and comes inside the fence, wanting . . . she doesn't know what. To catch a further glimpse of the life Tesoro has chosen to replace theirs: a sweet little boy, a white Cubana with pretend-blond hair, a house with a yard and a toy dog. It all makes sense; what doesn't make sense, it never does, is to be the discarded one after a lifetime together. Why? she asks the little boy who's chomping away at his candy, green goo coming out of the sides of his mouth. He reaches out his little hand for another mentica.

Perla thrusts her hand in her satchel to give him another treat. Her fingers graze the dish towel with the knife sandwiched inside.

The woman has come to the door again, the dog slipping out between her legs, barking up a storm. ¡Cállate! she yells at the animalito. You want la necia next door to call la policía? Like the dog is going to answer her.

Vitalina stands on the top step, looming above Perla, as if she's a goddess from Pepito's book. It takes only seconds before she is screaming at Perla. What are you doing? Ay, Dios mío, she's poisoned him!

Poison? It's only candy, Perla could say about the green goo coming out of the little boy's mouth. But Vitalina doesn't give her a chance. Oro! Oro! the mother is screaming like a furia, leaping down the steps toward her little boy.

Perla has to prevent this imposter from taking the boy, who has suddenly transformed into Tesoro himself. He is hers! She shoves Vitalina away, at the very moment the mother is scooping up her child. The shove proves more deadly than Perla intends as there's a knife in her hand—how did it get there? It sinks into the child. The woman's horrified screams are deafening. Perla can't think straight.

She swings again, slashing her rival's throat to quiet her, and then because the little dog is furiously barking, Perla stabs him into silence as well.

Blood is everywhere. What has she done? Perla can't breathe. She feels faint. She stands paralyzed for a few moments, trying to thread the needle of what to do, how to escape. She looks up and down the street warily. Has anyone seen her? It's the middle of the week. The yards are deserted. She has to get out fast. Before someone drives by. Before Tesoro wakes up and comes out of the house or returns from his errands. But first, she has to finish the job—Vitalina's eyes are opened, rolled up as if pleading with God. Perla closes them and then mercifully, she thrust her knife one, two, three, four times into the mother's chest, and then the boy's, just in case, to end their suffering. She never meant to hurt them. The dog is already dead.

Perla flees down the street like a madwoman. A few blocks away, there's a small park with a water fountain, a set of swings. Behind a tree, she takes off her dress, wraps it up with the knife. Her uniform is still in her work satchel, she slips it on, wipes her arms and hands with the towel she wets at the fountain. Her heart is beating in her throat, her breath short and rapid. Is it she who's sobbing? She looks around. A squirrel observes her from afar, a bird calls in the trees. What could have possessed her? That's what it felt like, a possession, like santeras back home, taken over by spirits. It has to have been. Perla would never have done such a brutal thing.

She goes back carefully over what has happened: she is coaxing the boy with candy to endear herself to him; she is entering the yard to take a further look around; next thing she knows the woman is screaming at the top of the steps, the little dog is barking, nipping at her heels, the knife sinking into the boy's chest, blood spurting out.

But wait. How did the knife come into her hand? Perla remembers that just before stabbing the boy, a picture flashed in her head from the book Pepito used to teach his mother to read. A woman stirring the severed limbs of a child in a cauldron of stew to feed the father in revenge for his betrayal.

Is that where the idea came from? A storybook? Back when she first encountered it, Perla remembers asking Pepito if such things really happened. Stories tell the truth of secret passions in people's hearts, he had answered. So, was this vengeance lodged inside Perla all along, compelling her to thrust the knife into Tesoro's mistress and child? Or did the story itself put the murderous possibility in her head, allowing what otherwise Perla would never in her life have considered, no less carried out?

⚊ Ruins

Pepito is sitting in a kafeteria in Aleksandropolis, staring down at the clotted coffee grounds, wondering what future they foretell, when his little brother reaches him. The WhatsApp connection is terrible. But it doesn't take much bandwidth to transmit terror.

Their father has been taken into custody. A person of interest in a murder case.

And Mamita? Is she okay?

His brother must not have heard him. Where are you? George Washington is asking. I can hardly hear you.

I'm in Greece, remember? No need to offer a specific location. For all his traveling with his work in pharmaceuticals, GW is terrible with geography.

Mamita missing . . . the police . . . a call from Ramírez to let him know . . .

Pepito can barely make out the tangled story. Something awful has happened to their mother, he is sure of it. Why else won't George

Washington just come out and say who the victim is? Pepito can see his mother's bloody body so vividly, he shakes himself. Maybe that's what the clump of dark grounds signifies?

I'm headed back to Nueva York. I'll know more when I get there.

Where are you? Pepito echoes his brother's earlier question. With cell phones you never know. He can't assume his successful brother is sitting in his brightly lit office in Manhattan, negotiating a deal with one of his accounts in South America. Or at home in his Harlem apartment in boxer shorts, about to go out to a bar with his girlfriend du jour. When will you get back?

But before George Washington can answer, the call has dropped.

Pepito pays up and heads for his Airbnb, his head swirling. Has his father done something to his mother? Pepito doubts it. Like most hard-working immigrants, Papote is a pretty clean-nose guy, but he does fool around. His mother seems to be clueless, thank god. She's jealous of the very air he breathes. It's as if all her vital organs are inside Tesoro's body. Her heart beats in his chest, her ideas are cooked up in his brain. She doesn't believe she can live without him.

It's all well and fine to love someone, but this lack of confidence in herself is debilitating. His father feels burdened by it, too. More and more, he grows distant and absent. His mother complains and nags, which only makes matters worse.

Pepito has caught his father any number of times with different women. Several times at a movie theater, once on the train. These women are definitely younger, or at least better preserved than Mamita, who has let herself get heavy. They dress sexily, makeup overdone in the way Latinas seem to like. The last time Pepito spotted his father, Papote was coming out of a clinic with a younger, pale-skin woman, attractive for sure. They seemed to be arguing. So maybe his father has gotten in over his head? Perhaps he has done something to free himself from Mamita. But what? Papote has a temper—but he's no murderer. A man who feels faint at the sight of blood.

Pepito has often thought of confronting his father, but Pepito has his own secrets to hide. He has never come out to either parent, his father's homophobia is vocal and vicious. Pepito would tell Mamita— she might scold, but ultimately, she would "forgive" him—but since his mother has to run every thought by her husband, she might blurt it out, causing further problems between father and son, whose relations have always been fraught. So, Pepito hasn't told her—a bone of contention with his partner, Richard.

Back at his Airbnb, Pepito rings his parents' apartment landline. No answer. Next, he tries Mamita's cell phone, and it goes right into voicemail. Back and forth, apartment, cell. He googles the news, tries calling GW back, but his brother isn't picking up either. Maybe George Washington is on his way home from—did he ever say where he was?

Finally, in desperation, Pepito reaches his aunt Lena.

Your father didn't do it! Tía Lena sobs before Pepito can say a word. Tesoro has been taken in, a prime suspect in the murder of a mother and child. Tesoro called Ramírez from jail, asking if his boss could please inform his sons and his sisters in the DR.

Tía Lena is sobbing again. I tried calling you, but I couldn't get through. I did reach your brother. He promised to call me once he got back to Nueva York.

Nothing to do but call Richard, who was fed up with ruins and stayed behind sunbathing in Paros while Mamita was visiting. The couple will meet up at the Athens airport and fly back to the ruins awaiting them in Nueva York.

Persons of interest

As Tesoro turns the corner, right away he sees the crowd in front of the small house, an ambulance, the lights not flashing, the siren silent—all bad signs, urgency no longer necessary. He crosses himself as he was taught to do as a child—even after all these years in Nueva York, where the wailing of ambulances is almost as common as birdsong.

It was a bad fight, lasting days, beginning with Tesoro wanting to go to the airport to pick up Perla on her return from Greece. Vitalina had gone crazy, blocking his exit, crying like la Llorona in that story his Mexican coworkers have told him. Tesoro has never been able to resist a woman's tears, and yet he's always making one or another cry. And so, he complied, leaving a message for George Washington to go pick up his mother. But it turned out Jorge was traveling and never got the message, so Perla had to find her way home on her own to the empty apartment. Just as well he wasn't there because what would he have said?

Perla, por favor, try to understand my situation. My mistress told me she was protected, but she wasn't. When she got pregnant, she refused to get rid of it. So, now I have a little son who needs his father. I gave most of my life to ours, now it's his turn.

He doesn't need Vitalina to tell him this is a bad plan.

But then his boss, Tony, called Tesoro. Perla had come to the office. She was distraught, threatening to hurt herself. Tesoro owed her and his sons a face-to-face explanation. That was the honorable thing to do, Tony advised, and Tesoro agreed.

Vitalina wouldn't hear of it. First it was the airport. Now a meeting. Next thing, Tesoro will have to go over to fix her sink, celebrate her birthday. ¡Olvídate! You go out that door to see that woman—

She's still my wife, he reminded her. ¿Pa'que fue eso?

Vitalina flew into a rage. Get out! Get out! she screamed como una loca de remate, the dog barking away, the boy bawling. Just the kind of scene that would trigger the nasty neighbor to call the police. So as not to cause further complications, Tesoro jumped in his car and took off.

He drove around for over an hour, not knowing what to do. Vitalina isn't the kind of woman like Perla to hurt herself over a man. ¿Pero quién sabe? Women still mystify him—even after his years of grazing new and verdant pastures, nibbling all kinds of tender and ripe fruits.

Now on the way back to Vitalina's after the bad fight, Tesoro is no sooner out of his car, but the unfriendly neighbor next door is pointing and shouting, making up for the silent siren. That's him! That's him! Before Tesoro knows what's what, the police are twisting his arms behind his back and shoving him into a squad car.

What's amatta? he keeps asking, in the smattering of inglés he has picked up. It seems the occupant of the house has been knifed to death with her little boy. The neighbor reported hearing a big row this morning, screaming and yelling, and then the alleged suspect running out of the house and into his car.

Eh—slow down, he pleads. *Dead* means *muerto*, correct? *Knife* is *cuchillo*. No, no, no, no, no, he moans. There is some mistake. Maybe he has misunderstood? Maybe it's his bad English? He has to see for himself if the words he has heard are true. He would reach for the door handle except his hands are tied behind his back. Instead, he throws himself against the door.

The car is already moving. Por favor, he begs, sobbing, please.

The officer on the passenger side shakes his head. What a drama queen, he says to his partner. These brown niggers are the worst. The one driving keeps checking on Tesoro in his rearview mirror, a narrow-eyed look Tesoro will never forget. He has already been found guilty! But what is his crime? Fighting with your woman is not against the law. Sometimes when he drinks too much and loses his temper, Tesoro can get physical. A soft slap, a yank by the hair, holding her hands behind her back and pushing her to bed, having a little sex to calm her down. But Tesoro isn't the type of man who gets off on slugging women. As for the child, how can these officers think he'd be savage enough to hurt his own son, his treasure, whom he has named after the most precious of metals? Tesoro would have ended things with Vitalina, especially after she tricked him. But once that little nugget was born, Tesoro was willing to leave Perla and start over just so his son could have a father.

A boy needs a man in his life to teach him how to be un hombre macho. Look at what happened to Pepito being away from his father until the boy was almost five. Pepito doesn't fool him one bit. Tesoro has seen him at Mofongo, hanging out with a white pájaro. But it's too late to set his grown son straight. Here's a chance to start over. And having a woman twenty years younger at his side is—to speak without pelos en la lengua—an investment in the future, a nursemaid to take care of Tesoro in his old age. In the meantime, she will keep him young.

But still Perla's image has plagued him. She is the mother of his two sons, if nothing else. He wants to assure her that he will continue to help her whatever way he can, and their two successful sons will pitch in, too.

All these things are running through his head. What could have happened? Who could have done such a deed, if indeed it is true?

Suddenly, Tesoro feels a dizzying certainty, and before he can warn the officers or position himself so as to limit the mess, he vomits explosively all over the squad car.

From further down the street, Perla watches as a silenced ambulance goes by followed by a police car. Dios me libre, Dios me perdone. She makes the sign of the cross. In her clean dress, she has been walking in the direction of the traffic. She tries to look calm, purposeful, a woman who knows where she is going.

At a busy intersection, she spots a policewoman coming out of a coffee shop, her skin the same color as her beverage, her hair obediently tamped down by her cap. Perla's radar tells her this woman has to be una dominicana. El subway? she asks, although of course she has already seen the telltale pole with a globe on top. A wily move, as a guilty murderer would not be asking an officer for directions. The policewoman gestures with her chin, bunching her lips, a gesture that confirms she is indeed a quisqueyana. Ahí mismo, señora, she says, kindly escorting Perla to the subway stairs, explaining which trains to take to the Bronx. They chat for a few minutes, Perla como si nada, the young woman talking in Spanglish like Perla's Dominican York sons.

When Perla arrives at her building, she does not immediately go in: she circles her block checking to see if la policia have come. No cars. No cops. Upstairs, she burns the bloody dress and towel inside her big pot, washes the knife with alcohol, and packs hurriedly. Inside the zippered sofa cushion, she retrieves her wad of cash. La tarjeta de crédito is in Tesoro's name and she wants to leave no clues behind. In her purse, Perla finds Filomena's number. Lena had given it to Perla after la viejita died. Life is short, Lena had said. Hay que perdonar.

Perla had no intention of ever communicating with Filomena, but curiously she has kept the slip of paper in her handbag. Way back, Filomena destroyed Perla's peace of mind. The story has been buried so deep, it should have rotted into oblivion. But like Lazarus in la Biblia, it keeps coming back to life, a ghost that is not a ghost, but her own living breathing betrayer of a husband whose face she saw resurrected in the face of that darling little boy.

What has she done? What madness has possessed her?

Perla rings up her sister's number. A man's voice answers, bachata blaring in the background. A cash register rings. Perla is told to call back in a few minutes. She's already on the street, hailing a cab, on her way to Newark Airport, when she reaches her sister. Perla feels safe talking, certain that the driver wearing a turban will not understand Spanish.

I'm coming, not a word to anyone.

And as if thirty years have not passed, Filomena does not put up any argument. She asks only if Pepito is okay. Then she instructs Perla to come to a cemetery, as if Filomena already knows what her sister has done.

⟨ Regreso

Filomena arrives at el cementerio, still groggy from having overslept after a restless night. Doña Alma is already there, pacing the ground with the arquitecta taking notes. How about here? Or better still, there? The arquitecta has visited the cemetery several times during Doña Alma's absence; now she wants to see the place through the owner's eyes.

I am sorry I am late, Filomena excuses herself. She doesn't have a reason she can share. She hopes la doña doesn't think that her employee has been taking liberties because her mistress was away. I hope your trip went well.

Very well, thank you. She has sold her house in Vermont. No turning back now, she remarks. By the way, Filo, Doña Alma notes, gesturing, the place looks great.

Filomena tucks in her chin to hide her face, embarrassed at her pleasure in being praised.

While the two women talk, Filomena sets about her work, distracted, one ear cocked for a knock at the front gate or back door. She can't stop running the conversation with Perla in her head. What was her sister's secrecy and desperation about? Over the years, Filomena would hear Doña Lena whispering to her sisters about the problems the couple was having in Nueva York. Problems? But why? All their dreams have come true. They have worked hard, saving up their money, paying a lawyer a hefty fee to arrange their marriages with Puerto Ricans, then filing for divorces from their rented spouses after their green cards came through. Pepito and Jorge have done well, professionals both. So, what are the problemas about? As an eavesdropper, Filomena couldn't very well ask.

Filomena remembers her promise to return and listen to the rest of Bienvenida's story, but Doña Alma might get the wrong impression if her worker is already sitting down so early in the workday, after also arriving late. The visit will have to wait until the two women leave. Each time Filomena goes by the tomb, she touches the plaster head fondly. The hair feels soft and real. ¡Dios me libre! She must be imagining things again. Doña Alma has said that Filomena has a great imagination. The stories she has told to gain entry are classic. In another life, you could have been a writer. Filomena has yet to confess that she doesn't know how to read, much less write.

The architect is outlining shapes in the air with her hands. We'll have to move that one, she says pointing to the glass globe, where the first set of boxes that would not burn are buried. The globe is set on a pivot, so it rocks on its stand when touched—Doña Alma has demonstrated—sending a cloud of white flakes swirling up, then very slowly settling at the bottom. It's mesmerizing to watch them.

That's what it looks like in the winter where I used to live, Doña Alma has told Filomena.

This structure had to be commissioned from a glassblower, as Doña Brava doesn't work with glass or kinetic structures. It's the most expensive. Only the best for Papi.

After the arquitecta's departure, Filomena cautions her mistress about relocating el Barón's site. Like Pepito, la doña has been raised allá, and would not know. The first tomb in a cemetery belongs to el Barón, and it should not be moved without his permission. You don't want to get on his bad side and bring down bad luck, not just upon yourself, but on all others who visit here. Filomena doesn't mention herself, so as not to sound self-interested.

Doña Alma has heard from her friend Doña Brava about that cult. But again, she reminds Filomena there aren't any real people buried here.

El Barón wouldn't care. He claims the first grave in any cemetery.

Is that right? Doña Alma responds without much conviction.

Padre Regino also dismisses such beliefs as superstitions. Invasions into Christianity from the voodoo religion next door. But Filomena knows cases of people who offend el Barón and end up losing a lover or their good health. Not even San Judas, with his miraculous powers, can protect them. Filomena would recount these stories now, but there is a crease between la doña's brows, which Filomena knows is not a welcome sign, especially on the face of an employer.

For the rest of the morning, Filomena tries to keep her mind on her work. At noon, she stops by the colmado. There have been no further calls. She buys a packet of tostones and a little sack of maní and eats them, sitting in front of Bienvenida's tomb. Maybe the story will distract her. But the marker is unresponsive. Did Filomena imagine the voice? Or perhaps Doña Bienvenida is aggrieved at being cut off just as she was beginning her tale?

To encourage her, Filomena leans forward and whispers the very words the box at the gate asks petitioners seeking entrance to the cemetery: Cuéntame. Tell me your story.

The birds in the trees are still, resting in the heat of the day. The sun climbs higher in the sky. Filomena finishes her snacks, and still, not a word from Doña Bienvenida, and as if the two are somehow connected, no more calls from Perla.

Finally, Filomena gives up, folds her chair, and heads for the shed to retrieve her tools. Time to get back to work. As usual, she stops at el Barón's tomb, to pay her respects, making the sign of the cross, then laying her fingers on the glass. The touch sets the flakes flying. A voice commences recounting its stories, other voices join in, more and more, as if blown by the wind or flying in on the wings of the twittering cigüitas who alight on one marker or other—a babel of noise, like the colmado on a holiday, packed with people drinking, gossiping, all talking at once.

Filomena puts her ear to the glass and listens.

III

≈ Manuel

Mamá was forty-nine years of age when she gave me to the light. More abuela than mother, with canas in her hair and aches and achaques all over her body.

Her cheek resting on the globe, Filomena discerns this one voice drowning out the others. She assumes it's el Barón's, perhaps angry at the idea of being moved, until the voice clarifies as a certain Manuel de Jesús Cruz, his story pouring out in a torrent, as if this might be his one and only chance to tell it.

Mamá gave me that middle name because I, too, was a miraculous birth. Her reglas had stopped, with an occasional spotting now and then. I also had a father, but I might as well not have had one. Papá considered me a nuisance, a ñapa he didn't want. He'd already had ten children with his first wife, who died, amazingly not in childbirth, before he married my mother and had fifteen more, twenty-five total, not counting the poor bastards he had with one or another of his mistresses.

Filomena's mind wanders back to her own childhood in the campo, where large families were common. Their neighbor, Yocasta, had ten. That woman has a factoría in her womb, Filomena's father once exclaimed. Filomena recalls some smart tongue wagging back, Sí, señor, and some were assembled during your shift.

Are you listening? the voice asks, betraying the same impatience as Filomena's former profesores, frustrated when she didn't already know what she had come to school to learn.

¡Presente! she replies, as she used to at la escuelita.

Mamá more than made up for Papá's neglect, the Manuel voice continues. She showered me with all the affection my father withheld, too busy with his numerous affairs and negocios. When he did turn his attention to me, it was often in disapproval. It irritated him that I loved poetry, that I cried if told a sad story. He tried to beat my nature out of me, and when that didn't work, he shipped me off to a military school. The harsh discipline, the unquestioned obedience to stupidity—I was miserable.

Mamá interceded: she wanted her little boy beside her. Papá relented. He owed her after his latest mistress gave birth to twins, brought to our door for proof, his telltale silvery eyes on their little faces. I was allowed to stay home and be tutored by Mamá, who inspired me with her love of reading.

The drawback to being home was Papá. He made my life miserable. I cried myself to sleep so many nights, I could've filled the water jugs in all the houses on our street with my tears. Mamá would try to comfort me, retrieving some little treasure from her curio cabinet for me to hold, telling me its story (the inlaid silver thimble or the snow globe from Paris or the Spanish señorita doll with a miniscule mantilla and castanets or the wooden shoes tied together with a piece of red string). We read books together. *Twenty Thousand Leagues Under the Sea, Around the World in Eighty Days, The Three Musketeers, The Arabian Nights.* I also loved Dante's *Inferno.* Was there a circle in hell for harsh fathers?

Mamá hushed me, afraid Papá would overhear and come after me. She made excuses for him: Papá was disillusioned with the government. His health was failing him. Your father is just jealous of you because you're so special.

Papá punished me for the least infractions. A beating, a shaming, one time locking me out of the house overnight because I had disobeyed his command that I eat with my fork in my left and my knife in my right hand, the European way, rather than switching utensils like the malditos Americanos, who were occupying our country. It also irritated him that I was so attached to Mamá. He will grow up to be an effeminate, a pájaro.

Are you a pájaro, eh? He poked my ribs. For supper, we're feeding you only birdseed.

Mean enough as a joke, but my father was in earnest. He set a bowl of birdseed in front of me. When I began to sniffle, he threw the bowl against the wall—birdseed and shards of glass flying everywhere.

That night Mamá proposed we make up a charmed place to escape Papá's rages. A world where every single thing, not just people, tells a story. Drops of water recount their journey from a cloud to a spring to a river to the sea; the broken bowl assembles its pieces and tells of the argument that shattered it; a cigüita discloses what lies over the mountains in Haiti; a seashell, a murderer, a brokenhearted sweetheart, a star stolen from the sky by a bold princess. Together, Mamá and I stocked our secret world with stories.

We needed to find a name for it. Mamá picked Alfa, the first letter of the Greek alphabet. But it sounded too bare, Alfa, all by itself.

Every year before the cane harvest, Haitian migrants would stop at our farm on their way to the sugar plantations in the southeast. Like birds migrating, they knew where to alight on their route, places where there would be abundant kindness and food. Usually, these migrants stayed a few days, Mamá giving them whatever work there was to do, paying them, feeding them. At night, they lit campfires, played the tambora and pipe, sang and danced, performing their rituals. One of their dances, the Calenda, had been banned over in Haiti, the plantation owners fearing that it would stir up powerful passions that might spark a revolution.

Every time I heard that tune, it got under my skin. I leapt to my feet and joined the dance. I couldn't help myself.

Why not Calenda then? Alfa Calenda, we christened the place.

Filomena has heard those very words in the wind and has assumed they were some fulana's name and surname.

From then on, whenever my father came after me with a belt or an open hand, or shamed me with harsh words, or banished me out of his sight, Mamá slipped into my room and sat on my bed, wrapping her arms around me. Are you ready? Now, close your eyes! Había una vez . . .

And off we would go to Alfa Calenda . . .

Filomena is finding it difficult to concentrate. Her thoughts keep straying. Where is Perla now? The sun climbs; the weeds inch out of the ground; Perla does not appear.

Manuel's voice is growing faint, like a windup toy running out of time. Most of the flakes have settled to the bottom of the globe. A phone rings in the distance. Filomena braces for a shout, summoning her. But the call is for someone else. Where is Perla?

Shake me, the voice whispers.

Filomena considers disobeying; perhaps this might end the tale. But today is not the day to offend el Barón. Gently, she rocks the globe; the dust motes cloud the air again.

Reinvigorated, the voice recounts how as a young man he joined a group of dissidents, listing names as if Filomena should have heard of these people. This is nothing new: as a servant, she has often been privy to conversations about people she knows nothing about.

The Manuel voice launches into a rant about the brutality of el Jefe. And I thought Papá was harsh. No wonder there are many circles in hell!

Filomena is not about to contradict el Barón's protégé, but according to her father, el Jefe was the strong leader the country needed.

During his rule, there was order, respect. A man could put a peso outside his door and the next morning it was still there. Perhaps Don Manuel's friends were thieves who stole money left lying around?

The globe shakes in disagreement, furious with flakes.

Someone in our group betrayed us. My comrades were rounded up. I, and two others, managed to escape across the border, boarding a steamship in Cap Haitien, bound for Puerto Rico. My friends stayed there to coordinate an invasion. But I was done with dictators. I went on to Nueva York.

Does everyone in the world end up there? Filomena wonders.

I was already a licensed medical doctor but los Americanos disrespected me, my accent, my brown skin, my foreign credentials. They who had been occupiers of my country were now telling me to go back to where I had come from. I am here because you were there, I'd curse them under my breath. Don't let my later success fool you, I never felt welcomed there.

What has it been like for Perla? Filomena wonders, her attention drifting again. She always assumed that her sister would find happiness allá. Everyone spoke of the United Estates as if it were Padre Regino's paradise. But maybe Perla has also been miserable? The few times Filomena has caught sight of Perla from a distance, she looks unwell. Maybe some of the problems Tesoro's sisters alluded to were similar to the ones Don Manuel is recounting. Has Pepito been called names because of his brown skin? But look at how well he has done. Filomena is so proud. Her would-be son has proven to be an exceptional student, earning scholarships, even becoming a teacher. Just because Don Manuel had difficulties doesn't mean everyone does. Not all stories turn out the same, Filomena reminds herself. Look at her life compared to her sister's. But now, at last, they will be together again.

By the time Filomena tunes back in to the voice, it is faltering again, the flakes are settling to the bottom of the globe.

Filomena backs away, afraid that even her footsteps will stir it up again.

⁓ Filomena

Filo! a voice shouts from the other side of the wall.

For a moment she believes Don Manuel is calling her back to listen to the rest of his story. But it's the salón owner, Lupita, on her way back to work after the midday hiatus. You have a call. Hurry, they're holding on.

Filomena rushes out, forgetting to lock the back door. Her face falls when she hears the voice on the other end. Doña Lena. Has Filomena heard from her sister? Just like that, Perla is *her* sister, not Lena's sister-in-law.

What can Filomena say? Perla has sworn her to secrecy. No one must know Perla has called and is headed to her sister's casita.

Why? Is something wrong?

Lena recounts the shocking news. There's been a murder. A mother and her little boy. Tesoro is under arrest. But he didn't do it. The police are looking all over for Perla.

Filomena feels faint. She leans against the counter breathing through her mouth. Bichán is in the middle of ringing up a customer. He glances over at Filomena. You okay? She collects herself and nods.

And Pepito? Jorge Washington? Are they all right?

Thank God and la Virgencita, Pepito and Jorge were both traveling. They are hurrying back to Nueva York to be with their father.

And their mother? Filomena ventures.

Don't talk to me about that monster! They're looking all over for her. In case you hear from her, call me right away! Doña Lena speaks in the commanding voice of a mistress. Has she forgotten that Filomena no longer works for Lena's family?

Years of habit kick in, and now there's the need to keep up her subterfuge. Yes, Doña Lena, of course, if I hear anything, I will let you know.

Back in the cementerio, Filomena finds the door ajar. Inside, her neighbor Florian sits on Bienvenida's marker, grinning like a truant boy.

You shouldn't be in here! Filomena says sharply. Her heart is thundering in her chest. She needs solitude to absorb the news. Doña Lena implied that Perla committed the murders. How can it be?

Get out! Filomena shouts at Florian and at the thoughts clamoring in her head. So different from her docility with Doña Lena.

Ay, Mami—

I'm not your mother. What do you think you're doing in here?

It's my day off from putting out other people's fires. I came to put out mine. He laughs at his own cleverness.

If you don't get out, I'm going to start screaming for help!

Ay, Filo, don't be that way. Come here, buenamoza, Florian coaxes. You get better-looking every day, you know that? His voice is cloying, like the oversweet dulce de leche Bichán sells that she can only eat in tiny nibbles. I wanted to see who it is you're talking to in here.

Filomena picks up her folding chair and comes toward him, swinging it like a machete.

Florian lifts his hands placatingly and backs away. The truth is, wagging tongues don't wag in vain. You're going crazy in here!

Filomena swings, Florian trips and scrambles up and away. She bolts the door and leans back on it. On the other side lies the world that keeps disappointing her, as it does all who don't take hold of their own story. Look at Perla. Some horrible thing has happened and no doubt Tesoro will lay the blame on her.

Filomena feels a heaviness overcome her.

She has no energy to finish her work today. But she can't go home yet: it would arouse suspicions. Set those wagging tongues wagging some more. Already, Bichán and his colmado regulars are buzzing with gossip. ¿Qué será lo que le pasa a Filomena?

She leans against Bienvenida's sculpture, baptizing it with her tears.

☟ Bienvenida

The groundskeeper is back, weeping. She must have heard sad news. Ya, ya, I whisper with the help of the breeze and twittering of birds. Nothing seems to help. Sometimes the best handkerchief is a story.

Did I ever tell you how I met el Jefe?

The groundskeeper stops her sobbing, startled by my voice. El señor, she says, pointing toward the glass globe. He was just now talking about your Jefe, too.

Filomena wipes her face with her hand, momentarily forgetting her story to fall inside mine.

Everyone came to know my Jefe. But I am recalling a time before he became everybody's Jefe.

I would soon be turning twenty-two. Already there were whispers, pobrecita, she's bound to be a jamona, for I had never had a beau—or rather, none that I would accept. I was an incurable romantic, awaiting my prince. Mamá blamed my cousin Joaquín, who was always putting novels and poems in my hands. I was also realistic. I knew I was no beauty. Short and plump—I never could seem to keep the weight off. Still, I was sought after by young men who had suffered enough under the sway of some beauty, I had a gentle, kind demeanor and what was considered an asset in our border town, pale skin and what people called "good hair." I also came from one of the top families in Monte Cristi, which wasn't saying much as ours was a hot, dusty town in decline. In fact, we were considered hicks by the people in la capital, which was fast becoming the center of culture, money, prestige, everything mi Jefe aspired to.

He was already an important man, head of the national guard, traveling the country, lining up support in his grab for power. When he was coming through Monte Cristi, the town council of which my father was a member arranged for a reception to pay their due respects. Even though Papá was no supporter of this gangster, as he called him, our presence as a prominent family was required.

That night was magical. Let me put you there, shall I?

Our groundskeeper leans in, listening.

An early spring evening: our Centro Cultural is lit up by gas lamps that hang from the ceiling; the jalousies are thrown open on the court-yard side, a fragrant breeze is blowing. The town fathers have chosen a Spanish theme, eager to prove our untarnished heritage despite our proximity to the border. The men look so elegant in their high-waisted pants and silk sashes, the women dressed up with combs and mantillas. As our Jefe enters, the band starts up with our national anthem. Next comes a waltz, followed by a slow bolero, "Linda Quisqueya," always a favorite. Then another waltz—interrupted when el Jefe lifts a hand for silence. The band stops playing. A ripple of fear runs through the gathering. El Jefe is displeased.

Why this foreign nonsense? We have our own music. Play me some merengue! One thing you can say about el Jefe, he returned us to our native rhythms.

The band lets loose. More than one matron is shocked. Merengues are still considered risqué in polite society, the close proximity of man and woman, the hips moving with the rhythms of desire—how would I know of such things? I confess, my girlfriends and I enjoy dancing together as we sing the lyrics in our shuttered bedrooms.

I'm standing by the refreshment table with my friend Dinorah, both of us trying hard not to sway our hips to the catchy rhythms, when we see el Jefe's lieutenant headed in our direction. I reach for Dinorah's beaded bag to hold while she dances. But the lieutenant addresses me. El Jefe would like the honor of this dance. Even Dinorah looks surprised.

Filomena can hear that merengue, as if she were at that party. Although she is no rich girl, has never been courted, never found true love, and knows nothing of poetry—still, she, too, loves to dance, if only with her broom.

I might not have been the prettiest girl there, Doña Bienvenida continues, but—and excuse me for boasting—I'm an excellent dancer, light on my feet. El Jefe repeatedly asks me for the next and next dance.

Bienvenida Inocencia, el Jefe whispers my name, lifting my face to look into my eyes. So, is it true, are you an innocent, welcoming girl?

I smile what the ambassador from Italy will later call my Mona Lisa smile. Of course, any number of people have made that same remark about my name, but never a handsome colonel with a chest ablaze with medals. I explain to el Jefe that the year before my birth my parents had lost my oldest brother to typhoid fever, so I was a consolation to them, a welcome innocent indeed.

A charming touch, to feel complimented every time someone says your name.

I feel a rush of unseemly desire. I bow my head to hide my blushing face.

During the slow boleros, el Jefe recites in my ear. My two favorite things—poetry and dance—how can this love not be meant to be?

The following morning, and subsequent mornings, a contingent of soldiers comes to our house with baskets of flowers: white lilies, roses, and my favorite, sunflowers. Our parlor is like a garden! You mean a wake, Mamá mutters. Each bouquet is accompanied by a love poem, signed by el Jefe, with lines I recognize from Rubén Darío's *Poemario*, a gift from my cousin Joaquín, our family intellectual.

Each night there is a serenade. I can't show my face, but I linger behind the curtain at my bedroom window.

A week into this wooing by proxy, having set the stage for his entry—a sense of drama the whole country will soon come to know— el Jefe himself makes an appearance. He's been touring the rough border towns, inspecting his troops; even so, he looks fresh as a flower in a bouquet like the ones he has sent me, and so handsome and manly in his uniform and high riding boots. Our whole family has joined us in the parlor, as respectable young ladies are never left alone with a suitor, especially one the family does not approve of.

Filomena irons the wrinkles in her skirt with her hand, as if she were making herself presentable for the gathering. Now that she is doing outdoor work at the cemetery, she wears her old clothes, saving her nice dresses for mass on Sundays. Doña Lena always insisted on uniforms, and unlike the new maid, Filomena never minded, as it helped conserve her small wardrobe. But Doña Alma has never required Filomena to dress any particular way.

We are all sipping our limonadas. Doña Bienvenida is so swept up in her reminiscence, she can taste that lemonade. And so can Filomena.

My sister Yoya, always the gregarious one, keeps the conversation going. I do hope you don't mind, Colonel, but Bien has shared some of your verses with me. You are quite the poet! She knows very well el Jefe is not the writer of those lines, as we've read those very poems by Ruben Darío in my poemario. I'm almost sure Mamá has set her on to prove to me that my beau is not who he appears to be.

Thank you for the honor of laying your lovely eyes on them, el Jefe replies, giving her a gracious bow. I've always had a talent for writing but I haven't had time lately with my many duties.

What a shame! Mamá and Yoya flash me a meaningful look: *Do you finally see now what an imposter he is?*

Who cares who wrote those poems! What matters is that el Jefe cares to impress me.

As I mentioned, Mamá and Papá are set against him. A man with no principios, thinking he can remake himself, hiding the sun with a finger. He fooled the gringos who kept advancing him through the ranks of the national army they created before they finally left the country, but not Papá.

From some private inquiries my father finds out a piece of shocking news: el Jefe is married, with a wife and daughter!

I am distraught and shut myself in my room, crying my eyes out, indisposed next time el Jefe comes calling. But just like Papá, el Jefe has ways of finding things out and learns what my upset is all about. He sends an emissary, a prominent lawyer in our town, who explains to our family that el Jefe is no longer married. As a young man, he made a foolish choice, but he soon came to his senses and terminated the marriage. A civil divorce, granted, but it is perfectly legal. The lawyer presents a copy of the notarized document as proof.

Mamá snorts at this explanation. Every Catholic knows there is no such thing as divorce.

But el Jefe is no mere man. In fact, he is appealing to the pope in Rome to annul that first marriage. As for the rumors that mi Jefe is eliminating his enemies, plotting a takeover, I explain to my parents what el Jefe has told me: he is reluctantly taking control of our unruly half island to establish order, something even Papá has complained about. What this country needs is a strong man. I quote Papá's words right back to him.

That is what my father said about el Jefe, too, Filomena offers, allying herself with Bienvenida.

I've never stood up to Papá before. I've always been known as una masa de pan, a mass of dough, easily manipulated by others. But I resist all efforts to break up our romance, surprising even myself.

Most of the families in town boycot our small wedding, which takes place unceremoniously in the living room of el Jefe's acquaintance, the prominent lawyer. Of course, I would prefer a church wedding, but that ceremony can't happen until el Jefe's annulment is granted. The only family member present is my cousin Joaquín, who recites a poem he has composed for the occasion. El Jefe is impressed. I could use a silver tongue like yours in my campaigns. Joaquín is hired on the spot. So begins his own long career in politics.

I still remember every line of that wedding poem: "Bienvenida Inocencia. Welcome innocence, welcome happiness, welcome sweetness and grace and light."

A nearby bird joins in the recitation, singing with all its might, outdoing itself, until Filomena is laughing with delight. How can words do that?

During our wedding there's an awful storm, like a hurricane blowing in from the ocean, thunder so loud I can't hear my own voice confirming my vows. Immediately after the civil ceremony, el Jefe ushers me into the waiting car, refusing to spend even one night in this godforsaken town. Go ahead and cry, Monte Cristi, he addresses the pounding rain on the roof of the car. You are losing your loveliest jewel. From then on, and for three decades of his rule, he will never forget the indignities he suffered in my hometown, seldom deigning to visit, always deciding against Monte Cristi when it crosses swords with other municipalities.

The car sloshes through the muddy roads, the wind howling, the rain pelting the windows. We ford several rivers and the floor floods with water. Later, I will think back on this storm as a sign of the heartbreak that awaits me. For the moment, I am the happiest girl in the world. I have lost everything but gained this pearl of great price, el Jefe's love.

At the mention of *pearl* Filomena is jolted awake. Stop right there, she wants to say, before you lose your pearl, too!

But Doña Bienvenida cannot stop; her story is a rushing river flooding its banks, spilling over in tears running down the plaster face, and it's Filomena who now reaches out to caress the marker, murmuring, Ya, ya.

⌇ Perla

Perla waits in a cell in Nueva York for whatever is going to happen next. She doesn't care. Most of the other women are darker skinned, only one other light-skinned Latina like herself, and two big white Americanas, full of swagger. When Perla can't stand their bullying anymore, she snarls, ¡Putas Americanas! which the one with stringy beige hair and a snake tattoo winding up her left arm, the tongue licking the neck, misunderstands. Damn right she's pure American! Perla spits on the floor by way of translation. The woman slams Perla against the wall, her friend adding a few kicks for good measure. Perla passes out.

She wakes up in the infirmary with a bandage around her head and a terrible headache. Once she recovers, she's put into solitary confinement for attacking another prisoner.

Perla could tell her lawyer what exactly happened. But she has already made up her mind. The officers who apprehended her as she was trying to purchase her ticket to the DR at the counter recited her rights in a monotone, repeating them in Spanish: she has a right to remain silent.

When asked for her story, she will remain silent.

When her trial comes up, she will not defend herself. She will not say that she wants nothing more than to exchange her own life for that of the little boy. If she ever sees Tesoro again, she will not berate him or throw in his face that he brought this on himself.

She will remain silent.

The lawyer Pepito hires informs Perla that she is lucky: New York has done away with the death penalty. Even if convicted, she won't be facing execution. But Perla prays that death will come soon. In the infirmary, she looks around for anything she could use. The staff is vigilant; the empty beds are kept stripped, no sharp objects or medications or even a pen in sight.

Pepito visits, explaining the next steps. The lawyer is working on getting his mother deported. Filomena Altagracia Moronta never became a US citizen; her green card does not protect her—permanent residents who commit crimes of moral turpitude can be placed in removal proceedings.

This is a lucky thing, too, Pepito says. It will go easier for Mamita back home where the law is more forgiving of crimes of passion. With cash, strings can be pulled and braided together into a strong rope to haul Mamita up out of the pit she has fallen into.

But the only rope Perla wants is a noose around her neck. She is tormented by what she has done. It's as if a swarm of hornets are chasing her, all of them with the little boy's face. She keeps shaking her head, trying to scare them away. No one can save her. She is already damned.

She cannot stop thinking about that story in the book Pepito used to teach her to read. A man who killed his own mother was pursued by vengeful spirits. Isn't killing a child and its mother even worse?

Mamita, Mamita, Pepito keeps pleading, remember: you are more than the worst thing you've ever done. Where did the boy learn to talk like that? Lovely words on a high shelf Perla cannot reach to avail herself of their beautiful comfort. He probably got them from a book as well.

This is not the end, Mamita. Te lo prometo. As if that is anything someone can promise.

Perla looks at her son, a look that does not need words to convey her love.

➤ Bienvenida

Three years into our marriage, el Jefe becomes president, and I am thrust into the role of primera dama with a round of official duties. Often, I'm invited to preside over numerous functions, a stand-in for our busy Jefe, Joaquín at my side. A splendid first lady, the papers report. I host endless receptions and dinners, never laughing too loud or voicing an opinion or embarrassing my husband in any way. I supervise the menus, arrange the flowers and settings at the table, deciding where to seat each person—in short, I make sure everyone is happy. Most of all mi Jefe, the center of my life.

I am learning to master that second language of all devoted wives. I read my husband's expressions for the slightest hint of displeasure—the lift of an eyebrow, tightening of a smile—and act accordingly. In photographs from that time, I am seen standing behind mi Jefe, my face radiant with love. This may sound vain, but I believe I become more attractive. It helps to have a superb seamstress who knows which styles best suit my stocky figure and a stylist who fixes my hair and works magic with creams and makeup. Not that I care a whit about attracting any eye but my husband's.

Often, after a successful event, mi Jefe praises me. You live up to your name, Bienvenida.

When the American First Lady comes on an official visit, I do everything possible to make her feel welcomed. Behind every successful man is a good woman, she compliments me to mi Jefe. She should know, traveling the world for her husband who has polio. That is why he could not come himself, she explains, but she will give him a good report. Mi Jefe catches my eye and winks.

From time to time, stories reach me. Mothers pleading for clemency for their jailed sons. Families needing help to leave the country. I try to be a gentle influence on mi Jefe. But others, self-interested lackeys, incite him to harsher and harsher measures, including—I'm ashamed to admit—my cousin Joaquín. I do what I can quietly, often sending these petitioners to Mamá and Papá, who I know will aid them.

You have too soft a heart, Bienvenida, el Jefe sometimes complains, scowling with impatience.

I want only to protect you, mi Jefe. You know I would give my life for you.

But there is one thing I cannot give him: an heir. My problem is not infertility, I keep getting pregnant, but after several months, I miscarry.

Specialists come and go to my quarters at the presidential palace. They prescribe all sorts of treatments: vaginal enemas, a bland diet, a quiet schedule, no outings, no gatherings, no public appearances. I'm fattened up, dosed with drugs and home remedies. My maid who fancies herself a curandera brews me teas, manzanilla, campeche, té de San Nicolás. A santera is brought in to exorcise whatever demons are keeping me from bearing a child. Everything I do is carefully monitored. I begin to feel like a prisoner in a golden cage. I weep in his arms on his rare drop-ins, which just serves to drive him away. No one is allowed to visit my quarters without his approval—to protect my health, I'm told, and my life. El Jefe has so many enemies.

The one exception is Joaquín, who checks in regularly in his new capacity as el Jefe's right-hand man, a post he owes to my introduction and recommendation and to his own grit and wiliness. He keeps me informed, a reliable magpie, bringing bits of news. There is a rumor circulating that el Jefe is having an affair with a woman who is jealous and possessive, with a will equal to his own. A serious rival, not just el Jefe amusing himself like all men. Joaquín is worried about *his* standing should I fall into disfavor.

My death knell comes when this mistress gives birth to a son.

Filomena shivers. Evening is coming on. The sun is low in the sky, casting strange shadows behind each tomb. Soon it will be dark—a moonless night ahead. But Filomena cannot leave, the voice holds her with its urgency and grief. She, too, wanted a little boy. She, too, lost her Pepito.

Bienvenida plunges ahead, ignoring the groundskeeper's moods and silent musings. She, too, is in the grip of her story.

One day Joaquín arrives with what he says is good news, his voice full of false excitement, his words belying the strained expression on his face. *A man who will save himself above all else*, the phrase used by that writer I've mentioned to describe him. More and more I sense a certain distance in his affection. Joaquín informs me that I will be visiting Paris, where I am to see a world-renowned fertility specialist.

My first reaction is a surge of happiness. Finally, I will have el Jefe to myself! We can rekindle our love, crossing the ocean, watching the sunset from the deck of the ship. When do we leave? I ask Joaquín, like the innocent I still am at heart.

Bien, you know that's not possible. El Jefe has no time for leisure. He has work to do. Joaquin quotes one of the maxims of the regime, which he himself drafted for el Jefe. *Mis mejores amigos son los hombres de trabajo.* Men who work and women who obey, Joaquín adds with a grin.

Within days, I am on board a steamship bound for France. At Le Havre I'm met by the ambassador, who delivers the blow. During my absence, the congreso has passed a law rendering a marriage null and void if there has been no issue after five years. Of course, this is only possible because ours is a civil marriage. El Jefe's first marriage, in the church, only the pope can—and will in a few years—annul.

I collapse in his car en route to my hotel.

Filomena wipes the tears streaming down Bienvenida's cheeks. The old people in the campo claim that on the second day of November, the stones weep in the killing fields, where the Haitians were cut down like cane years ago. But the Day of the Dead has come and gone.

Ya, ya, Doña Bienvenida, Filomena soothes. She should spare the poor woman from reliving these sad memories. But Filomena wants to hear this tale to its end. A kind of exorcism, and not just for Bienvenida, but for Filomena as well.

I am admitted into House of Serenity, a convent in the outskirts of Paris that also serves as a temporary home for unwed pregnant women and girls. A kindly old nun, Soeur Odette, attends to me, urging me to accept what cannot be changed.

But I did everything right, I plead my case, as if it's within Soeur Odette's power to change my situation. I gave him all my love. How can he not see that?

We can never understand God's ways. The elderly nun sighs, betraying a lifetime of bafflement. The veil of innocence is slowly, painfully being stripped from my eyes as well.

Soeur Odette dries my tears, her hand lingers, caressing my cheeks, a question lingering in her eyes. What I don't understand is how a good woman like you—Soeur Odette stops herself, but I complete the thought in my head: How did I end up with a man like el Jefe? It's a question not even the writer of my story will be able to answer for me.

⚞ Alma

Alma is intrigued by Filomena's obvious affection for Bienvenida's marker. The caretaker visits the others dutifully, stopping to do her obeisance to el Barón at Papi's snow globe, rocking it and watching the flakes fall. But she lingers in front of Bienvenida's sorrowing face, absorbed, sometimes reaching out to stroke the plaster cheeks.

Brava has noticed this affinity as well, but she is not surprised. People do this all the time with art, she says to Alma. At galleries, museums, you sometimes see someone unable to tear her gaze away from a certain face or scene depicted on the canvas, framed, hung on the wall. A Diego Rivera mural will make a jaw drop in awe at all the anonymous hands that make the world run. A Van Gogh will bring back the field of sunflowers outside a childhood home.

Bienvenida's story has definitely touched a nerve in Filomena.

Not the story itself, Brava doesn't think. More likely, the face or attitude of the sculpture. Because how would Filo even know the story? Brava herself had only learned about it to satisfy her curiosity when Alma first commissioned the work. Ask any person on the street about Bienvenida Trujillo and I bet you there's not a single one who will know who she was. They might recognize the name Trujillo, but that's as far as it goes. Erased from the history books. Brava makes a sweeping gesture as if painting over a figure on a canvas that doesn't suit her.

Brava is right, of course, no one remembers Bienvenida. After el Jefe divorced her, the new wife and former mistress, Doña María, removed all traces of her predecessor: no more Bienvenida Ricardo Schools; no Avenida Bienvenida—nice ring to it; no playing canciones composed for her on the radio or at fiestas. El Jefe had married his match.

Maybe Filomena has learned the story in other ways, Alma hints. Maybe the characters in the cemetery are releasing their stories, and

Filomena hears them. I brought them here to lay them to rest, but maybe that's not what they want. Alma is testing to see if Brava can tune into the voices, too.

Brava looks thoughtful. A bird calls relentlessly from a nearby laurel tree, the distant roar of traffic out in the carretera is punctuated by the wail of a siren, a car's muffler backfiring nearby. So, if Bienvenida wanted to be known, why then couldn't you tell her story?

She didn't trust me, is all Alma can guess.

So, she trusts Filo?

Maybe Filomena's a better listener. She won't make use of her story the way we artists do. There's a kind of violence in art. Alma thinks of Mami, her fury at being misrepresented. *But it's fiction* didn't work for her. Alma recalls a friend sharing that his own mother was upset about a farmwoman protagonist in one of his novels: You gave her my life without my permission. You put her in that horrid dress I would never wear.

Violence? Brava couldn't disagree more. I call it surrender, I call it love.

Hard to argue with that, Alma thinks, but still, she does. Their back-and-forth banter on matters great and small is how their friendship makes its own kind of love.

≈ Bienvenida

A few months into my exile, I'm still staying in the House of Serenity. I spend my days in the sitting room, surrounded by tall windows, writing letter after letter to el Jefe, pleading for one more chance, blaming my infertility on the pressures of being a supreme leader's wife. I tear them up, appalled at my groveling, and thereupon write angry ones, berating him for his treatment of me, and tearing those up as well.

Even though I've picked up quite a bit of French, I keep to myself. It's painful to be surrounded by all these young women about to become mothers. Not that these girls are any happier, knowing they will be forced to give up their newborns for adoption.

Soeur Odette suggests I consider taking one home. A child might help your heart to heal. Someone to love with all your heart.

But I don't have a home to take her to. Doña María has made sure of that. Our island isn't big enough for us both. There have been stormy scenes at the palace, Joaquín keeps me up to date on the chismes. Where am I supposed to go? How will I live? These decisions are out of my hands. Under these circumstances, how can I provide for a child? But I promise Soeur Odette, If I ever do have a little girl, I will name her after you.

One afternoon, Soeur Odette comes to my room and announces that I have a visitor. I assume it is the consul, who occasionally drops in to check on me with saludos from the ambassador. I'm no longer worthy of a visit from the top dignitary.

Sister shakes her head. *Your husband,* she whispers, refusing to say "ex," as the church does not recognize divorce. I have not had the courage to explain to Soeur Odette that ours was only a civil ceremony.

Hurriedly, I change into a fresh dress, gather up my hair. No time for anything else. El Jefe is not a man to be kept waiting.

Right away I know something is wrong. His face is drawn. There's a haunted look in his eyes. His story comes out. He has been diagnosed with cancer and has traveled to specialists in Paris, desperate for a cure. I am his good luck charm, he says. It was during our marriage that he took charge, rebuilding the country after the terrible hurricane of San Zenón, hospitals, schools, roads. A grateful country elected him president. All these good things happened with me by his side. But since our divorce, his luck has turned. Doña María has cast a spell on him. El Jefe wouldn't put it past her. A voodoo priest is a frequent visitor to the palace. His security police keep him apprised. He would cast her off, but their son is still so young and attached to his mother. Maybe she has him under a spell, too?

It was a mistake, getting entangled with her. I regret it, I do. I had to marry her for the sake of a legitimate heir. My country insisted, my congreso forced my hand. But my plan has always been to divorce her and come back to you.

The clouds part and a blue sky spreads over my life again. I move into his suite of rooms to devote myself to his care, accompanying him to his medical appointments, nursing him through all his procedures, soothing his fears. Morning and night I pray my rosary fervently. The hotel provides me with a prie-dieu like the ones in all the rooms at the House of Serenity. Sometimes I spot him kneeling there as well, something I never thought I'd live to see, my Jefe on his knees! We are intimate again as in the first days of our marriage. The former wife is now his mistress, and the former mistress, his wife! I thought such things happen only in the novelas I love to read.

A few weeks into our reunion, el Jefe receives some good news: The deadly cancer turns out to have been a mere inflammation of the prostate. The treatments have eradicated all signs of infection. The doctors give him a clean bill of health. Their patient is free to travel home as soon as he wishes.

The first piece of news sends me to the mountaintop, the second dashes me down to hell. He is going back, and though he doesn't say so, I finish the sentence in my head with dread. Going back to *her*.

I told you that you are my lucky charm! he exclaims, giddy with joy, like a boy who has just been given a wished-for toy. I catch a glimpse of who he might have been in another set of circumstances.

He promises we will be together soon, and although I should know better, I again surrender myself to him. My body is a fertile field ready for his seed. Indeed, I am convinced that is the night we conceive our little Odette. Several months later, when I'm less afraid I might miscarry, I telegram mi Jefe from Paris with the happy news. He's pleased but makes no further mention of divorcing his wife.

Stay there for now. I want you to have the best medical care. Once the child is born and you can travel, I want you to come back.

I return to Serenity House. Soeur Odette comforts me with one of her favorite sayings. When you can't have what you love, love what you do have. She lays her hands on my swelling belly. The good Lord will safeguard this pregnancy. You hear that Odette? she whispers. Odette kicks back in response.

⟅ Alma and her sisters

Alma's sisters call often, wanting to know how things are going. Alma is so caught up with her project, she seldom has time to shoot the breeze. Everything's fine, she reports, chats for a few minutes, then cuts out, blaming it on the signal.

Her news, like nonjuice oranges, is nothing juicy, not even newsy. So, what are you doing with yourself these days? the sisters persist. As casual as you please, the slant way to squeeze a drop out of her.

Not much of anything. Taking walks, soaking up sunshine, remembering, remembering. That's what she loves most about being here: everything triggers a memory. The island is mined with madeleines. So many stories!

So, are you writing again? Piedad always knows where the hot-button issue is.

Not every story has to be told, Alma snaps back, irritable at being reminded.

Doesn't sound like you, Soul Sister. Just saying. Piedad backs off.

At least, she has hired a caretaker. That's a relief. They don't have to worry about her alone in that bad neighborhood. But wait! What if this individual is connected to criminal elements? Did you get references? Where are you staying anyhow? You're not sleeping there, I hope. They're on a conference call, the sisters all talking at once. Alma can't tell who's asking what. They all sound the same; they all sound like Mami.

I'm in the cuzzes' beach house for now.

So, what comes after "for now"?

How should I know?

Her sisters break into Amparo's theme song, now transferred to Alma. *How will we solve a problem like Sherryzad?* A chorus of explosive laughter.

Glad you guys are having a good time. What's up? They rarely call all together. Usually, it's one on one.

Piedad gets down to business. Back when Papi died, Piedad had volunteered to be Daniel in the lion's den and serve as the liaison with Martillo. The Hammer wants to see us in person once the documents are ready.

What for? Alma is sure this is a trick. I thought we were finished with Martillo. Only thing left to do was sign off on the divided properties, which I've already done.

Not so fast, Martillo says we all need to sign our deeds in person— the DR authorities won't accept DocuSign. A bold-faced lie, but if Alma indeed can't even get a good phone signal, she's unlikely to have the bandwidth to call up Google and check it out.

We can stay a few days, have that sistercation you promised.

Alma balks. She has missed her sisters in theory, but she's not sure she wants them concretely in her life right now, full of argument and opinions. Making her second-guess her choices. When were you thinking of coming?

As soon as you can host us.

But I don't have my own place, Alma reminds them.

There's plenty of room at that beach house. Face it, you could put a small village in there.

A village might be easier than her spirited sisters. You're always welcome, Alma hedges. But why not wait, though, you know till my project's done, then I can show it off?

What project? You mean that weird burial place for your characters? (This from big-mouth Consuelo, thank you very much.)

It's more like a . . . sculpture garden, Alma says, launching into a description of Brava's creations. Whatever it takes to avoid further interrogation.

The sisters agree to postpone. Piedad will contact Martillo for an estimate of when the final documents will be ready, so the sisters can come collect them in person. If he gives her his usual, "in no time," she will press him: You've been saying that for over a year. Our time is worth money too, you know.

It's a pity that Baby Sister has never learned to put her prickly emails in the draft folder overnight before she hits *send*.

Bienvenida

Years pass. I mark them by Odette's milestones.

When her baby teeth come in, we move to el Jefe's house in Miami. It's not home, but at least it's closer than Paris, where we've been living with the nursemaid el Jefe sent to help me out.

The spring Odette starts talking, she meets her father for the first time. He is free to travel now that he is returning to private life after the international uproar over the disastrous massacre at the border—a decision soon to be overturned upon the death of his puppet president.

The autumn Odette enters school, we get word that we can come home. We are installed in a sprawling ranch house in the outskirts of Santiago, away from the bustle of the capital and the vigilance of Doña María, el Jefe's jealous wife, whom he has not discarded despite his promise.

One day, while Odette is at the convent school, el Jefe's black Cadillac pulls up to the porte cochère, as I learned to call the entry-way in France. Usually there's a call ahead alerting me, followed by a procession of cars, El Jefe's agents, checking out the property; only after the all-clear does el Jefe himself appear.

Today, surprisingly, there's only the lone car, and instead of el Jefe, it's my cousin Joaquín who disembarks from the back seat.

I had begged the clinic not to notify the palace of a recent incident. But there's no hiding anything from el Jefe and his spies. And woe to you if you try—a sign that you're conspiring against our supreme leader. Why else would you keep anything from his all-seeing eyes? Citizens, wanting to ingratiate themselves, are now painting their allegiance on the roofs of their houses: TRUJILLO AND GOD, in that order.

No surprise then that el Jefe has learned about the attempt on my life by a thug who broke into the clinic while I was being examined. Thank God that the fellow was none too bright, as many of them aren't—after all, the job requirements call for obedience, not intelligence. The confused man ended up in the wrong examining room, knife drawn, holding the nurses hostage until la policia stormed the clinic and arrested him. Under interrogation the man confessed he had been sent by Doña María and his intended target was me.

Joaquín has come to inform me that el Jefe is sending me to the States for my own safety. Arrangements have been made: the nuns have agreed to let Odette board with them.

A wave of dizziness sweeps over me. At the clinic the doctors discovered I'm suffering from diabetes. These fainting spells are becoming more frequent. But this time it's not the sugar in my blood but the news I've just heard that's making my head spin. I must talk to el Jefe myself. I will not leave without my daughter.

Bien, Bien, Joaquín coaxes, using my childhood nickname. During my time as first lady, my cousin was the model of deference and courtesy, addressing me always as Primera Dama Bienvenida, as if we had not been raised together. Please, don't make this any harder.

Any harder for whom? How can you think I'd accept this? I must speak to el Jefe.

Something in my voice convinces my cousin that Bien—impressionable, malleable, accommodating Bien—has hardened her resolve.

The next day the Cadillac is back, this time the property crawls with guardia. Joaquín in tow, el Jefe enters the house. He greets me in a chilly voice that does not bode well.

Jefe, please take a seat. Joaquín gestures toward the galería with its comfortable rocking chairs. Would you like a refreshment? He speaks in that ingratiating way he assumes around the powerful, which once included me.

But el Jefe lifts his hand in refusal. You wanted to see me?

My legs feel too weak to hold me up, but I refuse to sit and have him look down at me. Granted, even standing, I'm barely five feet tall. El Jefe is not much taller himself, but the thick heels on his custom-made shoes push him four or so inches above me. I've taken off those shoes, washed those feet, putting each toe in my mouth. Anything to please him. Has he forgotten?

I've never asked you for anything, Jefe, I remind him. But I'm asking now—please don't separate me from our child.

It's what's best for Odette, he says, his face a blank, not a trace of all we've shared. It's the face I've seen him wear when eliminating a dissident, silencing an opponent. But those are his enemies. I was once his wife, and afterward, to my shame, his mistress, enduring the scandal of bearing an illegitimate child.

The child is only seven years old, Jefe, I plead.

This is my decision for my daughter, he concludes, as if he'd given birth to Odette all by himself.

In desperation, I throw myself at his feet, begging him to reconsider. I'd rather you take my life than my daughter. By now I'm sobbing, my face contorted in a grimace. I know how unattractive I look. But then, I've never relied on my looks to get me anywhere with men.

Tears might evoke pity, but not from el Jefe once his mind is made up. He turns and glares at my cousin, cowering behind him. You called me here for an "emergency"? He doesn't wait for an answer. Make the arrangements, he says in that small, cold voice of his, more frightening than a shout. Without another word, he exits the house, leaving Joaquín to mop up what's left of me.

Bien, Bien, my soft-spoken cousin tries to console me. Don't despair. No hay mal que por bien no venga. God doesn't give us a burden without also giving us the strength to bear it.

I want to reach out and slap that smug look from his face. To think I recommended him years back when El Jefe decided to hire him as his speechwriter. What can my cousin know of despair or a mother's devotion to her child? A confirmed bachelor with seven sisters and a doting mother, Joaquín doesn't know how to give, only how to receive love. A man who will save himself above all else. The road to some people's hearts only goes in one direction.

Filomena

Now that construction is underway on Doña Alma's casita, the cementerio fills with workers. The barrio is grateful for the influx of jobs, the foreman happy to be back on site. Filomena's duties have picked up, cooking for the crew and cleaning up after them. It's dark by the time she leaves. Not yet light when she arrives.

Whenever she has a moment's peace, she tries to keep up with her listening visits to each marker. But only Bienvenida's tale seems to hold her attention. Pobrecita, having to leave her child behind. Filomena shudders, imagining the suffering Mamá endured that finally drove her to leave her two young daughters behind. Papá was not a powerful jefe, but he could be cruel and violent. Ay, Mamá. What you must have suffered!

Her mind is a wasp-nest of worries. Perla is sitting in a jail cell in Nueva York awaiting trial for murder. Pepito is working with a lawyer to get his mother deported. Pepito worries that she'll languish in a gringo prison, isolated and confused, not knowing the language. But the lawyer assures him that the prison system is full of Dominicans. His mother will have plenty of paisanos to talk to, if she ever decides to speak.

Pepito calls his tía daily with updates—easy enough now that Filomena has accepted Doña Alma's earlier offer of a cell phone. She has never asked her nephew for details about the charges against his mother. She doesn't need to: the story is all over the news. On Bichán's radio, on Lupita's little TV where her clients catch up with the world while their hair is being blown straight and dry. Filomena doesn't believe it! How on earth could Perla, a mother herself, commit such a horrible deed? If it is true, and the evidence seems to point that way, then her sister must have lost her mind. And the culprit is none other than the sinvergüenza she married. Un hombre sin principios. Look at what he did to Filomena, his wife asleep with his son in her belly. Not that she excuses herself either, but she was still a child. And here he is a free man, after having wrecked everyone's lives. She'd like to stab him with her butcher knife right through his wicked heart. Better yet, like that long-ago news story everyone was talking about, cut off his privates.

¡Dios me libra! Filomena makes the sign of the cross on her forehead. Here she is, plotting bloody murder herself! The truth is, people are capable of anything. Don't all the stories Filomena has heard in the campo, the barrio, and now in this cemetery confirm that?

≈ Bienvenida

A few days after my audience with el Jefe, I am bound for Nueva York. I had hoped that el Jefe would at least send me back to Miami, as I'd be that much closer to Odette. But Joaquín informs me there's a new favorite occupying the Florida mansion, a former beauty queen. Doña María cannot keep up with her rivals.

It's 1942 and the United States is at war. Everyone is nervous about the German submarines patrolling our waters, as we are allies of our neighbor to the north. Trujillo allows elections and wins by a landslide. We need a strongman to defend us. The Germans might decide to bomb us to gain a foothold in the Americas.

The consulate has arranged for a suite of rooms at the Essex House on Central Park South. A prestigious address, an important detail for el Jefe, who has always aspired to be a part of the small circle of fine, respectable families—one of my attractions, I can see that now. And though I might be the ex-wife, I'm *his* ex-wife. Even what he throws away belongs to him.

I again spend my days writing letters: dozens to el Jefe begging him to reconsider and allow our daughter to join me. The ones to Odette are filled with little stories she might enjoy: the snowfall that has blanketed the park like frosting on a cake, the store filled with toys, porcelain dolls and dollhouses she would adore, the pretty dresses in the shop windows. Always the same close: Write me, mi adorada hijita. Tell me everything. But what can a seven-year-old write that might fill the emptiness in her mother's heart? The ink runs so many times, I have to rewrite whole pages.

I try to structure each day to keep my sadness at bay. Mornings, I take walks in the large park across from the hotel with scraps from my breakfast to feed the birds and squirrels. Tuesdays and Thursdays, I head for the consulado to deposit my letters in the diplomatic pouch that goes out Wednesdays and Fridays. The consul comes out officiously to greet me. Any complaints, Doña Bienvenida, be sure to tell me first. Everyone is afraid of incurring El Jefe's ire. I hope the hotel is a comfortable place for you.

I don't spare him my complaints. Every place is hell without Odette at my side. A daughter, especially a young tender girl, should be with her mother.

This is what's best for the child, Doña Bienvenida, what el Jefe wants, what we all want—isn't it? Obviously, I will find no support from him.

Essex House is pleasant enough: fresh flowers in the lobby, a well-trained staff, the ambience hush-hush as if not to excite the residents. The place reminds me of Serenity House, except that instead of pregnant young girls, my floor is occupied by older women, long-term residents, bereft divorcées, widows, abandoned mistresses, well-heeled spinsters who never made matches for themselves. The few male guests seem to be Europeans, diplomats most likely.

I have yet to run into any Spanish speakers among the inhabitants on my floor, or if there are, they never let on. Everyone keeps to herself, as the rich tend to do. The only people I speak to are Sandrita and Chela, two Colombian sisters who clean our rooms and fill me in on the hotel's comings and goings, my fellow residents, their lives in this cold city. There's also a Puerto Rican, Arístides Ramos, a nice-looking older man, extremely polite and kind. A former undercover policeman, he has been hired by the management "to protect the hen house"—Sandrita, the more gossipy and irreverent of the sisters, tells me. He's now retired on a good pension, so he doesn't really have to work, but—again according to Sandrita—Arístides has taken on the night job because he recently lost his wife. His two sons are overseas in the army, he's worried about them. Keeping busy is his calmante.

One day in the elevator, I overhear one of the diplomats speaking loudly in French (I picked it up in France) about negotiations to get some important Jews into the United States.

In different circumstances I might have boasted about my own country. Poor as it is, it has stepped forward at the conference in Evian, offering to take in a hundred thousand Jews. Joaquín has been involved in the negotiations. At first, neither el Jefe nor my cousin was keen about allowing in Jews. The Spaniards threw them out of Spain for good reason. But finally, el Jefe waved away his misgivings. The important thing is that the Jews are white and likely to intermarry, thus advancing el Jefe's campaign to cleanse our blood of the African invasion from next door. Not to mention that the country needed a humanitarian boost after the disgraceful massacre on the border.

I heard about el corte, as it was called, from my sister, Yoya, in a letter posted from Nueva York, where she had gone with her husband, a Marine she met during the Occupation, to visit his family. It was during my absence in France, everything hushed up, so it was hard to get news. The killings were widespread around Monte Cristi, she reported. She and her husband Harry had hidden their Haitian maid and her children under a pile of laundry when the guardia barged in to search the house. According to Joaquín, el Jefe did not know about the massacre. But nothing happens on our little island that our supreme leader doesn't know about. Mamá and Papá had warned me that el Jefe was capable of anything in his grab for power.

But he is also the father of my child. His eyes gaze back at me from her little face: I see him in the assertive way she carries herself, her willfulness, her outbursts of temper, her sly smile as if she's holding something back. For my own sanity, I hold on desperately to the official story: this unfortunate incident was a popular uprising by angry campesinos, sick and tired of raids from across the border. After all, if it had been el Jefe's military, they would have used bullets not machetes.

Despite all my efforts, my daily routines, the stories I tell myself to avoid the facts, I can feel myself losing hope. I'm convinced I'll never be reunited with my daughter. The only unpardonable sin, as Soeur Odette often reminded me, is not trusting God to find a way. If so, I am damned. Life has become unbearable.

In desperation, I act—a secret I never wanted Odette to know, which I carried to my grave. I can tell it now. Our groundskeeper is un alma de Dios, as we say, a discreet woman who keeps her counsel, unlike the writer who wanted to give me a voice. I did not want a voice. I wanted my privacy. I wanted silence.

One night, a dark mood overtakes me. I reach for the bottle of pills for my nervios I obtained back home, where pharmacies will sell you whatever you will pay for. I swallow them one by one as if they were candies, the mints I love. I draw a warm bath as a backup: my plan is to lie in it, so that if the pills don't complete the job, I'll pass out and drown. I forget to turn off the water and the guest in the apartment below calls the front desk. Her ceiling is leaking. It's late, the handyman has gone home, so the front desk clerk sends Arístides up to check what's going on.

He knocks, then pounds on the door, calling out my name. When there's no answer, he tries to get in with his master key, but I've taken the precaution of sliding the chain in its groove. Arístides rushes down the hall onto the fire escape, crawls on the ledge, and climbs in through a window, rescuing me just in time. I'm rushed to the hospital, where my stomach is pumped. Arístides stays the night by my bed in case a translator is needed.

The next morning the alarmed consul shows up at the hospital. The palace will have to be notified. It wouldn't do to try to keep my overdose a secret. El Jefe is sure to bite off my head, the man complains bitterly. How are you doing? he asks as an afterthought.

Please leave, I answer in as steady a voice as I can manage.

Doña Bienvenida, please understand, I've come out of concern. He adds that Essex House has already notified the consulate, who pays the bills, that it is responsible for all damages to their property; the sodden floor will have to be repaired. More complaints. Furthermore, I will no longer be welcomed at the Essex; the consul will have to find me new accommodations. What a nuisance my despair has created for him.

I lose control. Get out! I shout. I almost feel sorry for the man, scurrying away like a scared animal.

Arístides has been sitting outside my door, not wanting to intrude. When he peeks in to see if I am all right, I tell him about the hotel no longer willing to host me. *Host* you? he snorts. For five hundred dollars a month! Until then, I didn't know how much el Jefe has been paying for my accommodations.

I spend a few days in the hospital before being released. Arístides visits daily, Sandrita and Chela swing by on the way home from work. Another visitor is a young Dominican who works on my floor as an aide while he waits for his foreign medical credentials to be approved.

Dr. Manuel Cruz, he introduces himself. When I mention there was a doctor by that name at the clinic where I get my care in Santiago, his face tightens. I never had the pleasure of meeting him, I add, but I heard him highly praised by the staff.

Cruz and Manuel are common names, he reminds me, dismissing the coincidence. This Manuel Cruz is vague about his family: his father is deceased, his siblings have scattered, he doesn't keep up with his relatives—all of this is very odd for a Dominican. But perhaps, he, too, has fled a painful situation. My questions must be opening old wounds, making him more guarded in my presence. We foreigners can be uncomfortable about personal questions from Americans. But it's common enough to ask other Latins stranded in this country where in the Americas they've come from.

Another Spanish speaker at the hospital is an older woman with a long, narrow face that reminds me not unpleasantly of a horse and cropped white hair—that genderless look of older American females. Dr. Beale served in an ambulance unit during the Spanish Civil War, where she picked up her heavily accented Spanish. She has never married (by choice, she adds—something I've never heard a woman openly admit), instead she is wedded to her profession: medicine is her love. She is well past the age to be working so hard, but she will never retire. What else would she do with herself?

She drops in one afternoon, having heard my story from Dr. Cruz.

Dr. Beale turns out to be a woman who is unafraid to speak up. She gives me quite the scolding. Someday, I will be reunited with my child, and little Odette is going to need a mother more than ever. Oh yes, she says, she knows all about el Jefe. I will only compound the child's suffering by doing away with myself, leaving her an orphan, morally speaking, given the monster I was married to. This puts steel in my back. I'm determined to stay alive.

Dr. Beale gives me her card and invites me to visit her consultorio whenever I need to talk. Before leaving the hospital, I want to thank Dr. Cruz for his care. He has not been by in a while, perhaps my questions have driven him away. I suspect Manuel's professional ambitions are not the only reason for his extended stay in Nueva York. According to Arístides, there are quite a few Dominican dissidents in the city.

My last day, I see him hurrying down the hall, accompanying a moaning woman on a gurney, about to give birth.

Dr. Cruz! Manuel!

He glances up, startled, and gives me the same wary look I've seen before, then waves brusquely, the way we do when we're both greeting and dismissing a person with the same gesture.

⇜ Filomena

Dr. Manuel Cruz . . . Filomena savors the name as if she were sucking a mentica to freshen her breath. Could it be the very same character who spoke when she rocked the globe at el Barón's spot? That Manuel was also a doctor who worked in Nueva York. For a moment, Filomena forgets Perla and the predicament she is in, Pepito and how he might be faring with his mother's tragedy. Whatever became of Manuel Cruz? Did he ever return home to his beloved mother? As Filomena goes by his marker later, she can't help giving it a nudge—the flakes fly, a whirl of white, and slowly they settle.

These stories are rekindling Filomena's own longings. She still aches for her Pepito, always a little boy in her dreams, and for Mamá to return as she promised. Occasionally, on trips back to her campo, Filomena has asked for any news. Bits of gossip and cuentos had been saved up to tell her: her mother was spotted in Jarabacoa getting out of a carro público; she has been working for a German family at Playa Dorada; selling billetes in the streets of Puerto Plata; drunk, dancing in a barra in Cabarete; remarried with a little son, in Nueva York. More stories than there are Altagracias to live them!

Each one a trickle of hope flowing into a river, overflowing its banks until Filomena is sure she will drown in sadness. She tries to forget, burying her hopes deep in her heart. She must not give in to despair like Doña Bienvenida.

Ay, Mamá, Filomena murmurs as she goes about her work. Ay, Mamá when she cuts her finger on the pruning shears. Ay, Mamá. On the radio in Bichán's colmado, she hears a report of yet another moreno Americano killed on the streets. Eight minutes, forty-six seconds, the police held him down, and what did el pobre hombre cry out as he was dying? *Momma, Momma*—how they say Mamá in English. Jesús, too, cried out for his mother on the cross, according to Padre Regino. Even God needs a mother!

Nights, she pulls out the cigar box from under her mattress and studies the only photo she owns of her mother. Papá had torn it up and thrown it away in the trash, but Filomena rescued the pieces and taped them back together. The image is full of creases like the lines on Bienvenida's marker, but Filomena can still make out the sweet brown face looking so much like Perla's but with Filomena's deep-set eyes. She kisses the photo, then takes out the other keepsakes: Mamá's mantilla for wearing to mass; her rosary with its white beads like perlas, the paint peeling off; three pebbles with rings around them, signifying good luck; and finally, a tiny medal of la Virgencita de la Altagracia—Filomena kisses that image as well.

As a child, Filomena had to hide these treasures from Papá, who was infuriated by the mention of esa sinvergüenza puta porquería. As for Mamá's promise to return, Filomena never dared speak of it to anyone except Perla, who dismissed it as a silly dream.

Now, working at the cementerio, Filomena hatches the idea of burying her treasure box, maybe alongside Doña Bienvenida, or better still, Don Manuel, where it would have the added protection of el Barón's oversight. ¿Y quién sabe? Perhaps el Barón will use his powers to reunite Filomena with her mother. Filomena considers asking Doña Alma for her permission, but what if la doña starts picking apart the request with questions? What is this all about? Who is the woman in the picture? What did she tell you when she left? Filomena could not bear it. The wound is still tender. Besides, la doña doesn't need to be bothered with one more thing.

At the first opportunity, Filomena will bury her box beside Don Manuel's box. In exchange for this accommodation, Filomena promises Don Manuel to be as faithful to his marker as she is to Bienvenida's.

She puts her arms around the globe and kisses it into activity.

⇜ Manuel

I have to read the name on the patient's chart several times to believe it: Bienvenida Trujillo! I'm curious but cautious. As a man on the run, I have learned to be careful. Everyone knows somebody who knows who you are on our little island. If it were to leak out that Manuel Cruz is alive and well and working in Nueva York, not rotting in the jungles of the Cordillera Central in his failed effort to escape to Haiti, my family back home would suffer the consequences. And it wouldn't end there. The regime's long arm stretches far into the exterior. Dominicans have been killed or disappeared from Mexico City, Havana, Cuba, and from this very city.

St. Vincent's doesn't have many foreign doctors, as our credentials aren't readily accepted here. But due to the war, medical professionals are scarce, and thanks to Dr. Beale's intervention, I've been hired as her aide, filling in wherever there's a need. Dr. Beale has presented my case for review to the board, and she is hoping I can earn my license by passing the examinations. Once that happens, she plans to employ me openly as a physician on her staff.

Meanwhile, she turns what she calls a blind eye on my taking care of her patients. Just keep it under wraps, another expression I haven't yet learned in the free English classes at the library, but its meaning is clear enough. Having to sneak around is demeaning when I'm already a full-fledged doctor back home, on the staff at the very clinic in Santiago where Doña Bienvenida used to get her care. We never crossed paths there; she was in exile in France; by the time she returned and the attempt on her life was made, I was gone. A good thing we never met, given that we are now face to face in her hospital room in Nueva York.

She's a nice lady, sencilla, without pretentions or arrogance, just as I'd heard from my colleagues. But history will scratch its head at how such a good woman could end up married to the devil himself. Of course, she's now an ex-wife. Even so, I'm not about to let down my guard. She might betray me even without meaning to.

Doña Bienvenida has occasional visitors, some I suspect might be el Jefe's spies. The most frequent one claims to be a Puerto Rican who recently retired from the New York police force. The more questions this Arístides Ramos peppers me with, the more uncomfortable I become. Whenever I have business in Doña Bienvenida's room and Ramos is around, I'm brief and efficient.

Dr. Beale understands my caution, of course. She was in Spain during the civil war—infiltrators, traitors, secret agents, the dead thrown into mass graves—she's seen it all. She feels sorry for the woman, however. An innocent to the slaughter—by her own choice to be sure. But sometimes you've gone down the road too far to open your eyes and live with yourself. Dr. Beale falls silent, looking at some view visible only to her. What is her story? I wonder. Not the stories she has told me—medical school, the war, ambulance driving, but the story we keep to ourselves or even from ourselves about who we are and what we love and whether our lives reflect that.

Dr. Beale is worried about what will happen to our patient once she leaves the hospital. A fragile soul, that poor woman can't bear to face the truth. Just a glimpse would kill her, as it almost did this time. Sometimes we need our stories, even if they are lies.

Of course, I feel for Doña Bienvenida's predicament, trapped like Mamá in a marriage with a cruel man. What stories did Mamá tell herself to survive? Perhaps Alfa Calenda was as much a refuge for her as it was for me.

Bienvenida

The suicide attempt—hushed up as an inadvertent overdose—turns out to have its silver lining. No hay mal que por bien no venga. Even insipid sayings from the mouths of Joaquín and others sometimes prove to be true.

El Jefe is concerned, Joaquín reports when he calls. It's finally hit home that I'm willing to take my own life rather than lose my child. Additionally, there have been troubling reports from the nuns that little Odette is a handful. She has bitten one of the girls. She refuses to do her homework, to make her bed, to clean her plate. She is losing weight, she throws tantrums. These things combined would probably not be enough to sway him, but el Jefe is distracted by the war. A German submarine in our waters has sunk the cargo ship *Presidente Trujillo*—something I'm sure el Jefe, superstitious as he is, must take as a sign.

In June he plans to visit Nueva York, the consul informs me later. Now that Europe is at war, his medical checkups are being done here. He will be bringing Odette with him. It's only the beginning of March. But once again, the consul says, el Jefe knows best. Odette must finish out her school year in Santiago.

By then, you'll be in your very own home, he adds. Since I am no longer welcome at Essex House, el Jefe has asked him to purchase a house in a quiet suburb with a Catholic school nearby for Odette to attend. There is also the option of Montreal, where other Dominicans have settled. But Canada is too cold and even farther from my beloved country.

Queens is where Arístides lives. There are reasonable houses for sale near his place in Astoria, he has told me. But when I mention this to the consul, he vetoes that choice. El Jefe prefers a tonier place, like Jamaica Estates.

I end up in Forest Hills, a pleasant cottage on a quiet street full of identical houses, as if no one wants to stand out, like the cowed citizens of my own country. More and more my eyes are being opened, but with my daughter as hostage, I squeeze them shut. It's April when I move in, flowering bushes are in bloom, azaleas and forsythias, Arístides teaches me their names. Many lawns have trees called dogwood and another known as weeping willow. My weeping tree is in the backyard.

I feel more isolated here than in Manhattan, where I could walk in the park and distract myself by talking to Sandrita and Chela and visiting the consulate for news of home. Here, my neighbors seldom show their faces. A few call out "hello" and wave, collecting their newspapers or inspecting their lawns. Just as well. If they were to speak to me, I'd have to shake my head, no English.

Arístides drops by often. He has left his job at Essex House. He wants better hours, work closer to home. I wonder, though, if his decision has anything to do with the management's treatment of me.

One afternoon, I'm in the backyard under my willow, so I don't hear his knocking at the front door. When he doesn't get an answer, he comes around back. That's where he finds me. Are you all right? he greets me. I think he still worries that I'll despair and harm myself.

Nothing to worry about, I assure him, forcing a smile. Odette will be here soon.

And then, what will you do, Bienvenida? We're now on first-name terms.

Bueno, let's see. I answer playfully, pretending I'm a santera, reading my fortune from a coffee cup. Odette will enroll at Immaculate Conception Academy, learn English, teach her mother how to speak it. She will take lessons in music, piano and voice, and dance, something I used to love and haven't done in years. In no time, she'll be having her quinceañera. We will have the party here in the garden. The more I grasp for happy possibilities, the emptier I feel. I'm giving my daughter a future in exile. How lonely a life that will be. By the time I have her married and living with her husband and children in this very house, the fantasy won't hold.

Colorín colo—I bow my head to hide my tears. I can't complete the spell to end the story.

How about a different ending? Arístides's voice is intimate, a caress of sound. He lifts my face so we are eye to eye. You have your own life to live, Bienvenida. It can be a good life for you, too.

My life will always belong to him. I will always be the mother of his daughter. He can take her away at any moment. He can hold that over me.

Not if I have anything to say about it. Arístides stops himself as if aware he has gone too far.

I'm intrigued by this boundary he has almost crossed. What do you propose to do? I ask.

We can marry. I can adopt Odette; we can raise her together. She'll have two older brothers to protect her, and we can have each other.

What an imagination! He, a retired policeman, pitting himself against our powerful Jefe! David battling Goliath! I laugh in disbelief and delight. You're very sweet, Arístides, but that sort of happy ending only happens in novelas.

And who's to say novelas can't come true? He kisses me, a tender, tentative grazing of the lips. Enough to light the fire I thought had gone out. Later in my bedroom, I feel awkward. All I know of lovemaking, I learned from the only man I've been with. I kneel to take off Arístides's shoes, as el Jefe liked for me to do. But Arístides pulls me up alongside him. I want you at my side, not at my feet, he whispers.

⁀ Filomena

Pepito keeps his tía apprised of the progress of his mother's case. On one of his calls, he mentions that he will be visiting Perla at the jail where she is being held in Nueva York.

Filomena yearns to hear her sister's voice. Can I talk to her?

I'm not sure it's allowed, Tía. And even if it is, Mamita won't talk to anyone.

She talked to me.

When was that?

She called to tell me she was coming as soon as she could get on a plane.

That must have been before Mamita was arrested at the airport. Since then, she's refused to speak to anyone. Not to her lawyer, not to the social worker, not even to me. Pepito's voice catches.

I will get her to talk, you will see, Filomena promises. As if she could ever get Perla to do anything her little sister asked for.

Pepito is hoping that his mother will be deported soon. Her American lawyer thinks there is a good chance. True, his mother has long surpassed the five-year limit in which a resident can be deported for a single crime, but she actually committed two murders—three, counting the dog—and that might qualify her for deportation. The lawyer is also citing the irregularities in her documents. Filomena Altagracia Moronta has been going by the name Perla Pérez for years, as reported by her employers and other witnesses. This does not constitute a crime in and of itself, just further evidence of her shifty character.

Pepito hates for his mother to be portrayed this way. But he'll go along with whatever story will make her sentence lighter.

You do know, Tía, that all of Mamita's papers are in your name? I hope it doesn't create any problems for you in the future.

Future? Who cares about the future? Filomena wants to help her sister now. She offers to confess that it was she who committed those crimes. I can go to prison for Perla.

Ay, Tía. It doesn't work that way.

It worked in the Bible. Christ died for our sins. Why can't Filomena do the same for her own flesh and blood?

What a good sister you are, Tía. But there is no need for such a sacrificio. Pepito has already contacted a lawyer in the DR. It'll be easier there. Maybe ten years, or less. Money can make anything happen. Mamita can still have some of her life left when she gets out. His voice breaks again. What a good son.

If she's here, I can visit her. I can bring her food, medicine, whatever she needs. I have my job. I can help with the costs.

You mean they didn't let you go after what has happened? Pepito is surprised. No, he hadn't heard that his tía Filo no longer works for his father's family. That news didn't travel north to him, but then his father is no longer talking to him.

So, where are you working now, Tía?

A cemetery, but not for the dead. Filomena repeats what Doña Alma has said about the place.

Her nephew is intrigued. Sounds totally Borges. What exactly do you do there?

Casi nada, Filomena admits. Sweeping, keeping the grounds clean, washing the markers. She feels sheepish getting paid so well when her tasks are relatively light. Only recently with construction has her workload increased. Even so, she gets two full days off. Paid vacations. The doña has asked about health insurance. She is from allá, where employers abide by certain rules.

Pepito wants to know more. So, she's una Americana?

Una Americana-dominicana, ni carne ni pescado, like you, she teases her nephew.

You know her name?

It's a strange one. I can never remember it, but she said to call her Alma, Alma Cruz.

If it's *the* Alma Cruz he's thinking of, Pepito actually teaches her books! Scheherazade is her writing name, one and the same person. In fact, he's been trying to interview her for years. Filomena hasn't heard her nephew laugh like that since he was a child. All their recent calls have been so grim. I definitely want to meet her when I come down with Mamita. If she doesn't run the other way, he adds.

She would not do that. She is very kind y *muuuy* curiosa. Filomena draws out the word like a tape measure to show what lengths Doña Alma's curiosity will go to. Sometimes Filomena can't get her chores done, la doña peppering her with question after question about her life.

I could ask if she will meet with you, Filomena offers. I could say you are my nephew who teaches her books.

Not a good idea. Best not to mention his name. He has made himself a persona non grata to her agent with his persistence. And you, Tía, how are you holding up? Such a thoughtful boy.

'Tamo vivo, she replies like they do in the campo. Things could be a lot worse. She will not burden her nephew with her cares and concerns.

Besides, as the building project gets underway, Filomena doesn't have time to mope and worry. As soon as she gets up, she downs her café con leche and pan de agua—no time to make mangú—says her prayers to the santo del día on the calendar, checks on her treasure box, and hurries across the street. Often, la arquitecta is already there, giving orders even to Filomena, who is not part of the construction crew. But Doña Dora's bossiness lights a fire under the workers. The casita goes up in record time, painted purple with pink trim, a covered porch and two rocking chairs like those in her viejita's house.

When her casita is completed, Doña Alma decides to throw herself a house party and invite the whole vecindario. The neighbors end up pocketing dulces and bocadillos by the dozen to take home for their suppers; plastic and trash are strewn everywhere; the children keep hitting the snow globe as if it were a piñata to watch the flakes fly, finally dislodging it from its base. It rolls away, coming to rest against Doña Bienvenida's marker, a hairline crack across the surface.

Still, Doña Alma declares the party a success. When Filomena points out the crack, Doña Brava assures her that it's easy enough to fix with a line of glue. The important thing, Doña Alma adds, is the good will of her neighbors. They'll now look out for her.

She means to *live* in the house! Filomena had assumed the small cottage would be one of those getaway cabañas people of means build for themselves out in the campo. A place where the owners can spend a lazy weekend day, sometimes staying overnight if the festivities end too late to take the highway back to the capital or if they get delayed with their queridas. These cottages are quite popular, but they're usually located in the countryside or quiet beaches and intended for outings, not permanent residences.

Doña Alma's casita is no bigger than the house Filomena and Perla shared with their father growing up. But la doña insists it has everything she needs: a bedroom, bathroom, sitting room, an outdoor kitchen.

Where is the maid's room?

I'm not planning on hiring a maid. Actually, Doña Alma backtracks, she is hoping that Filomena will consider doing a little cleaning and cooking from time to time. I'm a terrible cook. Doña Alma says it like a boast. Filomena's work should be much lighter now that the crew is gone, and all the markers set up. And if it is too much, Filomena can hire someone to help her.

Filomena can handle all these tasks easily now that the construction is finished. She has been feeling like a laggard again, sitting around, her jobs done by midday, stargazing at the markers—though la doña has said that is part of her duties. She's about to refuse help, but the thought occurs to her that when Perla is released, her sister will need something to do. A job will keep her mind off her troubles. It will be like old times in the campo, keeping house and working side by side—and both getting paid for it, besides.

While the globe is being repaired, the mounting reinforced, the ground disturbed, Filomena takes the opportunity to bury her cigar box beside Don Manuel's box of papers. Should anyone discover her secret, Filomena will claim she knows nothing about it. Some devotee of el Barón must have put it there. On Tuesdays and Fridays, these petitioners still find their way over the wall at night to make their offerings and brujerías. Here, give it to me, she will say. I will dispose of it.

She makes a sign of the cross to absolve herself for the lie she is planning to tell. Hanging around cuentos for months, she has learned to invent the truth, rather than just tell it.

⟿ Manuel

Do you have time for a story? I ask Doña Bienvenida. We've literally bumped into each other when my marker toppled over, thanks to children getting out of hand at the neighborhood party.

Yes, of course. She laughs. Endless time is all we have!

Soon after your departure from St. Vincent's, a young lady arrives in the emergency room on New Year's Eve. My dubious credentials have been overlooked, as the acceptable physicians are out celebrating. I'm glad to cover for them. My heart is still heavy with the loss of my mother this past November. I'm in no mood to celebrate.

The señorita has twisted her ankle dancing at a party thrown by one of her cousins at the Waldorf Astoria. She's quite talkative, her English as good as my teacher's at the library. Seeing me struggle, she switches over to Spanish. She wants to know where I'm from.

I knew it! She claps her hands like she just won a guessing game. I'm Domincan, too. Lucía Amelia Castellanos, a sus órdenes, she introduces herself with mock formality. My friends here call me Lucy, Papi calls me Lulu, Mami calls me a handful! Her laughter is a peeling of bells, ringing in my New Year. My mood has suddenly lightened.

She wants to know why I'm practicing in Nueva York. Did I go to medical school here? Do I miss home?

I've become quite good at evading questions by asking them. Where did she learn such good English? In boarding school, she tells me, near Boston. So, what grade is she in?

She gives me an offended look. What'd you mean? I graduated ages ago!

"Ages ago" turns out to be last year. After she completed her high school, she started in at Katie Gibbs right here in Manhattan, before her parents dragged her home. She leans in conspiratorially. They didn't like my American boyfriend.

I feel a surprising pang—of jealousy! I, with no claims on this pretty girl I've just met.

Now, they brought me on this trip to get me away from you-know-who. She won't say who, but I can guess. There's only one you-know-who in our country. And he has an eye for pretty young girls.

I'm always wary when first meeting a Dominican, not sure if they support the regime. But I can't resist this girl's charms. Before she leaves, I make sure I know where she is staying.

The next day I stop by the Waldorf Astoria to see how her ankle is coming along. And the next day, and the next, a little disappointed at how quickly it is healing, as I will soon lose my pretext for these house calls. Her parents are very grateful for my attentiveness and insist on paying me, but I refuse. My pleasure, I assure them.

During every visit, Lucía barrages me with questions. I end up telling her all about my early years, Alfa Calenda, my dear mother, the childhood nickname she gave me, Babinchi—That's what I'll call you from now on!—my father's little cruelties, the loss of Mamá this past November 10th—That's my birthday!, she exclaims. I tell her about my medical education at the university in the capital. You paid for it yourself?! She cannot believe it. We veer into deeper waters. How I had to flee the country after joining a group of dissidents opposed to you-know-who—I wink. She laughs. We are already creating that private treasure trove of stories, code phrases, inside jokes intimates share with each other.

I don't think I've spoken this much about myself since my bedroom confidences with Mamá.

Lucía is at the edge of her seat, listening. Be careful, I warn her, you don't want to fall again and twist another ankle.

Maybe I do, she laughs, then I'll keep seeing more of you.

She wooed me with her beauty and liveliness. I wooed her with my stories.

Mi Jefe did the same with his poetry, Bienvenida says in a dreamy voice.

His poetry? I doubt it! El Jefe was barely literate. That's why he hired her cousin, Joaquín Balaguer, to be his silver tongue. Of course, I don't say this, not wanting to hurt Bienvenida's feelings.

Lucía's parents, Don Erasmo and Doña Amelia Altagracia, are none too happy with her new beau. An exile, a man she wouldn't look at twice back home. You mean *you* wouldn't! she challenges them. Afterward, she reports these scenes tearfully to me.

They're right. Lucía is in demand. So many novios and boyfriends I will hear about in the years to come, so many other lives she could have lived. Even the dictator, as she had hinted, who spotted her at a party and asked for her name, which is why her parents thought it best to evacuate her from the country for a few weeks with the excuse of a health problem. Her visit to St. Vincent's was, therefore, fortuitous. By the time they return, el Jefe's fickle heart will have moved on to the next pretty face.

I'm not going back! She digs in her heels. She would rather die.

Her parents must have known what I will find out in the years to come: when Lucía sets her mind on something, there's no standing in her way. Finally, they give their blessing, Don Erasmo slowly warming to me, Doña Amelia Altagracia smiling through her teeth.

The wedding cannot happen right away, as I have no way of supporting a wife, no less one accustomed to the best. I live in a room in a boardinghouse in Washington Heights, eat my meals at the hospital cafeteria, buy my clothes at secondhand shops. I have nothing in the way of savings, but I do have my pride, which will not allow me to take handouts. The compromise we all reach is that Lucía will wait on the island until I get my license and can earn enough to set up a home for us in Nueva York. A matter of months. Doña Amelia Altagracia seems relieved with this plan, perhaps hoping her daughter's ardent love will cool with time. (I confess, I fear this, too.)

A few days after her departure, I receive the disappointing news: the board has rejected my Dominican credentials. Dr. Beale has tried twisting all the arms she can—but no luck. She recommends a temporary move to Canada, where requirements are less stringent. I can enroll in some review courses there, earn my Canadian license, which I can then more easily transfer to the States. Apparently, there is no other option if I'm to pursue my profession as an exile.

The "temporary" move ends up lasting three years. I don't know how I endured it. But we do what we have to do to survive. Lo que no mata engorda, I used to tell my daughters when they wanted to give up. What doesn't kill you will fatten you. They didn't like that saying as they all wanted to be thin. Americanitas, por fin. I tried explaining that in our poorer countries, to be plump is a good thing. We're in the US now, they reminded me, as if I could ever forget it.

⬱ Bienvenida

Así es la vida, Manuel, a lot of rain and a little sun. I remember that I met you right before you left for Canada. We ran into each other outside the hospital. You were in love, so happy, but also sad about the imminent separation.

You have sharp eyes, Doña Bienvenida!

Not sharp enough to see the downpour of sorrows el Jefe would bring into my life. Mamá, Papá, Yoya, they all tried to warn me. Papa Dios also joined in, sending rain the night of my wedding. But I can't complain. Even in exile, it was not all nubes y nieve. I often think back on those sunny moments, trying to relive them. . . .

Arístides and I are crazy in love. Como dos teenagers! I have my hair done in the popular style, victory rolls that add inches to my height; I slim down and dress up more. Arístides is gracious with his compliments. I now see it's not money that makes me prettier, it's happiness.

We plan a quiet wedding. A civil ceremony, as it is unlikely that the church will allow our marriage, once I confess I am a divorced woman. No matter. The church has become less of a comfort, more a confinement. How to contain the wild heart within a corral of ten commandments. I'm letting go of so many restraints. Perhaps I've learned a thing or two from living in a free country.

Somehow, *La Nación* catches wind of our plans. A short announcement appears in the society pages: Doña Bienvenida, former first lady, is to marry Arístides Ramos, a Puerto Rican, retired from the New York police force. The next thing I know Odette will not be joining me. El Jefe does not want his daughter to be raised in a house with another man. My allowance is stopped. I'll have to vacate the house, which is in el Jefe's name.

Move in with me, Arístides offers. But that will solve only one problem, the one I consider minor compared to losing my child. So, we don't get married—he tries another angle. We live together. No one needs to know. I shake my head sadly. He is the innocent, not me, thinking we can keep a secret from El Jefe.

The choice is clear: a life with Odette as well as a livelihood—no small matter since I have no money of my own—or a desolate life in exile with a man who can never fill the emptiness that will be left if I lose my daughter. That hole will swallow us both up and destroy what happiness we might have together.

Arístides refuses to accept my decision. He keeps showing up at the house with the excuse that I haven't answered his calls and he's worried about me. You're making it worse, I say, dismissing him at the door. It's too much temptation to let him in, and also I cannot risk it. Finally, Arístides disappears like the dissidents back home, hauled away in the middle of the night. I worry that el Jefe's agents have eliminated my ardent suitor. But from Sandrita and Chela I learn that Arístides has lost one of his sons in Normandy. I write him with my sympathies, but then I tear up the letter. Why add to his load by reminding him of another loss?

After I break our engagement, Odette joins me. The consul informs me that we can stay in the cottage, but I no longer want to live in a place haunted by so many memories of Arístides. The city itself is mined with his presence. When I was forced to relocate from Essex House, the consul had brought up the idea of Canada. A whole other country, a chance to start over with my little girl.

The consul looks relieved at the revival of this idea. No doubt he'd be happy to be rid of me. First, however, he must consult with his superiors on the island. El Jefe approves the move, perhaps happy to put some distance between me and my former beau as well.

Before leaving Nueva York, I go to say goodbye to Dr. Beale and thank her once again for all her attentions. I bring my little girl along to show off.

Dr. Beale is curious as to why I am moving to Canada. Who do I know there and what will I do? I mention there are actually a few Dominican families living in an area called Westmount, where the Montreal consul has already found a house for me and Odette near a good school and a park. I do know French from my years in Paris. It will be a nice change. I chatter on, evading the real reason for my move.

Dr. Beale is studying me closely. I can tell she's not convinced this is my free choice. She brings up Dr. Cruz. Remember that young doctor who helped take care of you? She's about to say something more—but stops herself as if recalling some confidence she mustn't disclose.

And what of that nice fellow who kept a vigil at your bedside while you were in the hospital—whatever happened to him?

My mother isn't allowed boyfriends, Odette speaks up. Neither am I, she adds.

Dr. Beale seems amused by the pert little chaperone at my side. Is that a fact? And who, might I ask, has made this rule?

Odette looks at the elderly woman as if she has been hiding under a rock. El Generalísimo, she says. My father. When I'm old enough, boys will have to ask Papá first. She nods righteously.

As we kiss goodbye, Dr. Beale whispers, You got her back just in time.

Outside on the street, we run into you. This time you do not hurry away but greet me warmly.

And who is this? you ask, as if you can't tell. Even as an infant, Odette looked so much like her father. She also has his will, as the nuns at her convent school discovered. I hope that with time and gentle persuasion I can tame her character as I was never able to do her father's.

Odette Altagracia Trujillo Ricardo, she rattles off her full name. And who are you?

Her pluckiness makes you playful, ¿Yo? *Yo soy el aventurero*—you sing a few lines of the popular canción. We chat for a few minutes. I ask about your licensing exams. Your foreign degree cannot be validated here. Dr. Beale has pulled in every contact, but she can't change the policy.

You do have some good news, you add. You've met the woman you are going to marry! No, not a norteamericana, but a dominicana— you are very coy about sharing her name. Her parents don't want to announce the engagement until closer to the date, as you and your novia will have to wait to marry until you are able to obtain a license. Dr. Beale has advised you to try Canada. She is making the arrangements with a colleague at the University of Montreal. You are waiting to hear back.

We're going to Canada, too, my self-possessed daughter interrupts before I can tell you the news myself.

But I heard that you had bought a house in Queens. That you were going to marry—

My look stops you short. All in the past, I say, my eye on the young girl, the way we clue in someone that we can't talk openly in front of a child. Please do look us up in Montreal. The consul will know where we are.

At the mention of the consul, your face tightens up. Yes, of course, you say noncommittally.

I can see you are hiding more than the name of your novia. You have your reasons for wanting to remain incognito, reasons Dr. Beale must know about.

It gets very cold there, Odette rattles on. You will need warm clothes.

Ay, Señorita, if you bestow one of your smiles on me, I won't need any more warmth.

Odette lifts her little chin, dismissing the compliment. On the ride back to Queens she interrogates me about you: Who was that, Mamá? Is he the boyfriend Papa told me about?

I make a mental note to read all her letters home before I post them.

≈ Manuel

I have to laugh, remembering that little urchin.

Speaking of letters . . . I resume my story, having left it in the middle so Doña Bienvenida could catch me up on hers.

Those three years in Canada, Lucía's letters and cards are my lifeline. Even in wartime, they arrive regularly. I read and reread them.

Later, I will give my daughter Alma the box of her mother's letters and cards for a book she wants to write about us. But Lucía will veto that idea. You can write all you want about your father but leave me out of it! Ay, Mami, I plead with her. Don't Ay, Mami me. She'll dig up every damn secret, exaggerate it into an untruth, and blab it to the world. That gives me pause, for sure.

Finally, my Canadian license in hand, I pass my review board in Nueva York, and I am reunited with my love. Our long-awaited wedding takes place. We settle into a small, dark apartment with bars on the windows, like a jail, Lucía jokes, a joke that soon enough sours into complaints. For the first time in her life, she is having to watch her spending and make do with what I bring home. She is homesick and tired from having to clean and cook (boil and burn, I joke once, and never again)—no maids to attend to her. When she gets pregnant, the pressure mounts.

My in-laws have returned to the island, and they want their daughter and future grandchildren nearby where they can help us—an insult to my ability to take care of my own. We can live there in the lap of luxury. Their lap. I keep refusing, pointing out that as a dissident I'll be seized the minute the plane lands. Maybe that's what your mother wants? A comment that results in another round of fights.

Now that the war has ended, the US can turn its attention to its own hemispheric mess. Under pressure from los yanquis, el Jefe grants a general amnesty to all his detractors and promises to hold free elections; opposing candidates are welcomed.

Lucía is elated. Now we can go back!

Don't you know it's all a show for the gringos?

No, it isn't. You just don't care about me.

Back and forth we go. World War II has ended. World War III is in full swing.

I hold off as long as I can. But Lucía's unhappiness wears us both down. When she miscarries our first child, I realize I have to choose: it's either divorce Lucía or swallow the bitter pill. If the king in Britain can renounce his throne to marry his divorcée, I can give up my American dream for my wife.

Lucía's father manages to obtain a personal pardon for me, further guaranteeing my safety, by arguing that my earlier dissidence was just the reckless politics of youth. The country needs my talents. A well-trained doctor, with a newly earned license to practice in the States, I have so much to contribute to el Jefe's regime. It works. Money can open doors, all right.

We return, moving into a house provided by my in-laws, their car and chauffeur at our disposal, as well as a beach house where my wife and our growing family can enjoy weekends with their cousins and grandparents. El Jefe doesn't dare touch the oligarchs unless they mess with him, and none of them do. It's not sycophancy as much as superiority. They're above the dictatorship.

Being in that bubble of privilege, while many members of my own family and colleagues are being rounded up, proves to be another kind of exile. I can't bear it. And so, I make "the stupid mistake," my wife's words, of falling in once again with some dissident colleagues. Soon my family is under surveillance; periodically, I'm brought into headquarters for questioning, Don Erasmo always managing to get me out. Lucía's brothers, too, are implicated, for I've gotten them embroiled in my underground cell. When the arrests start, we manage to get out, my wife and our girls, on a bogus fellowship fina-gled by none other than Dr. Beale, who's on the board of Columbia Presbyterian. We leave behind my wife's family to suffer the conse-quences of my indiscretion. Their status and connections will protect them, I tell myself. Even so, I don't think Lucía will ever forgive me for what "you put us all through" those last horrid years.

This second exile is much harder. Now I suffer not just my home-sickness and grievances but those of my wife and four young daugh-ters. My license has expired after ten years away, so I work night shifts as an orderly, studying for my boards again. I know that Lucía is receiving infusions of cash from her parents, transferred into an account she opens on the sly. I've seen the statements, but I turn a blind eye. How can I refuse when I owe her so much for the troubles she and our daughters have endured?

A few months after my arrival, I get my license. I work seven days a week to provide for anything my family needs. We move around a lot, a sublet in Manhattan, then the Bronx, briefly in Brooklyn, finally buying our own small house in Queens. Wherever we go, my girls complain about being bullied in school. Every day it's a scene just to get them on the bus. My wife finally contacts the fancy boarding school she attended, and with a subsidy from her father, the girls—reluctantly, at first—go off to Massachusetts, one by one, once they are old enough. Soon, they're all acting as if they were born and bred here.

I feel gratified to see them all thriving, but I miss them terribly. My wife does, too, at first, but in time, she also escapes the empty nest, volunteering at the Dominican Mission in the United Nations. Now that the dictator has been toppled, she has become a fierce advocate for her country. With her fancy surname and fluent English and charm and connections, she's more than welcome. Our ambassador much prefers the city's other attractions—the shows, the restaurants, the shopping—to the tedious work of being a nobody from a "banana republic." Lucía steps in to fill the vacuum, attending all the committee meetings, drafting and typing up "his" reports and remarks. She leaves the house early in the morning and sometimes doesn't return until late at night. I admit I am secretly proud of her. I had no idea she could work so hard when it is something she likes.

My daughters also drift away. They try to hide it, but I can tell they're ashamed of their Papi: my heavy accent—which I try to correct with private lessons, once I can afford them.; my old country manners and attitudes; the way I dress; what they call my off-color jokes.

Is there anything about me you do approve of?

Come on, Papi, don't be that way.

I try to loop them back in, writing them long letters with stories of Babinchi—using my childhood nickname frees me to do a little invention. I never get a reply. When I ask why, the girls complain that they find Spanish hard to read. So, I make the supreme effort and write in English. Only Alma, my second-born, writes back, enclosing the original with correction marks in the margins. This passage is unclear. This word is not well chosen. And sorry, Papi, but Alfa Omega is too farfetched. Alfa Calenda, I correct. Whatever, she replies.

Just as my daughters always find fault with how I dress and behave, now Alfa Calenda will be subject to improvement. And so, I stop sharing my stories with them.

They complain about that, too. You never talk to us. When I do offer some anecdote, they roll their eyes. You already told us that story. Infected by the American taste for brand-new, as if stories have an expiration date.

Her first year at college, Alma requests that we not come up for her parents' weekend. She has too much homework. She needs to spend the time working on her term paper.

But your teachers, your friends—they will think you are an orphan.

Are you kidding? Most of my friends' parents aren't coming either.

Her mother and I decide to surprise her anyway. We load up the car with her favorite foods from the bodega near my oficina, Café Bustelo, fried tostones, and a tin of pastelitos made by the Dominican woman who cleans my office, a special treat Alma can't get in the campos of Vermont. We show up so pleased with ourselves. Our plan is to deliver our gifts and then leave her to her studies until suppertime, when we'll collect her for dinner at a restaurant. Just a couple of hours of her time. After all, everyone has to eat.

But Alma is nowhere to be found. Maybe she is in the library working on her term paper, I suggest to the young woman at the dorm's reception desk. The girl snorts as if I've just dropped in from outer space. Alma is off for the weekend with her boyfriend.

We don't allow boyfriends. Alma knows that.

We drive back to the motel. That night my wife has to take Valium—something she hasn't done since our escape. After she falls asleep, I dress in the dark and slip out of the room.

I drive to the school, circling the campus, as if I might see my daughter at her dormitory window, waving at me.

I don't know what I'm going to do next. I can't go searching for her. I have no idea where she is. And what good will it be to find her? The harm has been done. The tie broken. I drive and drive until I'm miles from that small town.

I'm tempted to keep going, disappear, let my daughters and my wife rebuild their lives without me. I picture them: Amparo with her big heart will make a good social worker. Alma will write her books. Consuelo and Piedad are less formed in my imagination. But they will be fine as well. Lucía will recover quickly, cushioned by her familia, marrying some distant cousin, one of those gay ones who hide in disguise marriages and make no requirements from a spouse except that she entertain and manage the house and servants. I'm bitter and full of self-pity, too.

I find myself thinking of Alfa Calenda, the relief I used to get from visiting this world of make-believe with Mamá. The faces and places of my childhood, the stories, the poems, the smells, the sounds, the voices murmuring in that lyrical mother tongue, memories and dreams—all that I left behind, all that was lost of me in English, lives on there.

I feel a loosening in my chest, the way the ice on the lakes would crack in those warming days of spring in Canada. I turn the car around and drive back to the motel; I let myself into the dark room and slip into bed; my wife stirs but she does not wake up.

Alma and her sisters

Alma's sisters wait until the last minute to call her. They're on their way! Tickets have been bought—not cheap since it's right before Easter week, the only overlapping time the three had free. They're all retired, aren't their schedules wide open? Alma knows better than to ask.

The Hammer needs to see us now, Piedad explains. Their parents' lawyer has concluded all the paperwork: the estate is finally settled, the separate deeds drawn. But Martillo has one final small matter they need to decide about.

Here we go again. What now?

We'll talk when we get there.

Alma has put them off long enough. At least now she has her own casita where she can preserve some measure of solitude. It's too small for guests—not that any space would be large enough to accommodate her expansive sisters. But they prefer the beach house anyway—right by the ocean, with a staff that includes a maid who cooks. Minorities in the States, they're not above living like the privileged on the island, another kind of minority.

When Alma announces to Filomena that her sisters are coming down for Semana Santa next week, the caretaker's face lights up. How nice that la doña has hermanas.

It's already April, but there's still snow on the ground in Vermont where Alma used to live. She nudges the globe for a live show. The two women watch the flakes fly and listen to the blizzard of voices. In windy weather at certain times of the day, the breezes carry the dull roar of distant highway traffic, punctuated by sirens and horns asserting rank: *Move over. Let me pass. I'm bigger than you.* If you listen harder, beneath the hullabaloo of traffic and the noisy barrio, you'll hear them, the diaspora of drafted characters returning to the ashes of their rough drafts.

Alma does have a special request. I'd appreciate if you don't mention the voices to my sisters. Filomena assures her mistress that she is not one to gossip. She doesn't add that it is how the devil spreads its lies, as she does not want to insult Doña Alma's sisters.

The next afternoon, as Alma is strolling the grounds, her phone rings. Piedad's name flashes on the screen. Alma accepts the call: Where are you?

Where do you think?! We're here at the door. What the hell is this place anyhow? A cemetery? I thought you said it was a sculpture garden. And this little contraption doesn't work. *"Tell me a story"*?! Piedad mimics the voice. Give me a break. Let us in, okay? She hangs up before Alma can answer.

Alma feels irritated, too. She has never liked being surprised. Jack-in-the-box was her nemesis toy as a toddler. She takes her time walking to the gate, ignoring her phone when it rings again. As she passes by each marker, she hears lines of old poems, sentences from stories, passages from abandoned novels. She had thought burning and burying all these manuscripts would silence them over time. But they fade only to return, lingering as if wanting to be told.

Just outside the front gates, a taxi is idling at the curb; her sisters wave it goodbye and turn to Alma, unsure of their welcome.

Refuge! Consolation! Pity! Alma greets them. Why, oh why, did their parents name them like characters in an allegory? Every time they'd ask, Mami would say, ask your father, who'd return them to their mother. A circuit of secrecy, bonding them together.

Soul, Soul, Soul! Are you really glad to see us?

Of course, she is. Alma folds them into her arms, overcome with tenderness, wanting to protect them from the worst in her nature. But why didn't you tell me you were coming today?

And have you run the other way? No way.

The truth of what they say makes Alma bow her head before they can see the confirmation on her face.

Consuelo has been inspecting the intercom, intrigued. She keeps pressing the button. *Tell me a story. Tell me a story.* How does this fucking thing work anyhow?

Alma sighs, trying to suppress her irritation. You press the button *once*. You tell a story. That simple, she doesn't add.

Consuelo leans in, her ear to the little box, as if the intercom were a seashell and through it, she will hear the sea. Everybody gets in?

No, not everybody. Not all stories are created equal.

Amparo can't resist a jab. I thought you were this champion of storytelling, the big table set for all, including our oral cultures—what was it you called it, *orature?*

Alma is a little surprised Amparo remembers. Maybe her sisters do listen when she talks. The problem, she explains, is that many people don't think they have a story. So, they tell you some canned telenovela plot or some imported Disney nonsense they believe you want to hear. It reminds Alma of how her students would complain they had nothing to write about. Instead, they'd hand in some predictable, hackneyed plot copied from a sitcom or film.

Let's see, what story can we tell to get in? Consuelo swivels her hips, her eyes are full of mischief. How about the time Soul Sister blurted to the general next door that Papi had a gun and almost got us all killed?

Piedad has a better one. Alma screwing that guy in college and Papi finding out about it. Piedad goes into juicy fictional detail. She is on a roll.

Okay, guys, enough, let's go. You don't have to bother with the box, Alma adds. You get in for free. Sisters with benefits, Alma says grandly, stepping to one side and bowing them in.

Wait! Consuelo is still fooling with the box. So, who listens and decides?

Who do you think? It's not like I have a staff. Actually she does have Filo. Alma has asked the groundskeeper to add the intercom to her listening duties. Often, they turn the box off except for specific hours.

Shall we? she repeats again, this time not bowing.

The sisters enter the premises, trailing their roller bags. What is going on here? Piedad asks, looking around. Did you make these?

They're by my friend Brava—remember I told you about her? She made them to mark where I buried my stories, Alma explains. People can also order replicas of whatever they want.

Amparo sighs. This is so sad. To think you wasted years on all this stuff.

Alma shrugs. What would I have done instead?

Maybe we would have seen more of you. A sweet thing for Consuelo to say.

They came here directly from the airport, as they want to swing by Martillo's law office. He's been trying to contact you. Says you never pick up. Anyhow, he wants to see us all together. Piedad emphasizes the last word in case Alma pulls her usual.

Did he give you a clue what it's about? In Alma's experience, lawyers are always drawing things out, biding their billable time.

He certainly did. Piedad holds a beat, savoring being the one to tell, a rare role for the baby in the family. Before distributing the funds and dissolving Papi's estate, he needs to know what we want to do about the automatic payments going out monthly to another account. I asked him for the name on that account and—imagine!— he says he's not at liberty to say. Not at liberty to tell us where *our* money has been going! Piedad is outraged.

Papi's money, Alma thinks but doesn't say, to avoid starting a fire on her property that even Florian and the bomberos can't put out.

All I managed to get out of him is that these are monthly distributions Papi set up with no instructions about termination. With his dementia, Papi probably forgot to clean up after himself. Or maybe he was purposely leaving tracks to the secret self he never would disclose. More questions piled onto all the unanswered ones they already have. And Alma no longer making up stories to fill in the gaps.

When the sisters catch sight of Alma's house, they ooh and aah. That's so cute. It looks just like the traditional casitas from their childhood. Is that where your caretaker lives?

I live there, Alma says right out. And please don't start in, the neighborhood looks out for me. In fact, I'm safer here than in some big house that signals someone worth kidnapping or robbing lives there.

Her sisters shake their heads, their rescue work cut out for them. They better head right over to Martillo before his office closes for the day. Tomorrow is Friday, and next week, Semana Santa, everyone will be on holiday. They pile into the pickup, exclaiming at how Alma's finally gotten the vehicle she always wanted. She's letting herself have things she always denied herself, never mind that they are weird antojos: a beat-up red pickup, a cemetery. As they head out toward the front gate, the sisters point out this or that marker. The giant eyeglasses that magnify the blades of grass; the urn filled with bird shit; the face with lips stitched by words, tears streaming down its cheeks; the scissors with sharp ends snipping at the air; the snow globe in the midst of a raging blizzard.

⟲ Manuel

I have something to confess, Doña Bienvenida. Something that must never see the light of day, or the pages of a novel, a secret I took with me to my grave.

I feel a stab of pain and look around wildly for the shore of silence to return to. But it's already too late. The undertow has pulled me in over my head. All that is left of me is the story.

Go on, Bienvenida says, by way of encouragement.

Remember, how Mamá and I would comfort each other?

I can sense Bienvenida remembering, *Alfa Calenda*, the words flowing back to me, waves breaking on a beach.

Over the years, as my wife becomes more and more involved with her United Nations and my daughters drift away—colleges, marriages, graduate schools, jobs in different cities—I return often to Alfa Calenda. I lose myself in memories, sitting at the office after everyone has left, or at home listening to music, waiting for Lucía to come back from one of her receptions. But with time the solace of my invention begins to fade. I realize nostalgia is not enough to run Alfa Calenda. Just as I did with Mamá, I need someone to share it with.

I mentioned the Dominican woman who cleans my oficina and has a little side business making Dominican food to supplement her earnings. Lucía is one of her loyal customers, ordering pastelitos, tostones, empanaditas, dulces, to send to the girls at their colleges and to serve at the receptions the Dominican mission throws at the UN.

I am spending long hours at the office, so as not to be alone at the house. After the staff have gone home, this woman comes in to clean. The first time she finds me, sitting in the dark at my desk, she jumps. The bucket she is carrying spills soapy water all over the floor. Ay, Doctor! What a fright you gave me! I did not know you were still here. I can clean your room later. Let me mop up this mess first so you don't slip.

No, no, I gesture her in. I was just leaving.

But I don't leave. I stay, watching her work, noticing her strong arms, her slender waist. A woman in her forties who has maintained her figure, not that common among my middle-aged patients. I should know her name, as Lucía has often mentioned it. But I've never paid much attention until now.

Altagracia, she tells me, touching the tiny medal on a chain around her neck. My mother-in-law's name, not one with happy associations, so I'm relieved when she adds, But everyone calls me Tatica.

When Tatica is done with her mopping, she again apologizes for disturbing me, and backs away toward the hallway.

I start asking questions to delay her departure. Where is she from? How long has she been here? When is she planning to go back home?

Tatica is circumspect in her answers, the way people can get when talking to their boss. It turns out she is from a campo in the mountains where I used to ride as a boy, hunting guineas with my older brothers. She listens as I recount our weekend outings, leaning on her mop. I'm encouraged and go on, one tale leading to another.

You must forgive me. It's not every day that I find someone to indulge me.

The pleasure is mine, Doctor. Your stories take me back. You know how we miss our country when we are far away.

The next afternoon, I find myself lingering, waiting for Tatica's arrival, but she never shows up. Perhaps her schedule is irregular. Next morning, I ask Linda, my office manager, how often the cleaning woman comes, not naming her to hide my interest.

Right now, she comes twice during the week, and then over the weekends for a more thorough cleaning. In between times, Linda and the staff do the tidying. Why do you ask? Linda wants to know. Is she not doing a good job?

I have no complaints, I assure her. But perhaps, she should come more often. The staff is working hard enough without having to add on janitorial duties.

And so, it happens, our visits become more frequent, our chats longer. Sometimes I return home after Lucía has arrived. A good feeling, to have my busy wife waiting and worrying and eager to see me.

In one of my reminiscences, I happen to mention Mamá's dulce de guayaba, licking my lips, relishing the memory. Next evening, Tatica shows up with a jar for me to share—con su esposa, she adds, careful not to overstep.

I don't believe I can wait, I say, taking the jar with me to the small kitchenette where the staff and I eat our lunches. I'm no comesolo, I add, as we call the selfish who eat alone, hoarding their food. Come accompany me. I pull up a chair to the small table. The mopping can wait. And so, we share our first meal, saltines with guava jelly, a feast eaten together.

These encounters become customary, treats she brings—habichuelas con dulce, kipes, more dulce de guayaba, which I supplement with a bottle of Bikavér, my favorite. Bull's blood, it is called in Hungary. She pulls back in disgust. Not really, I laugh. She prefers something sweeter, una coca cola spiked with rum. I start to keep a stash in my samples closet under lock and key.

I tell her stories of my childhood, the very ones my daughters complain they've already heard, sighing with impatience. My father's harshness, my doting mother, my studies, stories I've been telling you, Doña Bienvenida, inching further and further into deeper waters: my demanding wife, my Americanized daughters embarrassed by their father. I don't know when it is I realize that, without inviting her, Tatica has joined me in Alfa Calenda.

Each evening, I find it harder and harder to break away.

Often, in fact, she is the one to end our conversations. Doña Lucía will be waiting for you. She sends tins of treats home as gifts for my wife—a reminder to us both that nothing untoward is happening. I find out that in addition to my office Tatica cooks and cleans in the houses of several Dominicans. Weekends, after finishing my office, she puts in a shift at a little restaurante owned by dominicanos. All sin reportar: under the table, as they say here.

I also pay her in cash, adding a bit extra every time, as a propina. Usted necesita descano. I say in my professional capacity. You are working too hard, Doña Tatica.

Tatica, she corrects me. We are now on more familiar terms.

I begin to notice that all of Tatica's stories end in childhood, even after I've left my own early anecdotes behind to catch her up on more recent events. I probe just like my nosy daughter Alma. When did she leave Jánico? Was her father an agricultor? Did she have a novio? Surely, una señorita tan buenamoza has to have had a lot of young men after her?

She lowers her head, hiding her face from me, finally releasing a simple, You think so? Eh?

And there it stops, the gates of her story close.

⤳ Perla

Several times a week, Perla is taken out of her cell to the conference room to meet with Pepito and lawyers. The latest is a special deportation lawyer Pepito has hired. Usually, the lawyer's clients are appealing to stay, but this odd case wants to be sent back.

My parents are dominicanos. De pura cepa, he adds, trying to ingratiate himself, to get Perla to talk. It would expedite the process if she were just to confess to her crimes and to falsifying her identity, so she can be deported home.

Home? Perla has been gone for over thirty years. The only home she'll find there is with her sister, who has every reason in the world to reject Perla. And yet, even after all that has happened, her sister is willing to take her in. It brings tears to her eyes. If there's any salvation, therein it lies.

Sometimes her visitor is a social worker, una Mexicana-Americana, who is trying to ascertain if Perla has indeed committed the murders or if she's just fronting for her husband. The degree of her culpability. The murder charges can be mitigated by reason of insanity. Has there been a history of mental illness in her family?

It would be tempting to lay the whole crime at Tesoro's feet. But what good would that do? Perla will never rid herself of the horrible images in her head: the little boy in a pool of blood, his mother falling beside him, one hand trying to stanch the gushing in her neck, the other cradling her son, as if to comfort him.

I know it won't make it all go away, Pepito counsels. Since she is not speaking, he comes along to translate her expressions for the lawyers and social worker. Not only can he "read" her face, but he can also overhear her thoughts, feel her feelings with his heart. Pepito squeezes her hand. The sooner we get you out of here, the better I know we'll both feel.

Bless his heart to think that he can relieve his mother's pain. Sana, sana, culito de rana. As simple as that. If her son only knew what demons roam in her head, breaking and entering into her thoughts, into her dreams so she wakes up screaming. Her cellmates have complained. But Perla doesn't want to take away the illusion he can help. She has already robbed one boy of what's essential.

Perla has not heard a word from Jorge, but from Pepito's comments, she gathers that her other son is standing by his father, whom Pepito also does not mention. Perla does not blame Jorge or her husband. She does not want to be related to herself either.

Pepito tries to keep her spirits up. They are making progress. It looks like Perla might soon be deported and handed over to the Dominican authorities to punish her in whatever way their legal system determines. I'm going down, too, Pepito adds, so don't be afraid.

The owners of their apartment building have evicted his parents. When he was packing up the place, he found the first book he ever gave her. He holds up the small paperback. Her son seems to have forgotten the gruesome picture on the cover: a man holding up a severed head. Perla shivers.

¿Qué, Mamita? You like this book, remember? Pepito picks out a story and begins reading it out loud to her.

Perla finds it difficult to pay attention, the throng of horrible memories nipping at her heels. But slowly, the story enters her. She listens, feeling relieved, accompanied, her grief is being shared. Others have suffered. Others have done wicked things and lived to tell about them.

⟳ Manuel

It is a penance to tell this part of my story, Doña Bienvenida. I must ask you not to repeat it. I am ashamed of how horribly I behaved.

My lips are sealed, she assures me.

My wife and daughters note my withdrawal. Earth to Papi, Earth to Papi, they tease. Things must be hopping in Alfa Calenda!

If they only knew.

My daughters settle for the explanation that their father is his usual uncommunicative self. Papi is a grownup. He is responsible for himself. They have their own lives to live. All this advice courtesy of their therapists I pay for.

But Lucía has a nose on her all right. Her jealousy flares up. She listens in on my phone calls. Opens mail that comes to the house addressed to me. She has learned how to drive, and I've bought her a fancy car, so that she never has to ride the subway from late night meetings alone. One morning, she leaves for the Mission, but I catch her circling the block. A silver Mercedes tailing me to Brooklyn, well, I don't have to be one of el Jefe's SIM agents to figure that one out.

Finally, my wife is convinced. Besides, the world is keeping her busy. She's been named to a special committee on the rights of women and travels constantly to speak at conferences. Vienna, Copenhagen, Mexico City, even one in China, where she is to give a speech. You can come along, but I think you'll be bored. I'll be attending meetings all day. A lukewarm invitation that includes reasons for refusing it.

Usually, I would jump at the chance even if I know I'll feel like an extra, her manservant. But I have fish on my line, too. It crosses my mind that my resentment of my wife's neglect is part of Tatica's appeal.

And what would I do in Beijing, turn the pages of your speech? I counter. Sit with the nobodies at the little table while you preside on the dais, hobnobbing with world leaders?

She gives me such a pained look, my heart hurts with love for her.

Babinchi, she uses my childhood nickname, a sign of tenderness. You know I'd give it all up if you want me to. But I need something to fill my life, too. You've always had your profession. I don't complain when you come home late or work weekends, do I?

I look down, afraid my guilty secret will show. I have done nothing wrong, I tell myself. I have not gone beyond friendly conversation, but there is an attraction there I cannot deny.

The first few days after Lucía's departure, I go home immediately after work, leaving a note on my desk about a commitment. The next morning, I find it in the same exact place on my desk, seemingly untouched, unread. Finally, I ask Linda, if she has changed the cleaning woman's schedule.

Just that I told her to come more often like you requested.

That night, I stay late to be sure. I watch her let herself in, looking weary, heavy-hearted. Again, she is startled when I step forward to greet her. After an initial warm smile, she says she better get to work. She'll leave my office for last.

No sweets tonight? I joke to lighten the mood.

The ones I left in the refrigerator went bad. Her voice trembles. When she collects herself, she asks, Have I offended you in some way?

Why would you think that? Didn't you read my notes? Even if they were lies, I had the courtesy of informing her I was busy night after night. Receptions, meetings, events—all those excuses, as if it's me not Lucía in so much demand.

She shakes her head slowly. I didn't see them, no.

That night after she is finished, I invite Tatica to dinner at a Dominican restaurant up in Washington Heights where nobody knows me. Our waiter treats us like husband and wife. We laugh at his mistake. The place is a little slice of the island, flags and posters of our beaches on the walls, toothpicks on the table, the menus in Spanish. What would you like to eat? I ask Tatica, scanning the oversized plastic menu.

Whatever you are having, she says. I assume she is following my lead, not wanting to choose something more expensive she prefers, so as not to appear to be taking advantage. Order anything you'd like, I urge her. It's my bonus for the good job you've been doing. I point out this or that item on the menu, testing her, as I'm beginning to connect the dots: the unread notes, the demure refusal to order from the menu. Tatica is probably illiterate. Many of my patients don't know how to read and write, and not just in English. I feel ever more protective of her.

After several drinks, I again broach the subject of her family back home. I've told her so much and her reticence is beginning to bother me. It reminds me of my daughters' complaint that I am a closed book. Tell me about your campo? Do you still have family there?

When she doesn't answer, I fall silent, too.

¿Y qué te pasa? she asks, taking my hand, a new trespass. What is it you want to know?

Whatever you are hiding from me.

She lets go my hand as if it were a restraint, takes a swallow of her rum and coke, and launches into her story: how at fourteen an older man in her campo carried her off; how he'd beat her when he got drunk, how she endured for years, finally running away to the capital, where she worked as a maid for a rich family. On one of their trips to Nueva York, where they kept an apartment, they brought her along to help. The night before their departure back to the island, she slipped away. After several weeks, her temporary visa expired, but she managed to find work, a place to live among other dominicanos also without papeles. She has gotten by now for over twenty years. She has heard that the American presidente might forgive immigrants without documents and allow them to stay here.

But don't you want to go home? All alone here?

Something like Lucía's pained expression comes on Tatica's face. Tears form in the edges of her eyes. I reach out to blot them. Our waiter gives us wide berth, waiting to clear our plates. He must think we need privacy; perhaps the husband is breaking his wife's heart. Again, I have a fleeting image of Lucía sitting across the table from me.

Forgive me, I am saying this to both women. But it's Tatica's hands I reach for. Maybe, I can help you, with your papers so you can go back and forth safely.

Her face brightens. I would be so grateful. I will clean your office for free, any antojo you and your wife would like, whatever you require in payment. With this last offer, her look sharpens, like when I learn a word in English for a feeling I've known only in Spanish. *Interés*. There is interest in her face.

I shake my head. No need to repay me. This is what we do. We help each other.

She kisses my hands, a sign of gratitude, but from an attractive woman in these circumstances, I suspect it is also an invitation, a suspicion she confirms when she asks if I would like to come to her place.

My wife is across the world in China. An empty house awaits me. Any calls to my daughters, I will get their message machines. All I want is company, someone to talk to. But it is too risky to go to her room in an apartment she rents with other Dominicans, some of whom are my patients. I know how we are. It could get back to my wife. I don't want any trouble. Now that we've turned a corner in our relations, even being here in a restaurant owned by dominicanos is making me nervous. I run through places we can meet, alibis I can give.

I am thinking like a cad, turning into my father.

Oh, Doctor, I overstepped, perdóneme. Back to the formal. A blush wouldn't show on her soft brown skin, but an appealing glow spreads over her face. One that deserves a kiss, on the forehead, like I might bestow on my daughters. And this woman could be one of my girls with a handful of years added on. It is probably best to end the evening now. It is getting late, I tell her.

But it is already too late.

I drive her to her building, but as we are saying our goodbyes, we fall into each other's arms, kissing and fondling, giddy with naughtiness, finally migrating to the back seat like teenagers. Afterward, I feel both thrilled and terrified. It's a heady thing at this point in my life to open up the gates of possibility and let the impossible in.

The next evening we rendezvous in my office. Let me just say— and forgive me, Doña Bienvenida, for dragging you through this— examining tables have multiple uses.

When my wife returns from her trip, she asks how I managed.

I shrug. Fine, not adding my usual, I missed you terribly.

I missed you, she prods, watching me.

I lean in to kiss her forehead as I did Tatica's. A wave of shame washes over me. I have acted like a sinvergüenza. And yet and yet, I would do the same, given the opportunity, which will be given and taken, again and again.

Every time my wife leaves town, Tatica and I share dinners and part of the night together. Funny the little restrictions I place on myself to minimize my transgression. I can have relations with the woman, but I must sleep in my own house. I must wake up in the bed I share with my wife even when she is not there. I cannot invite Tatica to a restaurant where I have taken Lucía or where either of us might be known. As long I keep my connection to Tatica in that Alfa Calenda part of my brain, I can grant myself a certain measure of moral amnesty.

It is painful just to tell you this story, Doña Bienvenida. I hope you will pardon me.

Remember, Manuel, we all have a lot to be forgiven for. Her kindness brings tears to my heart. She quotes the Lord's prayer: "We must forgive others if we expect to be forgiven."

I am left wondering what exactly does Bienvenida have to be forgiven for?

She replies to my unspoken question with the clarity that comes from telling our stories. More and more, I've noticed, we can enter each other's thoughts.

I was a coward, she admits, willfully blind. I also committed the sin of despair, as you know.

I wish those were my sins.

They seem so small to you, Manuel, but they are huge to me. We sin as we live in character.

Even so, Doña Bienvenida, I'm mortified confessing all this. How could I have lived it?

A lot of men have these . . . relations, Bienvenida says from her enlarged point of view. El Jefe had dozens. She stops herself, perhaps aware that her ex is no one I want to be compared to. But she is right. I was no less cruel and thoughtless in my actions.

You are not the first, nor the last to break a woman's heart.

If it were only that, I tell her.

⮬ Alma and her sisters

The firm of Matos, Martínez & Martillo is located in an upscale neighborhood between an art gallery, ¡Mira!, and a bakery, Patisserie Pati.

Why would anyone call a repostería a *patisserie*? Spanish has a perfectly good word for a bakery. Piedad says she can feel the firm's charges rising, along with her blood pressure. *If I had a hammer*, she sings. Consuelo joins in, Amparo provides the sound effects, tapping a beat on the dashboard.

You guys, better zip it up, Alma cautions. Stay on message if we want to get out of there without breaking the bank. Simple yeses or nos, and where do we sign? Discussions, waxing anecdotal—all of it costs money. Remember last time? Papi was still alive, the sisters met with Martillo in regard to their deceased mother's estate. Martillo happened to mention his support of a recent ruling barring Haitians born in the country from their right to citizenship, and Amparo went into a rant about human rights, and oh boy, they all paid through the nose for her righteousness. Like the Hammer was going to listen to her.

The office building has a chic, industrial look, all sleek lines, steel and glass, like a facility where justice is made to order for those who can afford it.

The attendant posted at the entrance to the parking lot seems unsure whether to lift the barrier and allow Alma's old pickup into the gated community of Audis, BMWs, Mercedes, some purring like overfed cats with their chauffeurs dozing inside in air-conditioned comfort. Finally the attendant waves them in, a bunch of mujerotas after all. What's the harm?

The front door is locked; an intercom asks only for their names—they can tell their stories inside. The reception area smells perfumy with a whiff of cigar. A dramatic arrangement of birds-of-paradise graces a glass coffee table. Consuelo checks, feeling up the leaves. Fakes, she pronounces them—in English, thank god.

The young receptionist with the looks of a beauty queen eyes them—this time it's not their vehicle but their outfits that are suspect, wrinkled cotton tunics, loose-fitting pants, Birkenstocks, not the designer silk suits and stilettos of Dominican doñas. She ushers them through a warren of hallways to the dark, wood-paneled conference room. A maid in a gray uniform enters with a tray of cafecitos and shakes her head apologetically when Consuelo asks if she doesn't have anything stronger.

So pleased to see you again, Licenciado Martillo greets them, entering, a middle-aged man with black hair peppered with white and the slender figure of a bullfighter. He'd be to-die-for handsome were he not their sly lawyer. They expected a chilly welcome after Piedad's prickly communications and Alma stonewalling his voicemails. But Martillo seems oblivious to their opinion of him as he enthuses on and on about their late father (un caballero) and mother (una mujer ejemplar) and how privileged and honored he has been to take care of la familia's business all these years.

The sisters exchange a look, full of subtext.

Martillo advertises his firm as bilingual, but the sisters have no evidence from past communications that he really understands their instructions. Witness: it's now almost two years and their father's estate has yet to be settled. Piedad has already explained to Martillo countless times—and she's got the printed-out emails to show as evidence—that the real estate is to be divided in this and this way, the deeds retitled, all accounts closed, funds distributed among the sisters, end of story.

It is complicated, Martillo has replied: their father having held dual citizenship, laws here, laws there, often in contradiction with each other. These things take time to be settled correctly, if they are not to encounter problemas down the line, illegalities, penalties, possible jail sentences. He has listed an impressive number of scary possibilities.

Today, however, he is happy to report they are actually nearing the end of their legal relations. The sisters all make pouty faces—the irony lost on Martillo. The final deeds on the properties are ready. He calls the receptionist, Valentina, on the intercom to bring in four copies. Meanwhile all accounts have been liquidated except for the one in question in their father's name, which will also be closed once the daughters settle the matter of how to handle the monthly payouts. Should they want to continue the arrangement—

Absolutely not, Piedad cuts him off. I mean, why should we when you won't even tell us who it is is getting paid off?

It's not for me to say. Martillo shows them his palms as proof it is out of his hands. These were your father's instructions.

In that case, we say terminate. Piedad looks over at her sisters. You bet, Consuelo agrees. No ticket, no laundry, Amparo approves, the idiom lost on Martillo. They turn to Alma to confirm. Not so fast, her look suggests. Her three sisters glare at her, daring Alma to ruin a unified front.

Can't you at least tell us, Licenciado, Alma asks nicely as taught by Mami to do to get what you want, no names, no personal information, just what this was about?

I am not certain myself, Martillo says. I don't probe into my client's private affairs unless there is some illegality involved. But it is perfectly within the law to continue these kinds of arrangements past death. I once had a client . . .

Her sisters shake their heads at Alma: look what you got started. Billable stories.

. . . who arranged for bouquets to be sent to his widow the first of every month for the rest of her life, unless she remarried, in which case, the deliveries were to be discontinued.

Did she ever—Alma feels Piedad's heavy Birkenstock press down on her foot.

Martillo sends Valentina a message to bring in an additional form to terminate Don Manuel's account for the Cruz daughters to sign. Martillo checks the time on his wristwatch, superfluously as there is a large digital clock sitting at one end of the conference table with the date, day of the week, temperature, and humidity. Perhaps he wants to show off his fancy watch? Too late to fax over the form this afternoon, he says, but first thing tomorrow.

Valentina enters the room with a number of folders for the sisters to sign. Martillo's face brightens like a three-way bulb at its highest setting. Alma wonders if Martillo has a provision in his will to send flowers to Valentina until she takes on a new lover.

Alma scans the termination form. An account at Banco Santa Cruz in Higüey—not her parents' preferred Banco Popular, owned by a member of Mami's family. After signing, Alma asks for a copy of the form, along with the deeds. For our records, she adds, as even her sisters are giving her quizzical looks.

Outside, she outlines her plan. She's hoping to find a weak link at Banco Santa Cruz who might divulge the name of the recipient of the monthly payments before their father's account is closed and the trail gets cold. Alma's craft might have lost its potency, but she has not lost her craftiness. Tomorrow, first thing, they'll head to Higüey to be at the bank when the doors open and before the termination fax arrives from the capital.

First thing? Her sisters groan. We *are* on vacation in case you didn't notice. What's the big hurry?

Alma explains her urgency: the account might be closed if they delay their arrival. Semana Santa is next week. The whole country closes down. Let's just get all the legal stuff out of the way, so we can just enjoy ourselves. Sure, I can do it by myself, but what if it's something devastating. I need my posse along.

Nothing like the carrot of drama to incentivize the sisters.

They all have pet theories about the beneficiary of the account. Maybe it's as innocent as a pension allotment for a loyal former employee or severance pay for a litigious one? Or perhaps these monthly withdrawals were some form of protection money siphoned through a Dominican bank, which their father forgot to cancel when his memory started to fail him? Alma remembers working summers as a teenager in Papi's office. Two slick guys would occasionally show up. Linda had coached her that these men were to be treated with kid gloves, ushered right in to see her father. The gabby nurse lowered her voice: these men were collecting protection money to keep her father's office and his person safe from "accidents."

Whatever Papi was up to, the sisters are now on board with Alma's plan, equally game to solve the Papi puzzle—not that it will do much good going forward, except to give them one more story to talk about.

⟩ Perla

Perla arrives at Las Américas airport accompanied by a US immigration agent, seated beside her in the bulkhead. Outside the plane, Dominican authorities are waiting. Pepito, on the same flight but farther back in row 23, files past her on the ramp and hands over that first book he gave her. That is not permitted, the Dominican agents inform him. Pepito inserts a sheaf of dollars, a marca libro, he explains. The book is cleared; the bookmarks pocketed. For all his dreamy bookishness, her boy has street smarts.

I will be by with the lawyer tomorrow, he calls after her as the guardias escort Perla away.

The Dominican lawyer Pepito hired has made arrangements. For an extra fee, Perla is held in one of the less crowded cells, awaiting her hearing and sentencing. Her food is catered, a special service provided by the wife of the prison director. Filomena has offered, but Pepito insists this is better. A way to ingratiate Mamita with the muckety-mucks in charge.

All of this has to be costing a lot of money, Perla suspects. If she ever gets out of jail, she will work, night and day, until they put her in the ground, to repay her son. What she owes that little boy whose life she stole she can never pay back. Her soul is bankrupt. Forever and ever—until she opens the book of stories and recalls the healing balm of Pepito's voice reading to her, infusing calm into her body and filling her empty heart with hope.

She pores over it in her cell. Is that a Bible? one of the women asks. Read to us. I could use un chin de Jesús in this hellhole.

Now you're asking a muda to talk, another scoffs, shaking her head. You must believe in miracles! Why not ask for a miracle that matters? Get us the mierda out of here.

That night as they all lie on their cots, Perla begins to read out loud. A number of the women prop themselves up on their elbows. Even the disenchanted who threaten anyone experiencing a minor pleasure are surprised. The mute woman can now speak. The scoffer makes the sign of the cross.

The story is about a wild country girl who is pursued by a rapist. As he gains on her, the girl cries out for help. Some god takes pity and makes a miracle happen. He turns her into a laurel tree.

Is it true? asks a young inmate with the sweet face of a child. Is she even old enough to be imprisoned? Perla wonders. The girl readily admits she stabbed an uncle who had been raping her and her little sister for years. But all she was turned into is a prisoner.

We had a laurel tree out in the campo, another offers. Abuela always made a tisana with the leaves to reduce the cramps during menstruation.

A woman from the mountains near Jarabacoa wonders if that girl in the story was maybe a ciguapa? The city girls have never heard of

such creatures except in that love song by Chichí Peralta. But those
from the countryside know the legend. Beautiful and fierce, the ciguapas seduce men, then drown them in the river—

¡Silencio! the guard on patrol barks.

The next night, Perla reads a story aloud about a tribe of fierce
warrior women, no men, all excellent archers. They cut off a breast
so it doesn't interfere with their marksmanship.

¡Dios santo! But wait! How do they have babies if there aren't any
men in the tribe?

Perla does not reply. She is only a voice, reading these old stories
out loud to them.

≈ Manuel

The groundskeeper has grown more devoted now that her treasure is buried beside my box of rough drafts. She has a handsome
look: deep-set eyes, café-con-leche skin, a vague resemblance to my
Tatica. Could it be my confessions have resurrected the woman I
wronged?

But the groundskeeper is no product of a guilty imagination.
Vivita y coleando, as we say, alive and wagging, with her own secrets
in her keepsake box. One of her trinkets is a medal of our Virgencita
de la Altagracia, just the name is a glowing coal on my conscience. I
have not had a settled moment since she buried her treasure here—my
flakes in constant commotion.

Today as she walks by, I intercept her. I am feeling an urgency
to conclude my story, but I would very much like to spare Doña
Bienvenida the shameful details of what finally happened. Despite
her assurances, it must be painful for her to listen to the story of a
man betraying his wife just as el Jefe betrayed her.

As the groundskeeper goes by, I throw myself headlong into my story. She stops in her tracks, lays down her bucket, and gives me a wipe with her rag.

Months go by, I begin. Tatica is growing careless with our office encounters. In one instance, she forgets her slip. Linda finds it, draped on the examining lamp. One of my patients must have left it behind when she dressed back up in her street clothes.

As Tatica relaxes, I become more and more cautious. I am also gaining weight with the many treats she fixes for me—a problem I never had before, as Lucía never did learn to cook, only to order maids or takeout.

The groundskeeper has been listening intently, leaning in so close her breath clouds the glass of the globe. She wipes it again and again. My mother's name was Tatica, too, she informs me.

There are hundreds of Taticas, thousands, I remind her. Every other woman on the street is Tatica. A bit of an exaggeration, but it's a nuisance when you are telling a story and your listener gets stuck on some minor detail.

The groundskeeper is silenced by the reprimand in my tone. Perhaps she fears that I will refuse to keep her box a secret if she pesters me.

Shall I continue? I ask more gently.

Please do go on, Bienvenida speaks up. She has been listening all along. She is now inside the groundskeeper's imagination as well. We are in this story together.

As I was saying, months go by. I am beginning to grow nervous about our office meetings. One evening, I am coming out of my office late, and there is Lucía in her silver Mercedes. She gives a toot on her horn, laughing at my shock.

What are you doing here? I ask, examining her face. She doesn't know anything, I don't think.

What do you mean what am I doing here? Tomorrow's our anniversary. (Indeed, I already had it on my mental calendar: our thirty-third, to be exact.) I thought we could celebrate tonight as I have a reception tomorrow evening. By the way, is Tatica cleaning today? I want to order two dozen pastelitos and kipes for the refreshments. I've been calling her but no answer. My wife's eyes stray over my shoulder and her face lights up. What good timing. Tatica! she calls. Just then, Tatica is bringing out the trash. Something she has been told not to do—all the drug addicts end up tearing open the bags thinking there are syringes inside. The receptionist is on watch for the truck on trash days, and only then does she take the bags out. Another instance I'm noticing of Tatica no longer following my instructions.

I start to tally the little liberties, the chances Tatica can take as a single woman but I can't, the demands she is making, insisting we go places that are not within the purview of safety. How will this story end? I don't want to hurt my wife. Sometimes it takes the threat of loss to make us realize how deeply we love someone—I cannot bear the thought of life without Lucía. In fact, I was happier with Tatica when we were just exchanging stories.

I begin making excuses: I will be away this weekend visiting one daughter or another. I have to escort my wife to a reception. With my help, Tatica has rented her own little studio where we can have some privacy. The stairs are too much for me. I plead tiredness. I am nearing sixty-five. I complain about my health, something I have never done. We have to stop. But every time I introduce the topic, Tatica breaks down sobbing. She becomes more needy and bold; increasingly, I feel an edge of threat in her demands.

One evening, soon after the surprise pick-up by my wife, Tatica announces she wants a pregnancy test.

Why? She must think it's a stupid question, coming from a man who is having an affair, a doctor at that.

Adivina, adivinador! she replies in a sassy tone, arms akimbo. Take a guess.

I am not in a playing mood. Something I've not shared with Tatica, for it embarrasses me to admit it, as if I've been castrated: I had a vasectomy years back, when—after four daughters and pills that made her sick—Lucía insisted it was my turn. I am relieved to have this card in my back pocket now. If Tatica is indeed pregnant—and I have my doubts—if she is, it means she is double-timing me. It does not occur to me in the moment, that I am doing the same to Lucía with her.

You best tell the father if you believe you are pregnant.

But you are the father, she insists, bursting into tears.

I feel a pang for this woman sobbing in my arms with no one to turn to—actually, she has at least one other lover: the father of the child she is supposedly carrying. I forge ahead. It cannot be mine. If need be, we can have a DNA test.

The weeping Madonna turns into a fury. You think I am just your toy? she shouts. Just remember: this toy talks!

Tatica is what my daughters call a loose cannon; she will not hold back her fire. I don't know what to do, who to talk to. I have never had close friends in this country. At my work, everyone is my employee or my patient, only with Tatica have I crossed that boundary. Should I confess to Lucía, I know what would happen. My wife is not the woman to forgive a betrayal. A bitter old age awaits.

As it happens, I have two contacts who come to my office regularly for protection payments. I tell them that I need a job done. Do they know anyone who works at the immigration office? I have a troublesome employee who is undocumented. I prefer if my disclosure is kept in confidence as it would frighten away many of my patients without papeles if they were to learn that their doctor has broken confidentiality and turned someone in. No problem at all, Doctor, they assure me. They take down all the information, and a few days later inform me that the raid has taken place, the individual apprehended and soon to be deported. I change the locks on the office doors just in case.

Once I know she is safely repatriated, I make arrangements through my lawyer, monthly payments with the proviso that she remain silent. But like all guilty persons, I live in fear of being found out, especially as my daughters age and grow more curious about my past. Over the years, I've built up a wall of silence they cannot climb over. When I do speak, I repeat the same old stories they complain they've heard a zillion times. In my last years, these repetitions and my long silences convince them that, like their mother, I have succumbed to dementia, a common ailment on our island. Only Alma persists in scaling the wall of my storied self, peppering me with questions. She must suspect there is more on the other side.

You're torturing him, her sisters scold. Don't you see he doesn't remember stuff?

It *is* torture to be reminded of what I cannot forget or forgive myself for having done. Sometimes before I can stop myself, Tatica's face flashes before me and I call out her name.

≈ Alma and her sisters

Alma picks up her sisters at the beach house early the next morning for the two-hour drive. The offices of Matos, Martínez & Martillo open for business at nine, at which time Valentina, having refreshed her lipstick and applied a last coat of nail polish, will start in on her faxing. As he escorted them out the door yesterday, Martillo explained the process. Late morning the regional bank in Higüey will finally get the nod from the head office in the capital to close the account. The sooner they get to Higüey, the better chance they'll have of obtaining the information they want. The early birds are usually the lower-rung and underpaid, used to complying with a higher-up's orders or a client's demands.

Alma finds her sisters still in bed, annoyed at being woken up in the middle of the night. It's not the middle of the night, she informs them, pulling back the drapes as proof. It's after seven; we have to leave now. No way, José. They need their coffee. And what about their mangú con cebollitas they've been dreaming about since they landed? The cook hasn't yet arrived. We'll stop for breakfast on the way, Alma promises. Reluctantly, the sisters begin to dress, muttering complaints.

That won't work, Alma vetoes the comfortable tunics and T-shirts and loose yoga pants they are slipping into. They need to look the part of Dominican doñas if they expect a bank employee to pay them any mind, no less disclose information. We Dominicans have a muckety-muck detector acutely sensitive to class: gold jewelry, brand-name clothes, latest-generation cell phones, and lots of attitude. Alma should know. She's been living here now going on a year.

Her sisters exchange a sidelong glance. This was bound to happen. Alma's turning into one of *them*. Alma doesn't have to ask who *them* is, not one of *us* is sufficient offense.

I am a shapeshifter, Alma concedes. It's a professional handicap. Ever heard of negative capability? As she often told her students, writers are "always betraying someone," to quote Joan Didion. To get at a higher truth, Alma would add, so as not to sound like the schmuck who would throw Abuelita under the bus. As her own abilities waned and the stock market of her popularity plummeted, Alma began to lose faith in this chameleonlike quality, part of her disenchantment with the craft. But it had become a habit, being several people at once.

Her sisters sigh. Spare us the lecture. It's too early in the morning for Joan Didion. And when is Alma going to get it through her head, they're not her students?

Look, if you don't want to do this, I'll just go by myself. Alma picks up her handbag, digs out her keys, a repeat performance of their mother's ultimatum scenes, threatening to go off to Bellevue if they didn't behave. But later, don't ask me to tell you what I find out. I'll keep Papi's secret to my grave.

Who said we don't want to go with you? Her sisters quicken their pace, donning the black outfits they all pack in their suitcases these days. Seems like someone in la familia is always dying when they're on a trip.

It saddens Alma to think that, this far out from childhood, Mami's trick still works.

They stop at Krispy Kreme for large coffees and a bag of pastries. I can't believe we come all the way to the DR to eat First World food, Amparo grouses, as she bites into her jelly roll.

At least it's a guava jelly roll, Alma humors her. Plus, Americans know how to do *fast*. Dominicans are notoriously slow. You don't just order, you visit. She should know. She's been here going on a year—

You say that one more time, I'm going to puke in your camioneta, Piedad threatens. She's already carsick from being stuck in the back seat with Consuelo. And it's only been ten months, by the way. She starts counting off the months.

They sing some old camp songs, move on to the Dominican national anthem but abandon it, as none of them knows the lyrics past the first couple of lines. They do a little *West Side Story, Hamilton*. None of them has a decent voice. Alma turns on the radio, a not too subtle hint. But this alternative is just as bad: staticky bachatas, hip-hop, rock, or a broadcaster reporting the news in the hyped-up style that always sounds parodic to the sisters.

Are we almost there? they keep asking, like weary children on a car trip.

Two hours and half a dozen arguments later, they roll into the small town, renowned as the spot where the Virgin of Altagracia appeared to a little girl in an orange grove. The central strip in the avenida has been planted with orange trees. Pictures of the Virgin abound in the windows of stores. There are streets, schools, clinics, a pool hall named in her honor. Signage with her name everywhere, the town's version of boast plaques in hotels and bars: George Washington slept here, Dylan Thomas drank himself to death here. La Virgencita appeared here.

The bank is the only modern structure on the block of wooden casitas. With its large picture window of one-way tinted glass, the building looks like it's wearing sunglasses. Appropriately so: the sun is already blindingly bright and it's only just after nine. They find a parking spot right in front of the entrance. The armed guard posted outside nods them in, no need to check documents, their dress-up outfits and white skin are sufficient proof they have business where the money is. As for the old-model pickup, this is not the capital. Any vehicle boosts a person's status. The only surprising thing is that a woman is driving it.

The lobby is quiet, except for the hum of the air conditioner and occasional ringing of a phone. Their teller—Miriam Altagracia Pichardo, the name on the tag reads—is dressed in the bank uniform, a soft brown suit that matches her skin, with a white blouse and a tiny gold cross around her neck. Buenas, she greets them. Para servirle.

Do you speak English? Piedad cuts to the chase. She's less sure of herself in her native tongue.

Lamentablemente, no, Miriam answers politely, not a trace of indignation in her voice. But really, why should a Dominican on her home turf have to learn the language of a random client?

Alma steps in. Let me handle it.

You're the expert, Piedad says snidely, Consuelo and Amparo chiming in, She's been living here almost a year. Ten months, Piedad corrects again.

Alma explains to Miriam what they're after, give or take a few truths. Their father, Manuel Cruz, has an account here. He recently died, so they'll be closing the account. But an automatic deduction has been going out monthly, which payout they, his daughters, would like to continue, but they'll need to know the name of the recipient of their father's largesse.

Miriam is studying first one, then another sister. Her training, recently completed, never accounted for such a request.

This is a copy of our father's cédula and passport, his death certificate, and here's my passport and driver's license. Alma piles the proof on the counter. And this last document authorizes me as his POA on these matters.

Lamentablemente, Miriam is not acquainted with the legal form. We will have to wait for my supervisor.

Alma understands, of course. But they themselves are not asking for any changes in the setup. All they want to know is the name and contact information of the person receiving the monthly payouts. Nothing more.

Miriam hesitates before repeating her default phrase: I'm not at liberty to disclose that information without authorization.

But it's our account; our father is dead; we're his inheritors! Who said Piedad didn't know how to argue her case in Spanish?

Comprendo, Miriam says. Her own father died just last month. She has a tender spot in her heart for people who have lost their fathers. But still, she does not want to lose her job.

We won't let that happen, Amparo assures her. Miriam isn't convinced.

Alma has brought along her silver bullet, a clipping from the national newspaper. Brava wanted publicity for her work on display at the cementerio, and she enticed a reporter to visit "the new sculpture garden" with the added bait that the project was the brainchild of Scheherazade. There was a big spread in the papers, accompanied by an old photo of Alma getting a medal from the U.S. president: RENOWNED DOMINICAN WRITER RETURNS TO HER HOMELAND, the headline read. Alma nudges the clipping to her sisters to hand over, as she wants to appear modest. *One may smile, and smile, and be a villain.* Let her sisters be the braggarts.

Miriam's eyes widen. She looks at the photo, then at Alma, then at the photo again. ¿Usted?

Alma smiles demurely. I would really appreciate your help.

Miriam looks over her shoulder: her supervisor's office is still dark; the account is up on her screen, the monthly deductions; the details all line up. Quickly, she jots down a name. I'm not authorized to give out information on clients' accounts, she says out loud while slipping Alma the note. She, too, can play the smile-and-smile-and-be-a-villain game.

De acuerdo, Alma says, pocketing the slip of paper.

Is there anything else I can help you with? Miriam says, looking worried again.

No, thank you, the sisters chorus in a moment of rare unity.

Back out on the street, they check the note. *Sisters of the Sorrowful Mother Convent*?! Did Miriam trick them after all?

It sounds made up. Consuelo is shaking her head.

Not at all. Piedad laughs. She's got us pegged. We *are* the sisters of the sorrowful Mami!

Alma approaches the bank guard. Would he know the location of las Hermanas de la Madre Dolorosa? Yes, of course. The hospicio, he calls it.

Really? A nursing home in this country? Mami and Papi had said such a thing was anathema in their culture.

Maybe it's for old nuns? Amparo suggests.

The home is located in the outskirts, a stretched-out ranch-style one-story with a long galería in the front and a dozen rocking chairs looking out at the road—the entertainment must be watching the cars and pickups and donkeys loaded with sacks of oranges go by.

The galería is deserted, the nuns praying or doing whatever it is they do at this hour of the morning. The front door is open but blocked off by a folding barrier like those baby gates to keep toddlers from tumbling down the stairs. An elderly nun with a whiskery face in full habit, a white coif and veil on her head, comes to the entrance. Ave Maria, she greets them.

Buenos días . . . How does one address a nun in Spanish? Alma has forgotten. She introduces her sisters and herself, then asks for the old nun's name. Sor Corita is delighted with their beautiful virtuous names. We're the daughters of Manuel Cruz, Alma goes on to explain. Their father has been making monthly contributions to the hospicio. But now that he is deceased, the lawyers will be closing his accounts.

Ay, sí, Manuel Cruz, Qué en paz descanse. The old nun touches each of their faces as if to wipe away tears that are only in her eyes. She reminds Alma of Bienvenida's kindly Soeur Odette, in her failed novel. Such a good man, the nun reminisces. For many years he has been sponsoring one of the residents with a generous stipend, which has allowed the Sisters to cover the costs of running their home. So many of our viejitos are very poor. We are so grateful. We will miss his help. Though God will provide, to be sure.

And we will, too, Amparo speaks up. Her sisters nod agreement.

We just want to meet this person who clearly meant a lot to our father. When one of our old ones dies, we're left with so many questions. That's why we came, Alma admits sincerely for a change. We can no longer ask Papi to introduce us or say why he decided to help this person.

Something about the place—the sliding doors through which they can see from the entryway a yard planted with scrawny vegetables an old man is watering, the birdsong in the orange trees, the arched hallway, the cracked tiles, everything in the process of decay, but taking its sweet time, the gentle old nun, reaching for their hands, come along, come along, you, too, to the one she doesn't have a spare hand to hold—all of it quiets them, as if they have entered another slower, kinder dimension where the rules of the grab-and-go world do not apply. Alfa Calenda, Papi would probably call it.

A group of elderly residents begin filing out of the dining area, on walkers and makeshift wheelchairs, seatbelts made of rope and strips of leather. A tiny old woman with gums for teeth and a vague, beatific smile approaches. Mamá, Mamá, 'ción, 'ción, she pleads. Several other elders join in, asking for blessings, confusing the visitors for their mothers as well.

Ya, ya, off you go! Sor Corita shoos them away, watching tenderly as they shuffle out to the galería, holding hands like kindergarteners.

Sor Corita regrets that Reverenda Madre is on retreat in Santo Cerro. She would be the one with the information of the whys and wherefores of Señor Cruz's donations.

All we want is to meet this person our father was sponsoring. Would Sor Corita know who it is?

Yes, of course. Tatica, that's what we call her. I'm not sure of her last name. Reverenda Madre would know.

Tatica! The name Papi kept uttering when he was losing his mind. From writing stories all her life, Alma should have guessed as much. Can we meet her?

Sor Corita doesn't see why not. She leads them through the emptied comedor toward the back kitchen from which come sounds of clanging pots and plates and ringing silverware. Before they go further, she does have to alert them. Tatica's memory is very bad. Many of our viejitos suffer from dementia. I don't want you to be upset if she doesn't remember your father.

We just want to see her face, Alma assures the old nun. She is telling the truth again. This could become a habit.

They enter the large kitchen with its long aluminum counters, open shelves stocked with plates and glasses. Two young nuns, heads veiled, long habits covered with oversized white pinafore aprons, are washing and drying dishes in a deep sink; their sleeves are rolled up exposing their sudsy arms—something about being covered up makes these patches of bared skin delightfully intimate. Ave Maria, Sor Corita greets them.

Sin pecado concebida, they respond, curtsying.

In the pantry alcove, a gray-haired woman, slightly older than Alma and her sisters, or perhaps the same age—hard to tell in her faded, baggy batola—is manically wiping and re-wiping the counters with a dishtowel. Tatica, Sor Corita calls her. These friends are here to visit you.

Tatica seems oblivious that she is the person being addressed and continues with her wiping. Sor Corita lowers her voice. Tatica believes she works here, and we let her help as best she can. Ven, ven, Sor Corita says in an ordering voice. I have something for you to do. She winks at Alma and her sisters. The ruse works, Tatica approaches, rag lifted as if she means to wipe Sor Corita's face next.

Alma studies the woman, her damp hair tamped down with bobby pins but escaping in wispy flyaways where it has dried, the vacant look reminiscent of Mami and Papi. Those doctors at Columbia Presbyterian were not kidding. Alzheimer's is rampant here. When will it strike Alma and her sisters? What memory loop will each one get stuck in, like those rings of Dante's hell in that passage Papi loved to recite? What was it Tatica did that makes her think she has to clean the hospicio's kitchens? Was she a dishwasher in a restaurant? A maid in one of their cousins' houses?

Alma addresses the woman in a calm, soothing voice, lest she startle Tatica the way Mami would get frightened by a stranger—which, as her dementia progressed, became everyone. Hola, doñita. We are the daughters of Manuel Cruz, Alma gestures toward her sisters.

Tatica scowls at them, and after a moment's pause, turns back to wiping the counters.

Sor Corita intercedes. Tatica, la señora is talking to you. Manuel Cruz is your benefactor. You must say thank you to his daughters.

But Tatica is lost again to her cleaning, rubbing and rubbing a spot only she sees. One of the young nuns comes forward and yanks the towel away. Didn't you hear Sor Corita? No, I'm not giving it back until you thank these nice ladies who came to visit you. Tatica sets up a wail like a child deprived of a favorite toy.

It's okay, Alma tells the nun. Something in this insistence that Tatica remember their father feels cruel. We just wanted to meet her, that's all. She reaches to touch the woman's hand, but Tatica pulls back, perhaps thinking her dishtowel will be taken away again.

Does she have any family? Piedad wants to know. Maybe someone else can provide the clue as to why their father was helping take care of this stranger.

Sor Corita shakes her head, slowly sifting through what she has heard. When Tatica appeared here, her mind was already afflicted. She'd been living in Higüey for years. A former patient of your father, we were told, but we never had the honor of meeting him. He made the arrangements with our Mother House in the capital. A true child of God, no one but la Virgen and Papa Dios and your father to take care of her.

And you, Alma adds graciously.

Sor Corita bows her head, accepting the compliment in God's name. We are here to take care of each other. Would they like a short tour before they go? To see what their father's contributions are helping fund?

Alma glances over at her sisters; they, too, are subdued, quieted by the otherworldliness of this house of the living dead, perhaps wondering along with Alma if this might be the end that awaits them all. A half island of old people without memories. A blessing at times, given what can be recalled, like Alma's character, Mr. Torres, from another of her failed novels, who had tortured and disappeared so many. Dying with a mind haunted by the faces of his victims.

They tour the dormitories, one large room for the dozen or so female residents, a smaller one accommodating the handful of males. The little cots are lined up like those in the Madeline books. *In two straight lines they broke their bread. And brushed their teeth and went to bed.* The beds are made, some sporting stuffed animals or needlepoint cushions: YO ♥ ABUELA; DIOS TIENE EL CONTROL DE MI VIDA, gifts from the charitable women's associations who visit regularly or from family if they have families. Sor Corita points out Tatica's bed. Two baby dolls are propped up on her pillow. Sus niñitas, Sor Corita smiles, her little girls. Tatica has forgotten their names.

As they are leaving, the sisters assure the kind nun that they will be continuing their father's infusions. Sor Corita blesses them and again regrets that she was not able to help them more. If you would like to come back once Reverenda Madre returns, you are most welcome.

Her sisters are headed home to the States in a week, so it would be up to Alma to make a return visit if she wants to.

But Alma has seen enough. She is done believing she can unearth the mysteries of another's heart. No less her father's. Whatever stories Manuel Cruz refused to tell, it's not for Scheherazade to resurrect them. There are borders even Joan Didion would not cross. The untold is sacred ground. Whatever stories are buried there should be left alone. It's called *the afterlife* for a reason. Her turn will come soon enough.

≈ Filomena

Before Filomena visits Perla at the jail in the capital where she is being held prior to sentencing, Pepito warns his aunt that Perla still isn't speaking to him or to the lawyers. We are making progress, he adds. I hear she's reading out loud to her fellow inmates.

Filomena, too, has been learning her alphabet. Doña Alma insists. Filomena can now draw all her letters and write her name legibly so others can read it. She already knows every shop on her street, who owns them, what they sell, but she can now decipher the names on the signs. Bichán, for one, is always refreshing his colmado's name—it keeps customers on their toes, he claims. Colmado La Vitamina has morphed into Colmado La Milagrosa—for when the vitamins fail, he jokes to those who inquire about the new name.

Mamita has changed, Pepito reminds his aunt. Remember, it's been thirty some years.

Her nephew doesn't know that Filomena has caught glimpses of her sister as well as Pepito every time they've come for a visit. She has watched her muchachito grow up: child, adolescent, young man, each stage a bittersweet surprise, as in her dreams he invariably returns to the little boy he was. Over the years, Tesoro has maintained his handsome looks, a bit of salt in his pepper hair, a few more pounds; obviously, he is flourishing; Perla, however, appears increasingly unhappy and unwell: her hair dyed an unnatural black, the gray canas showing, her face puffy and set in a permanent scowl, her body misshapen with excess weight. What could it be?

Meanwhile, Filomena has been garnering more and more compliments. Not that she believes Florian's piropos, but others echo them. It happens: the beauty at fifteen fades into a crone while her contemporary, passed over in youth, turns heads in her older years. Just as the sisters exchanged names at the beginning of their lives, now in middle age, they have switched looks, Filomena has become the attractive sister.

Filomena dresses up in her Sunday clothes for the visit. Lupita washes and sets her hair, inquiring if her neighbor now has a novio.

¡Qué buenamoza! her nephew compliments her. The guardias will go nuts.

At the prison gates, the guards inspect the bag of treats and toiletries Filomena has brought, taking issue but then waving her in when she slips them a tip. The visiting room is a hot, noisy hall, lined with tables, guardias posted by the doors. When Perla is escorted in, Filomena is shocked. Her sister's face is drained of life, her eyes have no spark, her movements sluggish as if her body is a load she doesn't have the strength to carry. Maybe she is already dead, one of the zombies who come back from the other side seeking revenge. Filomena's heart sinks. She can't think of a single thing to say. She reaches for her sister's hand and keeps repeating Perla's name.

Alma

The last days with her sisters are tinged with tenderness. Bickering at a minimum. About time, in their late sixties, early seventies. Coming right up against the mystery of another—Papi, this Tatica person, Mami, for that matter—has given them pause.

Inside the airport terminal, they linger, blocking the entrance to immigration. Señoras, would you kindly step aside, the young guardia says, his order in the form of a polite request. They are his elders by almost a half century.

We're sisters, Piedad explains, as if that gives them the right.

In this country, it actually does. The guardia gestures to the bench beside his post where they can take their time. That's another thing

Alma loves here, familia as well as age are valid excuses, as are, on the negative side, crimes of passion. If their flight were on Dominicana Airlines, air traffic control would probably delay the departure until the sisters are done with their goodbyes.

But they're on the American Airlines flight to Miami, which is boarding now, no ifs, ands, or buts. Time to go. The sisters rock in each other's arms. Refuge, Soul, Consolation, Pity—beautiful virtuous names, Sor Corita had said. Everybody loves everybody more. No need to bring out the measuring cup.

Back in her casita, Alma lies down for a nap, having woken up early once again, to chauffeur her sisters to the airport. For the first time since leaving the States, she dreams of her writer friend: *Are you going to betray them, too?* Alma is about to ask, betray who? but a bird is relentlessly calling, midday when most self-respecting critters are taking their siestas. A songster who will not quit. She checks her guidebook for the name of a bird that sings at all hours, a name might cage it up, at least give her the pleasure and illusion of control.

Cigüita? Ruiseñor? Martinete?

The long day lies ahead with no interruptions. To secure her solitude, Alma has continued to use the excuse that she's writing. The gates, left open during construction of the casita to make access easier for the workers, are again closed, the story box reactivated, operating on a limited schedule, whenever Alma, or more often, Filomena, is free to listen.

Her project is finally finished: the abandoned manuscripts have been put to rest in the ground, dormant seeds that will never germinate unless a writer comes along and unearths a historical figure, like Bienvenida, and ends up writing the novel Scheherazade never could finish.

But Papi's story will definitely remain untold. Visiting Tatica, Alma realized how little she knew her father. Only the small nation of Papi in the large continent of Manuel Cruz. The guarded, daughter-proofed stories he dished out over the years turned out to be impediments to the deep country of whoever else it was he was.

So yes, to answer her writer friend in the unsettling dream, Alma is ready to move on to whatever lies beyond the groomed lawns of once upon a time. If that's betrayal, so be it. Still, it bugs her, her friend's implication that Alma is in the business of betrayal, "too," suggesting "in addition to others." Who else besides herself did her writer friend mean? Alma hearkens back to the last line of her first novel, *a black furred thing . . . wailing over some violation that lies at the center of my art.* Back when she wrote it, she had no idea what it meant. Readers would ask about the creepy ending, and all Scheherazade could say was, I haven't a clue. She still isn't sure.

The bird persists, the laurel leaves joining in, their rustling like stories whispered behind hands. The tiny glint of an airplane inside which her sisters doze, traveling north, adds its dull roar. The inching grass, the probing roots, the pebbles with rings around them, murmur their tales. Alma had no idea until she shut up that the earth itself was storying.

Very faint at first, then louder as her ear becomes attuned to subtleties, Alma hears the sounds turning into sense. She opens a drawer for a spoon to stir the milk in her coffee, and the utensils are recounting their journey from the bauxite mines near Pedernales, how their red materials were gouged from the earth, transported onto ships headed north to be converted to aluminum, molded into unnatural shapes and sharpness, the workers who handled them, the boxes they were packed in, the mouths they've filled with tasty treats, meats they've cut, sancochos they've been dipped in—

Alma bangs the drawer shut, rinsing the spoon to wash away the story, but the water, too, has a tale to tell: how it bubbled out of the ground on the mountains of the Cordillera Central, a rivulet, becoming a stream, trickling down, joining other streams, becoming a river, the putrid chemicals and trash dumped into its currents, the replenishing rains, the banks flooding the valleys, the insistent pressure to feed the sea, feed the sea. The shutters rattle; the wind picks up, blowing in from the ocean with the tale of where it has been, the sails it filled, the desperate travelers aboard yolas, praying to Huracán, the stormy god, and to Our Lady of Altagracia for good fortune, may we reach Puerto Rico before the coast guard detects us. Each one on board has a story the wind carries.

Filo! Alma cries out. Filomena hears la doña's desperation and comes running. ¿Qué? ¿Qué le pasa, doña? What is it?

Alma is at a loss what to say. Do you hear them?

Filomena tilts her head as if unsure what la doña means. The globe, the woman with the sewn lips? You told me to listen.

Alma is relieved by Filomena's report. She is not alone.

Alma complains to Brava. The stories are still talking to her, now joined by other stories, more and more stories. Something's wrong. ¿Talvez me estoy volviendo loca? Not far from Alma's thoughts are the specters of ancestors, shipwrecked in their imaginations, Papi, for one, trapped in Alfa Calenda, uncommunicative to his last days. That same blood runs in Alma's veins, after all.

Brava sighs with frustration. Mujer, stop thinking everything is a sign of illness.

But there are so many! And there's no room left in here. Alma taps her forehead.

Then write them down, Brava advises. El papel lo aguanta todo, she adds. Paper can take it, even if Alma can't.

But the blank pages of Alma's notebook have their own tales to tell. The seedlings planted in the forests, the decades of growing, the hacking down, the mashing into pulp, the pounding and rolling, the cutting and binding.

Alma can't help but listen. *Drawn? Compelled? Enthralled? Possessed?* She searches for the exact word to describe what she is feeling, still hopelessly, helplessly in love with naming things.

⟰ Filomena

Over the weeks since Doña Alma's sisters departed, Filomena notes a change in her mistress. Today she hollers for Filomena like the casita is on fire. Filomena drops everything, but all la doña wants to know is about the voices.

Filomena considers disclosing all she has learned from Don Manuel and Doña Bienvenida. But if a person or persons decide to carry their stories to their graves, is it her place to betray them? Does anyone in the new life her mother made after leaving the campo know her story? Every time Don Manuel mentions his Tatica, Filomena can't help thinking of her own mother. Did a similar situation happen to Mamá? Filomena will never know for sure why her mother did what she did. Or Perla. Why would her sister murder a child? Filomena understands the haunted doctor, the heartbroken ex-wife of a dictator, better than the people in her own life! How can this be?

She also will not mention the other voices she sometimes hears coming from the marker in the shape of a large machete stained with what must be blood, voices crying out in a language she doesn't understand, though suffering requires no translation. Doña Alma does not need more clouds in her sky.

La doña's moodiness might have to do with her sisters. Maybe she has had a falling out with them as Filomena did with Perla. But the little phone rings often, the sisters calling, and although Filomena doesn't know English, she hears no antagonism in Doña Alma's tone of voice.

Her own sister's case has yet to be decided. Faithfully, once a week, Filomena makes the trip to the prison. What joy to be together again! Just like when they were girls in the campo, the sadness of their mother's absence and their father's harshness easier to bear with the other nearby. Each visit to the prison, Filomena reminisces with the silent Perla, hoping to prompt a response: the sancochos and dulces they cooked, aromatic yerbas drying in bundles hung from the ceiling, the hammock and how they rocked in it together telling stories, cocks crowing, the smells of sofrito, the plantains boiling on the fogón, the mist coming down like a lid on their mountain valley, burning off in the bright sun of morning. Filomena mentions her job, how nicely she is treated, how well she is paid—perhaps Perla can also work there once she is home? Often Filomena talks of Pepito. What a kind, smart man he has turned into! A few times she has dared to bring up their mother, watching her sister's face closely to see what emotions register. I've given up trying to find her, she tells Perla so as not to upset her further.

Even so, Filomena can't help wondering, as she would do all those years of separation from Perla: What is Mamá doing right this moment? Is she safe, is she happy? Does she remember me?

How does God hold everybody in mind? Why does He allow sorrows to happen? To keep His creation interested in what comes next?

Ay, Filo, Padre Regino laughs, you have gotten very philosophical working for that writer. Some months back, he read the article in the paper about the author's return and her sculpture garden. That's when he put two and two together: this Scheherazade is none other than the Doña Alma Filomena mentions again and again.

Many saints, and sinners, have asked those very same questions, Filomena, and none of them has come up with a good answer.

Filomena feels gratified that she shares something with the saints, and not too much, she hopes, with the sinners. But she has been remiss in her confessions. She has yet to divulge all her secrets, the box she buried without permission, the voices she hears, the stories they tell her. And what about those other unintelligible voices, the shouting, the wailing—could they be demons? She doesn't dare mention them to the priest or he might urge her to burn her box of talismans, quit her job in that bewitched place. But this is where she feels happiest. Everyone needs a little happiness. Even Doña Bienvenida and Dr. Cruz found ways to bring some sunshine into their lives, Dr. Cruz with his mother and his invented world, and later with his pretty wife and daughters, and for a while with his Tatica; Bienvenida with her daughter, Odette, and, briefly, with Don Arístides. Sometimes bite-size is all one gets.

After her daily rounds outside, weeding, raking, washing down the sculptures, feeding her birds, watering her plantings, listening, listening, Filomena lets herself in the back door of the casita. She knows better than to small-talk or turn on the radio until she assesses la doña's mood. A mere glance, a tone of voice, a line between the brows, speak volumes. She sweeps out la doña's house quietly, takes away the trash, prepares the noon meal, which she later finds uneaten in the refrigerator. Her cooking has always been praised. In fact, Doña Lena used to complain that those days Filomena was on her enforced vacation, everyone in the house lost weight.

Filomena questions Doña Alma. ¿Es que no le gusta? Maybe her cooking does not appeal?

It's not that. I just get distracted.

La doña's face is pinched. Her clothes hang on her. You will disappear, Filomena admonishes.

To ensure la doña eats, Filomena decides to be present at mealtimes, serving the almuerzo, then standing by in case she is needed. But this won't do at all. Grab a plate, come sit down, Doña Alma insists. She's no comesolo. She doesn't want to eat alone.

All her working life, Filomena has fed her employers first, and afterward, while they are taking their siestas or enjoying their sobremesa, tranquilita, she serves herself, piling everything in a big bowl, using a spoon to scoop her rice and beans, and her own teeth for tearing the meat from the bone she holds in her fingers. All those utensils and plates are a nuisance. It would take away her appetite to be fussing with so many implements.

But she makes an exception, swallows her shyness, and joins her mistress at the table, as it seems to be the only way to ensure Doña Alma eats. Her own appetite flies out the window, though later, in her own house, she is ravenous, wolfing down the leftovers Doña Alma insists she take away.

Even with this indulgence, Filomena cannot get Doña Alma to clean her plate. She is too busy asking questions, recounting stories. Does Filomena know her name comes from an old story about a girl turned into a bird after her brother-in-law cut off her tongue so she couldn't tell he had raped her? Filomena drops her spoon in shock. ¿Es verdad?

Doña Alma laughs. Her readers were always asking that same question: Is it true? Did you make that up? You know how we say, Cuando el río suena es porque piedras trae.

Filomena is surprised. They say that allá, too?

En todas partes cuecen habas. Doña Alma quotes another popular refrán. Old sayings Filomena has heard since she was a child. In English we have them as well. Where there's smoke there's fire. It's the same the world over.

And does Filomena know that the utensils they are using were once red dirt in Pedernales? That monkeys are our cousins? That humans have stepped on the moon? The climate is changing and one day soon their little island will be under water from the melted ice caps. What ice caps? Filomena wants to ask, but it will only delay la doña from finishing her meal.

She swallowed a parrot, her neighbors say when someone can't stop talking. If so, la doña has devoured a whole flock! In order to encourage Doña Alma to fill her mouth with food instead of talk, Filomena starts telling stories like the ones she used to tell the box at the gate, stories about her campo, about the viejita she once worked for, about her neighbors in the barrio. When she runs out of memories, she makes them up.

≈ Pepito

Pepito is staying with his aunt, who keeps apologizing for the lack of conveniences. What do you mean? he reassures her. He loves being here, waking up to the crowing of roosters, the sun sifting through the closed jalousies, the smell of the coffee his tía makes first thing in a sock on an outdoor fogón as if the twenty-first century is still a ways off. All of it makes him ache for things he never even knew were missing.

Okay, full disclosure: he does miss the lack of Internet access, a decent bathroom with as much hot water as he wants, his blender for making smoothies—funny the quote-unquote First World things without which he feels deprived. When Richard arrives for a visit, Pepito books a hotel in a nearby resort, as Richard needs a beach, a good bed, saunas, massages, fresh fish. He can't wait for Pepito's sabbatical to be over. Even in Greece their time together was interrupted by visits from Pepito's mother and excursions to ruins. I miss you, Richard whines gratifyingly, as in the scale of their relations, Richard has always been the one less in love.

And Pepito does need to get back to work. He has abandoned his manuscript these last few months, caught up in his mother's trials and tribulations. It's not that he hasn't tried. But every time he sits down to write, he can't seem to stay focused, instead asking himself a dozen times a day, why did he ever choose this topic? *The Influence of Canonical and Classical Texts on Latinx Literature*—¡Por favor!

In his defense: back in the day, in order to get his dissertation topic approved, he had to tether so-called marginal writers to the canonical texts to make them worthy. Read this, it's like Homer. Get a load of this, it's so Shakespeare. Now he's too far along into the research and drafting to change topics; he just wants to finish the damn thing, send it to the university press, and move on to a new project. He would love to write a novel—a historical novel, as those tend to hold more weight with his academic colleagues.

There he goes, putting on the golden handcuffs again!

But he has to earn a living. His bank account is drained, mostly from the costs of Perla's lawyers and defense. By the time it's all over, his savings will be gone. Not that Pepito has ever been a high wage earner or a thrifty church mouse.

His brother on the other hand, though swimming in dough, is not all that magnanimous about helping with Mamita's expenses. In this whole fiasco, GW has sided with their father, who disapproves of Pepito's efforts to mitigate Perla's punishment. In fact, Tesoro is no longer talking to him. Pepito suspects that a lot of other antagonisms are fueling his banishment, including Pepito's sexual orientation—not that Tesoro would ever openly admit this. Better to be righteous, furious, and unforgiving.

The mainstay through this ordeal has been his aunt Filomena. She has even considered quitting her current job and working at the jail in order to look out for her sister. But Pepito encourages Filomena to stay where she is. The pay is much more than she would ever earn in a prison. If all goes well, Perla will get off with a light sentence and be released on parole sooner rather than later. Meanwhile, Filomena can always take time off to visit her sister. Doña Alma is very understanding.

Not to mention, Pepito mentions, he'd love for his aunt to ask Doña Alma to grant him an interview.

His aunt doesn't dare. Doña Alma has grown increasingly reclusive. No visitors. Tell them I'm writing, she instructs Filomena to say to whomever comes to her door.

Maybe she is working on a new book, you think?

Filomena wouldn't know. The only sign Filomena sees of la doña's writing is scribbles in a little notebook. Sometimes, the cuaderno isn't even open from one day to the next. Doña Alma sits at her small desk looking out the window as if she is listening to her voices. She bestirs herself only to give Filomena her lessons, another reason that Filomena is pushing herself to learn to read.

Such eccentric behavior only serves to sharpen Pepito's curiosity. What happens when a writer leaves the gated community of her established craft and instead goes feral? Maybe he can entice Scheherazade to write one more book, about that.

≈ Manuel

Bienvenida's voice lifts me from the stupor of remorse I've fallen into.

You kept us waiting for your visit in Canada, she chides me gently. Odette would often mention that handsome doctor she met in Nueva York. I believe she had a little crush on you.

Perhaps it was overly cautious of me, I admit. But I didn't dare register with the consulate and risk being tracked down by el Jefe's secret police. I steered clear of the Montreal Dominicans.

I had no idea I was the cause of so much concern to you.

It wasn't you, but the other Dominicans I was worried about.

You'd be surprised. Many of them were critical of the regime. At first, they were cautious in front of me, given my former role. But they soon realized I would not betray them. They were very kind, taking care of Odette during my many hospitalizations.

I heard that your leg was amputated, that you were quite ill.

My diabetes got so bad. Joaquín later told me el Jefe had a tomb prepared for me. Gracias a Dios, I did not have to use it! When I recovered, the snow and ice and cold were a danger. I was always afraid of falling and breaking my remaining leg, so we moved to Miami.

A difficult life, you had, Doña Bienvenida. I repeat something my writer daughter once told me—a Chinese curse like our fukú. *May you have an interesting life.* An interesting life makes for a good story.

Call it what you will, it was life. Over time, I learned to accept what I could not change, but it was very difficult for me and for Odette. I think that is when all her problems started—she just could never settle down. I stopped keeping count of her divorces.

Our stories are winding down. We are entering the past tense. I linger, as I did in Alfa Calenda, not wanting my storied life to end.

So, we never met again? Doña Bienvenida asks, uncertain.

Never, except in the story my daughter drafted about us.

Your daughter? Scheherazade, our storyteller, is your daughter?

Sí, señora. Our would-be storyteller. Scheherazade to you, Alma to me. I confess that at first, I was disappointed she didn't write that book about me she was always saying she would. But in the end, I agreed with her mother, did I really want our private lives put out there for the world to see and judge? Another form of death, isn't it, to be remade in someone else's image? And as you have heard, there are parts of my life I wanted to keep secret, parts of myself I couldn't bear to face until this moment.

I can sense a question forming in Bienvenida's head. I intercept it with my own. Even here in draft form I work by evasion.

I've always wondered, Doña Bienvenida, what kept you going? Besides Odette, I add, anticipating her reply.

Ay Manuel, Bienvenida sighs, her voice so low I could be imagining it. What can I say? Those long days in the hospital, the curious pain in my missing leg, the prosthetic that never really fit, several shades lighter than my skin. The winter so long, the snow falling and falling. Even now that it's all over, I feel the heaviness of those years. The happiest moments of my life were in the past. I was a ghost before my time. She laughs, trying to inject lightness into that sad thought. And for you? she asks. What was the happiest time of your life?

I always believed it was that month in Nueva York when I was madly in love with Lucía. But that love brought me so much heartache. I sought happiness with Tatica but that, too, led to more heartache. It was the end of Alfa Calenda as I had known it. The stories that were its air and sunlight and substance vanished. Sitting in that nursing home, watching the snow fall, those blond aides attending to me, I devised a whole theory: happiness is not a static state. Happiness is circulatory. If you stop the flow of blood, what happens?

The patient dies? Bienvenida guesses.

Exactly. By keeping myself to myself, I stopped the flow. Those last months among strangers in the home were among my happiest.

We are quiet for a spell. This, too, is happiness, I am thinking.

Bienvenida breaks the spell and gives voice to the question she has been holding back. What ever happened with Tatica?

I took care of her. A private arrangement. She was never told who betrayed her, but I am sure she figured it out. The curious thing: she never denounced me or tried to contact me or my family. I suffered my guilt alone. The memory of my betrayal was a private hell inside me, replacing Alfa Calenda, intensifying my loneliness.

Over the years, I kept up with her through a contact in Higüey, where she had settled. When I learned Tatica had been stricken by dementia, just like Lucía, I arranged for some nuns to take her in. As far as I knew, she had no family. I felt bad committing her to an hospicio, but when I ended up in a nursing home myself, I found it fitting and strangely soothing, that this was something we were sharing, parallel lives.

Now and then, her face would appear to me and I'd call for her. They say I died of a heart attack. I died of shame, simple as that.

I wonder, Bienvenida muses, if el Jefe ever felt any such regrets toward me? I remember how in Paris he said I was his good luck charm. But was it love? What do you think, Manuel? Did he ever love me?

That is a most difficult question. To answer Bienvenida I have to enter into the feelings of my worst enemy. But it is a small thing I can do to ease her suffering.

Ay, Doña Bienvenida, who can know? I push harder into my resistance and into that circle of hell, my oppressor's heart. Yes, I suppose, in his own way he did.

⁓ Bienvenida

I can sense Manuel's reluctance. Why am I still asking for reassurance, encouraging others to participate in my self-deception? Have I learned nothing from my life, would I make all the same mistakes again, I wonder? A life of wrong turns and dead ends.

Time and time again the abyss would open up before me. I tried to shield first Odette and later my grandchildren from the horrible stories of the regime we began to hear more and more about. I did not want them to feel self-hatred because of the brutal blood coursing in their veins. When el Jefe was assassinated, it was Cousin Joaquín who called to let me know. Do not speak to the press, he cautioned. We were living in Texas at the time, no one suspected that the sweet abuelita of three stormy adolescent boys and a quiet watchful girl had once been a first lady, the discarded wife of a powerful man. I hung up the phone and it was as if the door of my cage had been flung open, but I didn't know where to go. It was too late to start my life over. All I could do was go forward, not look back, or I would turn into a pillar of salt, like that woman in the Bible, from all the tears I would shed, and not just for myself, but for all of us, the many lives lost, the grieving survivors, the haunted collaborators. Get thee behind me, Satan! as our Lord said to the evil one.

But the past found me out anyway. One day, my granddaughter, born and raised in the States, came home from her history class with questions about the island's former "ruthless dictator." The things he did! Killing anyone who disagreed with him, murdering those Mirabal sisters and all those Haitians with machetes so he could blame it on the local farmers. Wow, Abuela, no wonder you divorced him!

I wished I could have claimed the moral high ground. Told her, oh yes, my eyes were opened, and I left with your mother. Instead, I confessed the truth to her as best I could. I fell in love with the story I wanted to believe about mi Jefe.

Don't torture yourself this way, Bienvenida, Manuel says softly. We have to live our natures out, for better or worse. And regrets are just a way to make the same mistakes over and over.

I suppose it is too late, even for regrets. It was too late the night I surrendered to el Jefe's charms. Perhaps that is why I abandoned the novel your daughter was writing about me. I would have to live my mistakes again. I went to my grave with the same unanswered question that I once had seen in Soeur Odette's eyes: Why was I drawn to such a brutal man? I still don't understand.

We hear footsteps approaching: our groundskeeper heading home. Today, like most days, she stops at el Barón's globe, gives it a nudge, then watches as the only snow she'll ever see falls and settles on the ground.

Tía, someone calls from the other side of the wall. Open up!

Our groundskeeper hurries to the back door, opens it a crack. Pepito! ¿Qué pasa?

The nephew is headed back to his home in Nueva York in a few days. He would like to meet the writer. Come on, Tía, he insists. I teach her work. I've been studying it for years. What harm can it do?

I could lose my job, that's what. You yourself said it's probably the best one I'm likely to get. Besides, as I told you, la doña hasn't been herself lately.

Okay, the nephew concedes. Just show me around then.

His aunt cannot refuse the smaller favor after having denied the larger one. They visit the different markers, the nephew whistling with wonder. Whose idea was this? he wants to know.

La doña, with the help of her friend Doña Brava.

By now they are standing in front of my tomb. So, it's true, the nephew says. I'd read that Scheherazade was writing a novel about Trujillo's ex. Why'd she choose such a plain, unremarkable woman? Una masa de pan.

Bread dough, people always said that about me. Docile, taking the imprint of any hand kneading it. That's been the story handed down. Who was there to correct them since I never spoke up? What difference would it have made? Who would have listened?

Our groundskeeper knows my life was anything but dull. But she must also know that any such admission would only incite the nephew's curiosity.

Sometimes the still, quiet waters have a depth to them, our groundskeeper says noncommittedly.

But the nephew doesn't need further encouragement. That night, I hear him as he climbs over the wall using a ladder, pulling it up behind him.

≈ Pepito

His tía's neighbor is cool about letting Pepito rent his ladder for a small fee. So, what señorita will he be visiting tonight? All jokey, like this is *Romeo and Juliet*.

You mean, señorito, Pepito should joke back. The neighbor has been watching him, trying to suss out what's Americano, what's pájaro.

Pepito could have slipped his tía's key in his pocket and let himself in the back door. But she wears it on a string around her neck until bedtime, when she hangs it on the hook with her rosary and saints' calendar. If she wakes up and it's not there, she will know. Why add more upset to her load? She's already heavy-hearted about Mamita and about Pepito's departure in a couple of days. Besides, breaking in is part of the fun. Like *Romeo and Juliet*, yes. Turns out he has a talent for stealth, perfected over the years, a handicap of living in the world of story, becoming this or that character with the turn of a page, breaking and entering others' lives. He once had a therapist who suggested that it was time that he leave those strategies behind. Find out who he really is. But how would he know what a true self is without a story to put the idea in him?

It's a moonless, star-filled sky. Pepito guides himself, gingerly touching the different tombs, heading toward the lit window of the casita where the writer sits, keeping vigil, though it's unclear what or whom she is waiting for.

Pepito knocks lightly at the door, not wanting to disturb Scheherazade if indeed she is writing. Who wants to go down in literary history—the circles he travels in, after all—as the person from Porlock who interrupted Coleridge in the middle of "Kubla Kahn"? Unfinished or not, it's a pretty good poem. So, maybe the intruder from Porlock did the poet a favor? Perhaps Pepito will write a monograph about that. His sabbatical year has turned out to be a wash, what with everything going on. He better bump up his publications if he wants to pass into the higher echelons of tenured professorship.

Yes? a weary voice answers from inside. A *yes* so heavily laced with *no*, it might as well be a negative. Who is it? she calls out again, this time sounding more annoyed than weary.

A chair scrapes the floor, steps approach the door. Pepito considers squatting behind one of the larger sculptures: the urn or snow globe or the one he recalls from earlier in the afternoon, of the woman holding out her right palm as if wanting someone to read her fortune.

But this might be his last chance on this trip to meet Scheherazade. It won't be until the holidays or maybe spring break when he can get away again. Richard left a week ago, griping about being a sabbatical widower a bit longer. And it's time to get back and prepare for the fall semester. He has done what he can. His mother has been convicted of the lesser crime of manslaughter, but by reason of insanity, not passion. She is now in a women's prison near Higüey, one of the nicer ones. The lawyer will keep working on her early release, fueled by the pipeline of cash from the loyal son up north. His client needs treatment; she needs rehabilitation, not punishment.

Tomorrow, his last day on the island, he'll be going to visit Mamita with his aunt. His father's family is none too pleased about their nephew's continuing association with "that murderer." Mamita, he keeps correcting them. She killed two people, they point out. *Mother* trumps *murderer*, he could say but they wouldn't listen. The tragic story has them in its grip.

When the door opens, Pepito is shocked. His tía is right: Scheherazade is wasting away—"a tattered coat upon a stick" comes to mind. True, the only time he has ever seen her was at a reading years ago. The photos on the jackets of her books—like most author photos—show an attractive, airbrushed woman, as if in addition to having talent, a female writer has to look good to sell books.

Who are you? What do you want? How'd you get in? One question rear-ending the other, a way of letting him know he is in her way. She stands waiting for him to explain himself.

Wisely, Pepito doesn't lead with, I'm a huge fan, the professor who has been pestering your agent for an interview. Instead, he mines a vein he suspects is loaded with ore: I'm Filomena's nephew visiting from Nueva York. He gestures with his mouth in the direction of el Norte. In some diaspora chat room he'd read that it was the Dominican way of pointing. Mi tía has told me all about you and how you've been teaching her to read. I'm so grateful to you.

Scheherazade's face softens. She peers into the dark over his shoulder. Did she let you in? Filo! the writer calls out into the dark.

Tía's gone home. She wanted to get to bed early. We have a long day tomorrow. Should he mention his mom in prison in Higüey? Better not.

Scheherazade cocks her head, unsure. So, how'd you get in?

Pepito recalls his aunt telling him about the intercom at the gate where visitors are required to tell a story to gain entry. I told a story, he lies, and the gates opened.

Strange, Alma thought she turned the intercom off. She'll have to remind Filomena to unplug the damn thing before she leaves at night. Of late, the apparatus seems to have a mind of its own, letting just about anybody in. Maybe the ghosts of her characters are taking over the cemetery! Poetic justice or whatever. More likely, this nephew is lying and his aunt gave him the key to the back entrance? Something fishy is going on, which makes for an interesting story in and of itself. Come in then, Alma steps to one side, another door opening. She gestures for Pepito to sit before taking a seat herself at her desk, turning her chair around to face him. So, tell me the story.

What story?

She scowls, suspecting his story is a story. The story you told to get in.

On her desk, he spies an opened notebook, the page is full of messy marks, words crossed out. What are you working on? he'd like to ask her. But if he wants to get anywhere, he better oblige her first with the story he supposedly told at the gate.

All he can think of is what has been happening in his own life right now, his mother, his father, the discovery of the affair. Why not begin there?

Scheherazade sits as still as one of Brava's sculptures. The expression on her face is hard to describe. Enthralled, compelled, a sponge soaking in his words, her eyes brighten, she comes alive.

You should write that down, she says, when he is done.

⌇ Filomena

She wakes up to the sound of crashing dishes. A burglar has broken into her house. ¡Coño! a man's voice swears. Not a thief. A burglar would not swear out loud.

Pepito? she calls.

The house is dark. The electricity out again. Filomena lights her hurricane lamp and hurries to the front room. Her nephew is on his knees, picking up shards by the light of his little phone. The table Filomena had set for early breakfast tomorrow before they leave for Higüey has been upended. Plates and silverware and sugar from the toppled jar all over the floor.

¿Qué pasó? Filomena wants to know.

Nada, Tía, nada. Sorry about this. He gestures toward the broken plates, the scattered silverware. I was just out walking. I needed to clear my head.

Poor boy, worrying about his mother.

It's just plates, she reassures him, kneeling to help pick up the pieces.

She, too, is worrying about Perla. And Pepito. The day after tomorrow, he goes back to Nueva York. He says his work has not gone well. He says he has wasted his year—his life, he adds, his head in his hands. Ay, mi'jo, she consoles him. No diga eso. It hurts to hear him say so.

From what she has gathered from their talks, his father is not speaking to him. His brother Jorge Washington sides with Tesoro. Except for his friend Ricardo, he seems to be alone in the world.

You have me, she reminds him.

On the way to Higüey the next morning, she tries to lift his spirits with stories of her childhood with Perla in the campo. She presents a better version of Papá, an embittered man, as she wants Pepito to have a good impression of the grandfather he never met. A pretend abuelo whom she would have liked for a father. She brings up Tatica. Your abuela, she adds because he seems not to know he had one. Everyone has an abuela! Laughter bubbles in her throat.

Mamita never spoke about her, except that she died so young, when Mamita was ten, I think it was. You must have been—how old?

She did not die, Filomena says straight out. She left the campo for a better life in the capital. She promised to come back for me and Perla once she was settled. Papá was furious at her for abandoning us. If she shows her face again, he'd threaten, I'll send her and her little putas straight to hell!

Pepito's head jerks in her direction. The car swerves. Hey, Tía, are you making this up or what?

Filomena shakes her head sadly. No mi'jo, that is God's truth.

But you said abuelo was a nice guy.

I made that up, Filomena confesses. Papá was a hard man, especially when he drank, which was often. I was six when Mamá left,

Filomena continues. That night she had woken up, sensing someone in the room, fearing it was Papá coming back from one of his parrandas, mistaking their bedroom, the way he sometimes did, touching them as if they were Mamá while they pretended to sleep. Perla always defended him. He's our father. He's just giving us affection. All the blame for her sadness Perla threw on their mother.

But that night Papá had not yet returned or Filomena would have heard him, stumbling and cursing, banging into things, breaking plates, glasses. And these were stealthy footsteps approaching, probably ciguapas coming to kidnap a girl child for their tribe, which lived nearby under the Yaque river. Mamá had told her stories.

The face came down close and kissed her. Mamá! She had pinned the medal of the Virgencita she wore on her brassiere on Filomena's nightie, and on Perla's finger, she had slipped her ring, which her older sister threw into the river the following day. *I will come back for you.* Like el Jefe's promises to Doña Bienvenida—Mamá's never came to be.

We never saw her again. Did she die? Did she forget us? Did she not love us enough? Filomena understands her mother's reasons with her head, but her heart refuses to accept the answers she comes up with.

People sometimes make cruel choices out of necessity, Pepito says.

Maybe her nephew is thinking of his mother and father, leaving him behind, but they did come back for him, breaking Filomena's heart. How does God decide who will bear the greater pain? Another philosophical question to ask the old priest.

You guys sure had a rough life, Pepito says, shaking his head. And now this. His mother in prison, her mind racked by what she has done.

A rough life, that is true. But then, who doesn't? if Filomena is to believe the stories she has been hearing in the cemetery. Seems like everyone who lives has endured some sadness, sometimes buried so deep inside them, even they don't know it's there.

And if you could hear other people's stories all the time, what then? Would you understand them better? Would you forgive them? What about el Jefe? Tesoro? Manuel Cruz was not such a nice man to his querida, but hearing his story, Filomena can't deny it, no señor, she feels compassion for his predicament.

Listening to all these stories has opened so many windows in Filomena's life. Don Manuel, Doña Bienvenida. But also the other voices that come and go with the wind—each one offering a different view of the world. Even the disturbing ones that frighten and confuse her—maybe someday she will understand them, too, and their anguished wailing will turn to birdsong. So much sadness, so much wonder, so much joy. Her heart is messy with feelings, her mind with possibilities, twists and turns. It was simpler before. And yet, she would not go back. Now there is room in her heart for everyone, or most everyone.

What did your mamita tell you about me? Filomena asks. Pepito must have felt abandoned when his tía disappeared from his life.

She said you tried to break up her marriage. Is that true, Tía? You never liked Papote much?

I never understood him, Filomena says with new understanding.

Join the club, Pepito says.

Pepito

By the time they return from visiting Mamita, the streetlights have come on. The fireman neighbor is waiting in front of his house on a chair, on the lookout.

Where is my ladder? Florian confronts Pepito.

Filomena scowls. What ladder? she asks in a quarrelsome voice.

No problem. I'll get it for you. Pepito turns sheepishly to Filomena. Will you let me in, Tía?

Filomena opens the back gate to the cemetery with her key, saying nothing.

That night over a bowl of boiled víveres with queso frito, Pepito confesses. He just had to meet Scheherazade—he persists in calling la doña by that strange name. And, Tía, you said she wasn't feeling well, but you didn't say she was so spacey. Has she been that way for a while?

Remember, his tía reminds him. La doña's head is packed with stories. Sure, everybody's head is full of memories, noticias, chismes, worries. But in addition to all of these, Doña Alma has welcomed so many stories in that small head of hers, it gets stuffed, like a nose when you have a bad cold. That's why she started her cemetery. And even so, they keep speaking to her. I've been trying to help her. With the listening, that is all, Filomena adds.

Pepito is tickled. So, his aunt is a santera! He suspected as much.

No, no, no! Filomena will have nothing to do with such nonsense. Padre Regino has told her that such brujerías are sinful. She is a servant who has been given a task and she is fulfilling it.

Got it, Pepito says, tamping down his smile.

Before he leaves the next day, Pepito asks his aunt to send him progress reports of Mamita but also of Scheherazade. Doña Alma, he corrects himself.

I'll keep an eye on them, Filomena promises him.

Over the days, months, and the years to follow, his aunt catches him up on her news. Doña Alma has been to the lawyers. She has signed a lot of papers, Filomena reports, about what is to be done when she is gone. Doña Alma's sisters and Doña Brava have been named the trustees of Scheherazade's estate. Upon her death, the cemetery is to be a park, belonging to the barrio, with Filomena as its manager, a salaried position, which means she can set the rules. Filomena has already decided: the gates will be opened to everyone— no matter what story they tell. All stories are good stories if you find the right listener, she explains to Pepito.

Who will administer her literary estate? Pepito wonders. His tía knows nothing about that.

With her help and recommendation, Pepito contacts Alma, ingra- tiating himself with his charm—he is not Tesoro's son for nothing!— introducing himself as a scholar of Scheherazade's work; in fact, he is writing a book about her work and those of other Latinx authors.

Alma/Scheherazade finally grants him an interview, rambling answers by voice memos to his emailed questions. Of course, this is only the thin edge of Pepito's wedging himself into the writer's life. As that life draws to a close, Alma begins taking his calls, at one point laughing at his nosiness, You could be one of my sisters! He also manages to convince Alma to name him her literary executor. Unlike her sisters, he can make informed, writerly decisions. Unlike her agent, Pepito is un dominicano. Representing her work is un asunto del alma, he tells her. The pun lands nicely. It helps that he is also Filomena's nephew. One provision no one can alter: all the papers that Alma brought down and hasn't destroyed must stay, not just in the country, but in the cemetery. The funds from Scheherazade's royalties and other rights are all to go to the maintenance of the park. Except for monthly payments to some hospicio in Higüey. Near where your mother was in prison, his tía reminds him.

As for his mamita, she is still not speaking, Filomena is sorry to say. Hay que aceptar, she counsels her nephew. But Pepito won't give up. He consults a trauma counselor with extensive experience work- ing with survivors of rape and genocide, many of them women who have seen their villages torched, their loved ones slaughtered. These women sit in the counselor's office, mute, as if their tongues had been cut off. They will not—or cannot—say what they have endured.

Do they ever recover? Pepito asks, grabbing for any hope.

Some do, the counselor reports. But only when they can tell the story of what has happened to them do they begin to heal.

How can Mamita get better if she refuses to talk?

There is another approach, his tía says, apologizing for her presumption as she is no doctor and has not had much learning. You listen. There are stories in the silence, too. That much she has learned working for Doña Alma.

⬳ Filomena and Perla

As Doña Alma declines, Filomena is having to provide more and more care, finally hiring Perla to help. In fact, Perla's probational release has been secured, in part, with the argument that she will be doing a humanitarian service. You can always quit later if you want, her lawyer confides.

It's a relief to Filomena to have her sister back under the same roof. A comforting if silent presence. At the cemetery she delegates the task of listening to the voices to Perla, who seems to enjoy sitting before each marker for hours, as if she, too, can hear these abandoned characters talking.

One day, a tiguerito wanders into the park. Perla beckons to him. He sits quietly by her side. She takes his hand and traces the writing on the statues, calls each mark a name. The next day, the boy brings a friend along, and soon the cemetery is overrun by the street kids of the barrio.

They troop from marker to marker, learning their letters by reading the words written on them. Their teacher rewards their progress with mints from the stash she keeps in her pockets.

≈ Pepito

As her literary executor, Pepito is invited to write or lecture on Scheherazade's work. He speaks of his friendship with the writer, her decision to withdraw from public life, her return to her native land. When questions arise about her habits, her public silence toward the end of her life, her personality, Pepito calls his aunt or Alma's sisters. If they don't know the answer, Pepito makes it up. Why not? Scheherazade herself was an invention of Alma Cruz, after all.

He often thinks back on their one and only meeting. Scheherazade hardly said a word. She sat quietly listening to Pepito's story. He kept peering over her shoulder, like a child determined to uncover a secret. Finally, he asked his burning question, What are you working on?

Scheherazade twisted around in her chair to see what her visitor was referring to. Oh that, she shrugged at the scribbles on the page, and handed him the journal. Her writing was not easy to decipher, so many words crossed out, alternates in the margins, and those crossed out in favor of newer versions. Every word not quite the word or words she'd been searching for.

He struggled to make sense of her handwriting: *Everything on earth stops me and whispers to me, and what they tell me is their story.*

A description of her affliction or a keepsake quote? He dared not pester her with more questions and risk being booted out. Was it his idea or hers that they take a walk outside?

The night though moonless was studded with stars. He offered her his arm as if he were escorting her onto the dance floor.

Just like el Jefe, she laughed. He asked what she was referring to. Monte Cristi, 1927, she replied. Before your time.

But you weren't alive then either, he reminded her.

I was when I was writing her.

She must be alluding to the unfinished Bienvenida manuscript. Pepito knew bits and pieces of the story from earlier interviews, in which Scheherazade talked at length about the novel she was research-ing, drafts now buried in this cemetery. Someone should really dig them up and try to reconstruct the abandoned novel.

They walked slowly, as the cemetery had no lighting. She was barefoot and the ground was full of sharp pebbles, discarded nails and bits of wiring left behind by the construction crew. He offered to turn on the flashlight on his phone to guide them.

She refused. My feet know the way by heart. She laughed, repeat-ing the words with each step, feet, heart, feet, heart, as if she were a child learning the name of her body parts.

They walked up and down the makeshift rows in silence. It took so long to get here, she said finally. A whole life. ·

Did she mean her return with her stories to their homeland or this silence under the stars together? He didn't ask, not wanting to break the spell.

Still there was something unfinished. Some dream she'd recently had that perplexed her. *A violation at the center of my art.* Was she quoting herself? Pepito wondered.

She had stopped in front of a sculpture. Pepito was glad for the distraction. He pulled out his phone to read the markings. It was the marker he'd visited with his tía earlier, the head on a long stem of a neck, the face scarred with letters, words scribbled across the mouth, like thick black thread stitching the lips together. He cocked his head to make out small print: *Bienvenida? Inocencia? el Jefe repeated her name in her ear as they danced.*

As he read Bienvenida's marker out loud, Scheherazade again grew agitated. You hear that? she whispered. That wailing sound?

He was about to say, no, further upsetting her. But mercifully, a bird began singing from one of the trees. You mean that bird? How could he not hear it? It was strange, a bird singing at this hour of the night.

Its name? she wanted to know.

The few birds whose names Pepito knew were from up north. Of course, there were always literary birds from the books he taught: Poe's raven and Stevens's blackbird and that robin in the Dickinson poem. Nightingale, he offered.

She swatted at his arm. You're lying again. The real name! Tell me! she insisted like a thwarted child.

Ya, ya, he said, stroking her hand in the crook of his elbow. She quieted, becalmed by his touch or perhaps the song itself.

Beautiful, she said, when the bird was done.

IV

Colorín Colorado

The gates are open all day. At dusk, before heading home, Filomena and Perla lock them. Even so, nights are busy at el Cementerio. Tigueritos duck behind the sculptures at closing time. After dark, lovers climb over the wall and unlock the back door to their beloveds. Where else to reconnoiter? The cheaper motels that rent by the hour involve a trek out to the highway. Better a straw mat on the ground or nothing at all. In the confusions of pleasure, the body forgets itself.

The lovers rarely spend the night. Illicit love requires waking up in legitimate arms in one's own bed. But for the drifters, beggars, street orphans, el Cementerio serves as home. Each group has its preferred territory: the smaller boys congregate around the markers for the children's books, folktales and legends Scheherazade meant to publish; the older ones gravitate to the burned drafts about lusty revolutionaries never liberated into story form; beggars take the ashy crumbs of whatever is left, lines of poems, rejected essays. There are open stretches with no markers where members of gangs have sown marijuana seeds, their efforts frustrated by the sisters' diligence in weeding.

Fires are lit for warmth during the cool winter months, but often as not, throughout the year, for the comfort of watching the flames. The smell of leña. Ears of corn roasting; víveres buried under the embers. Pan de agua, slices of queso frito, salty salchichas and bacalao make the rounds, end-of-the-day handouts at el colmado. Bichán might be un tiguerazo with an eye to his advantage, but he has a soft heart for the orphans who live on the street. They remind him of the boy he used to be, before the Jesuits got ahold of him and gave him enough education to score a job, finally set up his own business with his savings. About saving his soul, they were less successful.

After satisfying their hunger, they tell stories, a Mamajuana bottle making the rounds. Boys and several girls protectively disguised as boys recount what happened that day, what was filched, who was kind, where they roamed, exact locations left vague to protect territory, curb competition. Old-timers tell of hurricanes, massacres, dictators, as well as of golden times when the living was good, and there was so much to go around, people tied up their dogs at night with links of sausages. The young men boast about their exploits, girls they spied on, bathing behind plastic, see-through shower curtains, throwing buckets of water over their beautiful soapy bodies. *So many curves and my brakes are shot!*

The laughter dies down. The younger boys yawn. The night wears on.

The groups disperse to their posts, sometimes searching out new locations, as some markers have been known to stir up nightmares. Others incite wonderful dreams. Turf wars erupt. Newcomers are warned to avoid bedding down by el Globo—el Barón is still on a rampage after his marker was moved to make room for the small house. There are stories of transgressors waking up with a tail between their legs or horns on their heads. Never were they the same again.

Even more than el Globo, everyone but everyone avoids the machete marker that wails when the wind blows, voices shouting words no one can make out. *Ou te trayi nou! Ou te trayi nou!* Either the devil is sowing confusion or God is speaking Portuguese, French, Kreyòl, whatever that language is.

The streets beyond the walls empty, the air stills, the quiet deepens, interrupted by an occasional motor, a drunk stumbling home; the shops and barras shutter up; the lights go out in row upon row of casitas. The living sleep, their stories turning into dreams.

The fire is a soft glow of embers. It's that hour fittingly called the dead of night.

Now out of time, they rise up and roam the grounds, claiming the bodies given to them in their aborted stories. Some never fully described manifest only as a "waterfall of black hair" or "eyes so blue the spring sky is envious." A young woman with "the tender smile of a Madonna in a medieval painting" rearranges a raggedy jacket on the shoulders of a sleeping boy; an old patriarch, "with skin more speckled than a cowbird's eggs," kicks a thieving hand away from a vagabond's knapsack. A farmwoman, solid as an ox, but with an otherworldly look on her face, speaks to a crowd of believers. *Pray, pray hard. The enemy of God is all over America.* A large Black woman listens to a tow-headed fellow who jabbers away, his tongue loosened by drink. His "ropey arms recall the rigging of a ship," the skin cluttered with tattoos. He strews the woman's path with petals of sunflowers, wooing her with talk of his sea voyages, punctuated by snatches of shanties. She shakes her head indulgently. *A woman must tell her stories to save her life. I suppose a man must, too.* She steers him toward the marker others avoid, calming the howling with her listening presence. *Of their bones are stories made*, she rephrases a quote from a book he hasn't read. A young volunteer reads to a blind man in a novel never realized—only a slight, unsuccessful short story remains. This shriveled viejo, whom the girl pities, was once a torturer in his native land, erasing the stories of others. The scene in which she learns of his past never written down, the ashes of his burned drafts buried under an oversized pair of eyeglasses propped on their temples like a strange insect. The girl guides the hesitant hand over each marker, describing it.

Did I kill them all? he asks the girl. The blind eyes weep.

She reassures him. *These aren't real people.*

They never are. How else could he have applied exquisite instruments to their bodies and thrown them over the cliffs to feed the sharks?

A little boy with green stains around his mouth holds his mother's hand. She sings to him using the voice of the rustling leaves and twittering swallows. He joins in with his own cricket trill. No one hushes him. Who cares if he doesn't know the words?

Tonight, one of these unstoried will be leaving, her tale soon to be published by a rising star, a professor turned novelist. Every night there has been less of her as she undergoes draft after draft. She wants to be left untold, the bliss of anonymity. Doesn't anyone consider that the most popular of epitaphs is REST IN PEACE?

She strolls on the arm of an older man in a Panama hat who is trying to console her. Now people will see you. Now people will understand. He himself would give anything to trade places. To be relieved of the burden of the secret he carries with him. He feels better already having shared it just with her and the groundskeeper.

So, come with me, the fading woman says, we'll find a place for you in my story.

But outside their own narratives, these characters are not in command.

Perhaps this scholar writer, whoever he is, will give you a happy ending, the man in the Panama hat encourages her. No more Bienvenida. We will have to call you Despedida. He chuckles at his own joke, as he often did in his unfinished story.

Hasta luego, he calls out to her. Till we meet again!

Until then, the swirling waters of oblivion will keep one from the other, the known from the unknown. For these, the nameless, unseen, anonymous, there are no gaps on shelves where their tomb-tomes might go, no eyes misting over at their approach, no minds transformed by their example. No one pines for their stories, no one even knows they are there for the telling.

But no matter. Who would want to go back to narrative form? Back into the living stream to be reborn in distortion in the minds of readers? A few linger, the clingers, the aggrieved, holding on to that hope. The ones with scores to settle or burdens to release. Not a fate to be desired, shackled again, contained and restrained in chapter and verse. And how long does it last anyhow? Eventually, storied and unstoried join in mystery. Nothing holds anyone together but imagination.

Trust us, they would say if they had the words. We should know. We have died. We are in love with everything.

Este cuento se ha acabado.

⌇ Acknowledgments

This book is dedicated to Anon, in gratitude to all those people, often unacknowledged, sometimes unbeknownst, who have given me help, love, and support, throughout my life, on and off the page, beginning with the oral storytellers of my early childhood in the Dominican Republic, whose stories came with me into English, stories steeped in the rhythms of Spanish with splashes of sunlight and filled to the brim and spilling over the brim with the wild excesses that encourage generosity of heart above all things. The homeland that never quits giving.

To my sisters who first listened to my poems in our shared darkened bedrooms, reciting them to me decades later when I'd forgotten I'd written them, who at times have fought with me about what I could and couldn't write, thereby keeping me and themselves honest and forcing my hand (literally) to be true to what I was willing to hurt for. What gratitude, I know! But thank you, 'Manitas, the one gone and two present, siempre unidas.

To my teachers, oh so many, some of them I never met, writers whose work I adore, whose book covers I have caressed to fadedness, whose words I have committed to memory. The living as well as the never-dead, the Ms. Stevensons and Mr. Packs, the David Huddles and William Merediths, and the writer friends, in whose shadows I have stood and still stand: the glorious Gloria Naylor, the intrepid

Sandra Cisneros, the empathic and heart-swelling Helena María Viramontes, and the old-soul "youngsters," Edwidge Danticat, Angie Cruz, Manuel Muñoz, Liz Acevedo. I am forgetting many of you, but I remember you where and when it counts: every time I sit down to write and your guardian spirits stand by, righting my writing with your consejos and with the example of your own magnificent books.

To my fierce and generous agents/angels, Susan Bergholz and Stuart Bernstein, who have helped open and widen the way, not just for my work but for that of so many others. Without your fierce encouragements, Susan, I would not have undertaken the daunting task of daring to find a spot on the shelf of American literature. And without your faith in my work, Stuart, from the early sonograms of rough drafts, to the fully formed final (never say final!) proofs, I could not have written my recent books. You hear me better than I hear myself. Gracias abounding.

To my editors, whose voices and marking pens live in my heart, beginning way back with Shannon Ravenel, Andrea Cascardi, Erin Clarke, Bobbie Bristol, and now Amy Gash, whose questions and queries challenge me to understand and clarify what the story and its characters need and demand. And to all my publishing familia at Algonquin Books, starting way back with Peter and Carolan Workman (los abuelos), Elisabeth Scharlatt (la madrina), the amazing Michael McKenzie (the fun tío), Betsy Gleick (ama de casa, keeping us all in line), and to so many others whose work on my books might be "invisible," even to me, because—though they make every aspect of my books happen, they disappear, leaving no fingerprints, like fairies vanishing at the first light of publication.

To my cousin, aka "mi Google dominicano," Juan Tomás Tavares, author, activist, critic, thinker, cultural entrepreneur, who keeps me informed on matters in our homeland and beyond and who always and generously answers all my questions and indulges my curiosity, including traipsing through cemeteries and lighting up borders: immeasurable gracias.

To Papi, who never lost faith in his storytelling daughter, however quiet his support, as per his habits in the Underground, and whose own story is not at all the anguished, haunted one told by the fictional Papi in this novel.

To Bill, who has made the life that feeds the work (and the writer) possible. My North Star, and when the skies are too cloudy to see, the hand that touches mine, comforts and guides me.

And to all of you, mostly invisible and anonymous readers, without whom all my stories would have ended up in Alma's cemetery, thank you for the resurrections you have given and continue to give my books by reading them and using them to fertilize the ground your own creations spring from.